MISADVENTURES
WITH A
TIME TRAVELER

MISADVENTURES

WITH A
TIME TRAVELER

BY
ANGEL PAYNE

WATERHOUSE PRESS

ISBN: 978-1-64263-162-3

*For Thomas, my own beautiful prince
and the king of my heart.
Thank you for believing in this one!*

PROLOGUE

MAX

1789 – Angers, France

Time has turned traitor on me.

Angry shouts are followed by fiery swoops of pitch-dipped arrows. The reflections of the attack make their way inside, painting the stone walls in shades of red, orange, amber. The lights dance up and down the hall like gleeful wraiths of hell itself.

But the mob outside is not gleeful at all.

They are furious.

France is birthing itself into something new. The old ways—and every single member of the aristocracy representing them—are now seen as evil as Lucifer. And as is the way of birth, there must be blood.

Tonight, the rabble is out for mine. Furious whispers suddenly echo behind me in the corridor.

"By the saints. They are going to kill him," gasps Kavia. The servant who has always been like a second mother to me has never sounded so petrified, and I clench every muscle to fight the tangible pull of her fear.

"*Oui.*" Carl is no help, which comes as no surprise. Kavia's burly spouse has never been much for words. At a time like this, I am not certain whether to thank him or curse him for the trait. "Most likely," he adds. "And soon. Unless we do something."

"You mean unless I do something."

Kavia's comment has me pivoting back around to fully face them—but my scrutiny can't help me decipher the truth behind their words. They have spoken to each other like that, with meanings layered upon meanings, since the days Kavia was shoo'ing me and my wooden play swords out of her pristine kitchen.

"*Dieu!*" she spits into the tense pause. "This is *insanité*. Because the king is a dolt, they paint every landed man and woman in the country with the same colors?"

"*Oui.*"

As Carl returns to his brevity, Kavia huffs again. "How does this make any kind of sense?"

I admit my own dire interest in a usable answer to that. Our family can never be labeled as the idle rich. We have worked hard to give back to this valley, helping its denizens through births, deaths, and the crises between. Many of the furious faces in the courtyard are framed differently in my mind, still joyous from when we played together as boys and girls.

At last, Carl growls out an answer to his wife. "Hatred spurns fear—and panic."

"And sheep like to panic," Kavia mutters.

"*Oui.*"

"Hmmmph," she snorts. "So how do sheep know about screaming to cut off *both* his heads?"

I save poor Carl from having to answer that with my laughing bark. In the doing, I save the shreds of my own

ANGEL PAYNE

composure. For a few moments, my fear has something useful to do.

Yes, I am afraid.

And I sense that Kavia and Carl know it too, despite my feeble attempts to rebuild my emotional armor. The barriers are like tree bark now, ready to snap as soon as the mob outside becomes the mob inside—

And they drag me away.

Undoubtedly to the same fate they have given Mother, Father, and Bastien.

Or maybe they will not take me away. Maybe they will make an example of Lord Maximillian De Leon, meting a special death for a special nobleman. Drawing and quartering? Bayonet wounds and then salt bath? A forced drowning in the river?

I laugh again, but it burns now. The bile in my gut has become acid in my throat—but before I retch, Chevalier lopes up the corridor with impeccable timing. I drop to my knees and embrace my beloved wolfhound, burying my face in his damp fur. How did I barely flinch when hearing of my family's executions but clench back tears from a mere whiff of Chev's mangy smell?

Words. I need words. Finally, the salvation of the syllables comes. "You are the last of the family, Chev," I croak. "You will remember our legacy, *oui*?"

His soft whimper seeps through my senses. He too feels the crowd's rage on the air.

"My lord." Kavia steps next to us and gently shakes my shoulder. "Please. There is not much time!"

"Time?" Carl asks. "For *what*?"

The woman says nothing.

I clench my jaw to the point of pain.

She is right. This *is* all insanity. But I will not be alive to see much more of it.

Which means I need to be thinking about necks besides my own.

Though my legs feel like seaweed, I force myself to stand. My lungs join the burn of my eyes as a sickening *boom* shakes the walls and floors.

I grab Kavia by the arm. "You all need to leave. Right now." I jump my stare between her and Carl. "Both of you and the rest of the staff. Whoever remains. You have all been steadfast, and my gratitude has no bounds, but now—"

"Stop."

Shock causes me to drop my hold. "Pardon me?"

Incredible. Despite the dwindling length of my life, I am once more dripping with affronted arrogance.

"Be quiet, Maximillian, and listen to me."

Carl fills my stunned pause by wheeling around, already pinning his wife with a glower. "And what exactly will he listen to, woman?"

Kavia's eyes, always such a flat gray, gleam with unholy light beneath the dingy kerchief on her head. "I *know* what I am doing, gentlemen. Strong blood courses through my veins." She pulls in a formidable breath. "The blood of sorcerers and mages, of wizards and—"

"Gypsies." Carl spits the word. "You mean unholy village fair gypsies casting equally unholy spells."

I lock my glare down on Kavia once more, bizarrely fascinated with the growing gleam in her gaze. "What is he talking about?"

"Abominations," Carl spews before she can get a sound

out. "Spittle in God's eyes."

Kavia hisses like a cat in a rain barrel. "*Fermé!*"

"What—"

The fall of her hand atop my chest, as violent as the battering ram at our mansion's front door, commands me to new silence. "I am not the one who will save you, Maximillian." A strange heat spreads from her fingers, seeping across my heart and lungs. "*This* is what will save you."

I flinch but am unable to step away, impaled by her deepening spell. "B-By all that is holy." Or is Carl correct, after all? Is this enchantment a hex of the *un*holy? "Kavia? Wh-What are you doing?"

"Not me, my lord. *You.*" She steps back, but the coals in my chest remain. I can barely breathe. "Your heart, and the magic inside it, are why you will not die today."

"S-S-Stop." The command rasps from a throat turned to parchment, but I force more words to my lips nonetheless. "You will stop these deranged ramblings. *At once.*"

"But my lord—"

"I said at once, Kavia. There will be no more of this heretical nonsense. I shall face my fate with the honor of a De Leon."

"Honor?" Her pleadings are gone, replaced by a biting laugh. "What honor? Your family name is worth less than the mud trampled by that mob." She stabs a finger toward the window. Steps forward with equal defiance. Locks her gaze directly to mine. A week ago, all three acts would have seen her punished for insubordination. Today, I can only chastise her with a steady glower. "Do you want to live, Maximillian?"

I bare my teeth. "What kind of a question is that?"

She dips a serene nod. "All right, then. If you want to live, you must choose to do so. And you can only do that by listening to me."

"Kavia, by the blood of Christ Almighty—"

"No." Her gaze grows brighter, this time because of brimming tears. "By your own blood, Maximillian." She presses a trembling palm to my face. "And I cannot allow that to happen."

I blink hard. Inhale and exhale with even more force. A pressure I cannot ignore, in my head and over my heart, emanates from Kavia's fingertips as strongly as the heat did.

"Woman," I dictate from between locked teeth, "*what* are you about?"

"Keeping you alive, Maximillian. That is all I am about." Though her grip returns to its former urgency, her lips tremble. Her chin wobbles. "You...you cannot die today, Max. You *must* survive this...Your Majesty."

The mob grows louder. So does the storm that breaks free in my mind. My body goes limp. I am helpless to resist Kavia's frantic yank, urging me down the corridor. I stumble along as if in a haze—because I *am* in one.

Because my mind fights to wrap around that single, stunning word.

Majesty.

"Dear God." It is a whisper on my lips but a truth in my mind. *My truth*. Somehow, I have always known it but never believed it. Even now, after hearing Kavia declare it, I am not certain that I truly do.

"How...do you know..."

My words are severed by a violent clap of thunder.

Not from the sky.

From the front door.

Kavia pushes me into a shadowed bedroom. Once we're inside, I seize her by her elbows. "*Kavia.* Answer me! How the hell do you know—"

"Because I was there." Her emotional rush takes me aback. For all my righteous demand, I didn't expect this swift confession. "The night you were born, sweet boy," she blurts through tears that flow even harder. "The sole occasion that Louis, Dauphin of France, ever acknowledged you as his true son."

I wait, breath held, for the joy those words are supposed to bring. Instead, I am assaulted by a thousand more questions about my birthright. But I do not have the freedom to voice even one. The mob rams the door with greater force. The very air shudders, preparing for their incursion.

"*Mon Dieu.*" Kavia paces the room, her skirts swishing. "Oh, my God. Oh, my God. What to do? What to do?"

She eyes the bed on its pedestal, the wash bowl on its stand, the writing desk in the corner . . .

And dashes to the huge wardrobe in the far corner.

Without hesitation, she swings open the chest's heavy doors. Fabric, ribbons, and shoes tumble out. The thing is stuffed with gowns, which my mother had not yet distributed to her maids, along with the usual accessories—reticules, gloves, hats. How she loves all the extras.

Loved them.

Grief torches my soul and stiffens my body. She is gone, as is Christophe De Leon, the man who was father to me in every way but blood. Bastien too. *My brother. Holy God, how I miss you already, Bas.*

The admissions bring stark recognition. Kavia is right. Our family name—the only one I have ever known or claimed—

is now dust. I am posturing for no reason. And here is the gypsy maid who has adored a bastard prince since the day he was born, begging him to believe in her for a few moments in return. Though moments are all I have left, I can think of no better way in which to spend them. I owe Kavia that much. The woman has kept a secret that would have had me slain long before now.

"Get in!" Kavia drags me through the sea of frippery, all but throwing me inside the wardrobe. "Hurry, my lord!" She ignores the pained grunt I emit when my forehead collides with the top of the chest. Once inside, I am swallowed by a new mound of perfumed fabrics. The layers of silk and satin barely muffle the revolutionists' fury. I swallow hard, preparing for the agony of being their fresh target.

Until my terror is replaced by bewilderment as Kavia jumps inside the hiding space with me.

Her eyes are nearly aglow, but her fingers are shaking. She burrows in and tunnels her gaze to mine. "They are almost here," she says. "So listen to me well."

"No." I wrap my hands around hers. "You listen first. My fate should not be yours and Carl's—so I want you to get out of here. I mean it. Carl knows the way to the hunting lodge—"

"My lord!"

"I will not abide your misplaced loyalty," I state. "At this point, it is naught but sacrificial suicide. You are both to leave here. Do not think about saving me again."

The mob grows louder.

Kavia raises her chin. "I understand. I will not think of saving you again, my lord."

I release a heavy breath. "Good."

"Because I am saving you now."

"*Ventrebleu.*"

"Maximillian. *Please.*"

I look back up to her—but do not want to. In ten seconds, the woman seems to have aged ten years. Her cheeks are sharp and gaunt; her gaze shimmers with surreal light. My heart cracks. "Damn it, Kavia!"

"Please! You *must* listen to me!"

I lift a grim smile. "Have I not always listened to you?"

"*Fermé,*" she rebukes. "And do as I say, child."

The silvery glaze in her eyes locks me down like shackles. My hands plummet as if those bonds are real and my movements are no longer my own.

"Kavia," I choke out, consumed by the tightening grip of her inexplicable force. "What—are you doing to—"

"*Fermé.*"

I watch, mesmerized and horrified, as she rocks her head back. The whites of her eyes take over her sockets. Words command her lips, babbling a language I do not understand. She seizes my wrists and digs her fingers into the center of my pulse. She does not relent.

Tighter.

Tighter.

Tighter.

She burns her power into me...

Through me...

"By the Virgin." I yank back to cross myself, but the woman holds on. She possesses the strength of twelve men. Her grasp is a burning, conquering presence through my being. "Kavia!" I fight her, threatening to topple the wardrobe. "This has gone too far. I order you, as your lord and master, to cease—"

"*Au-delà du temps. Au-delà de la raison. Dans ton demain,*

confiance à ton cœur."

The words are understandable but illogical. *Beyond time. Beyond reason. In your tomorrows, trust your heart.*

"Kavia? What in God's name..."

But I am robbed of words as I gape at the freakish changes in the woman's countenance. Kavia's face is still there, but another's has been layered atop it. The new face appears as if she has worn a veil to church. And the face on that veil...

Is the most beautiful woman I have ever seen.

Skin like crushed pearls. Eyes like the depths of the forest, with catlike tapers at the corners. Feline lips, full and crimson. And her hair...

By every saint I can remember, her *hair.*

The thick black mane resembles billows of the finest Paris satin, rivers of the softest Italian velvet. I long to clothe my entire body in its luxury. To wrap it around my bare skin as I do other things to her naked form. To touch her everywhere...

Who is she?

The question burns as potently as my lust. Even now, in this moment of darkness and doom, with a mob raging for my destruction, I crave to claim her. To know her as no one else has. To possess her...

Who is she?

Every fiber of my being screams with need. Every inch of my cock pounds with desire.

Who is she?

I am not aware of actually vocalizing it until Kavia's gaze ignites like silvered sunlight. "You... you see her?"

"*Oui,*" I grate.

"Of course. Praise God!"

No. *Not* praise God. This is the devil's work, and the

fantasy woman on that wicked veil is his emissary. I can conceive no other explanation. This vision looks too much like heaven to be from anywhere but hell, spun from the fabric of my most sinful imaginings.

I struggle to cross myself.

"Saints help me."

As the truth ignites in me.

Kavia *is* a witch—and her witch's touch has granted her access inside me. And now she is using that weakness against me. To drag me to damnation...

And I do not care.

My chest aches. My blood burns. My hands are numb, as if the hounds of hell have already bitten them off.

I still do not care.

The sorceress resumes her mad chanting. But this time, the devil's beautiful emissary is channeling herself through Kavia. I somewhat recognize the tongue. The words sound English but bizarre.

"Those kicks are dope, but the pants are nope. You are seriously harshing my mellow, girlfriend. I can't go dancing tonight, and don't ask again. I'm behind by three vid posts. Deadlines are joy killers."

A high laugh bursts from Kavia—shattering the trance of her she-devil's face.

"No," I protest in a choke. "No, no, no—"

"*Maximillian.*" She raises those fiery fingers to my face, and heat spreads across my mind. Commands my very vision.

"Bring her back," I beg past numb lips. "B-Bring her b-back."

"You do not need her back," Kavia croons. "Because she is inside you."

"What?"

"Look inside, Maximillian. She is there. She will guide you."

"But who is—"

"No more noise, boy. Center your mind on her. Center your *heart* on her."

Her cadence lulls me. Surrounds me. Burns into me, illuminating parts of my being I never knew existed.

"Wh-What is this sorcery?"

"A thing of beauty, Maximillian—sent to this time, this space, this moment to help you see your beauty."

"What the hell?"

"There are forces you do not understand. You *cannot* understand. The powers of creation, of joy, of hope . . . of love." Though she has all but admitted to being a witch, an angelic smile takes over her lips. "Powers you must find in your soul if this is going to work."

My belly twists. "If *what* is going to work?"

Her smile grows. Despite that, I am terrified. But why? Kavia has always been there for me, guiding me, teaching me— but no lesson she's ever imparted compares to this.

"I need to let you go now, Maximillian."

"No!"

"It is time for your journey to begin."

"*No*. Wait!"

"My sweet Maximillian. I love you so. You know that, *oui*?"

"Kavia—"

But she has already left, swinging the heavy cabinet doors on me. Her tear-tracked cheeks and tremulous smile are my last sight before the thick darkness takes over. And the crushing heat. And the terrible solitude. Most exceptionally that.

"You love me?" I thrust my frantic fear into each bellowed syllable. "This has nothing to do with love, Kavia!"

"Oh, Max." Her voice is drenched in a muffled sob. She is still standing so close, I can nearly feel her breath through the fruitwood doors. "This has *everything* to do with love."

"Damn you. *Damn you!*"

"She is waiting for you, Maximillian."

"She . . . who? Wh-What is happening?"

"You will learn soon enough. But before that, there is one thing more. The most important thing."

"Which you have waited until *now* to tell me?"

"So you will not forget. You *must not* forget."

She drives in that importance by pounding her side of the door, and I press my fingers to the wood, savoring the strangely comforting vibrations from it. "I will not forget," I vow with tender sincerity. "I promise."

"She is waiting for you, Maximillian," Kavia states. "I know it with every strand of my being."

"Who?" I charge. "Damn it, of *whom* are you speaking, Kavia?"

"But once you reach her, the potency of the portal will start to weaken."

"The portal?" I shout. "To where?"

"I can only give you one cycle of the moon, Max. Only one cycle to completely win her."

"Win her? How? In what way? Using what—"

But time barges in on us—and so does the horde. Their clogs pound the parquetry floor. They are inside the château at last.

"Maximillian! Tell me you understand this. One cycle

of the moon. Twenty-eight days. Before it is done, she must declare her love for you aloud, before witnesses, or the enchantment will be broken and the portal will collapse."

"Enchantment...broken. Portal...collapses." Once again, I understand the words but comprehend none of their meaning. "And what happens if it does?"

An audible sob again escapes her. "Then *you* are broken."

"What does that mean?"

Silence answers my demand.

"Kavia?"

Thicker stillness.

No.

Emptiness.

"*Kavia?*"

But I can barely finish the syllables. I have begun to disintegrate...to transform.

I am a flicker of ash floating on the air.

I am a disembodied wing riding an invisible wind.

I am specks sifting through the cracks between the wardrobe doors...

Until I see Kavia again.

She is across the bedroom, crouching beneath the bed to hide. She is not there two seconds when the murderous crowd breaks into the room and, seeing me nowhere, sprint at once for the wardrobe. With triumphant roars, they yank back the chest's doors—

But do not find me.

I am ash. Wings. Specks.

And then not even that.

I am sparks. Then light. Transparent. Transcendent.

Until I am not.

I am in darkness again. I have *become* darkness. Alone. But still alive.

CHAPTER ONE

ALLIE

I'm in hell.

Fine. Not really. But the fairy princess castle before me, despite its soaring French grandeur, might as well be hell.

I may vlog about fancy dresses and rub shoulders with a lot of queens, but a textbook princess life is nothing I have the time, energy, or patience for. I don't need some dashing prince to wrap his gentle arms around my dainty waist just for the honor of sharing half my fortune. I'm a twenty-five-year-old writer and vlogger who likes gourmet burgers and real dressing on her salads, and a lot of readers and viewers spread across *a lot* of social media platforms happen to agree about that.

I gawk up at the mansion and wonder what kinds of dating woes were experienced by the women who actually lived in this place. Back in the day, were there other Allie Fines? Did they have to explain why they liked standing at the punch bowl alone? Why they were okay without anyone in the room complimenting their hair? Had they learned, when that hair was still in pigtails, that castles could look perfect from the outside but hide trapdoors that dropped to dangerous dungeons? Sometimes, where the prince himself waited . . .

So, yeah. Fairy tales and me? Not a match made in heaven. Or anything close to it.

"Do. Not. Leave." I grit it at my shuttle driver, adding with a smile, *"S'il vous plait."* After slipping him enough euros to ensure he'll comply, I raise a fresh frown at the six-story structure in front of me. Its regal construction and burgundy-roofed spires have me wondering where Rapunzel's braid or Belle's rose are hiding. The estate is attached to miles of gardens and forests.

"Ahhhhh! She's here!"

Crap.

I repeat it aloud as a dervish with flying red hair and brilliant green eyes launches at me like a kitten at a laser beam. Raegan Tavish strikes again, body-slamming me to the side of the car as the smirking driver fetches my bags out of the trunk.

"You're here! You're here!"

"So you've told half the Loire Valley." The quip is drawled by the wench who approaches from my right, twirling strands of her cobalt-streaked hair. Drue Kidman is the only person on the planet capable of rocking that look in this setting, dressed in a slouchy sweater, paisley-patterned tights, and stilettoed boots from three decades ago. She jogs a cocky chin when I give her gear an approving onceover. "Yo, wench."

"Who you callin' whaaat?" I finish with a grin as acerbic as hers.

"Get your ass over here and give me some sugar."

Our embrace gains more force as Raegan bounces over from behind, happily taking up position as our resident Tigger. "Surprise!" she cries, ignoring how I groan from being the filling in a bestie sandwich. "Happy birthday. You're a quarter of a century old. We wanted to do something more than cake."

"Raegan is out for more than cake," Drue corrects, just wry enough to secure her spot as our Eeyore stand-in. "I'm just along for the ride."

I flash her a wink. "What a ride I bet it was."

She winks back. "Who says it's over?"

"And the wench scores a comeback point."

"Stop calling me wench. Around here, they may use that as permission to put me in a corset."

"Now *that* I'm adding to the birthday wish list."

Raegan interrupts with a happy dance around the gravel drive. "Can you even believe this place? It's got six floors, seven bedrooms, three gardens, two pools, a croquet court, stables with real horses—"

"And prehistoric Wi-Fi." I glower at my phone and wonder if—*please God, no*—their internet is dial-up.

Like a sadist on a bungie jump bridge, Drue snatches the device from me. "Live with the dinosaurs for a few days, wench. I dare you."

I commit to a censuring glare. "Not. Fair."

"And the pace you've been on is?" she counters.

Now she's hitting real buttons. I scowl harder while crunching a divot into the gravel with my boot heel. Fortunately, the tension is cut when the mansion's massive front doors are swung wide. A man and woman appear, as regal and imposing as the portal itself. Both are dressed in this season's Prada, though he's opted for a blue silk cravat to finish his tailored cream suit, and she's accessorized her pink poplin dress with impeccable antique jewelry.

Wow.

I almost blurt it out loud, wondering if they actually have titles to match their noble allure. I've not been in such awe of a couple since first watching Grace and Rainier's wedding footage.

"Bonjour." The man strides forward, still in gallant knight-at-arms mode. "Bienvenue to Château De Leon." Along with the greeting, he lifts our hands and brushes kisses across our knuckles. "I am Monsieur Henri De Leon, and this is my wife, Pascaline."

Grace—errr, Pascaline—sweeps her head down as if preparing to be crowned. "But just Pasca to keep it simple, *oui?*"

"Just Pasca. Got it," Drue answers. "*C'est joli.*"

"*Merci.*"

As Pasca smiles again, I scoot closer to Drue. "*C'est joli?*" I challenge into her ear. "Don't tell me you're really going down the rabbit hole too."

"*Pffft.*" She flips her long mane over both shoulders, compelling me to stand back. "So it's a little over-the-top—but isn't over-the-top what you thrive on, Ms. Key Fashion Influencer?"

"Seriously?" Raegan snips. "Five minutes in, and we're already bringing up the girl's day job?"

"She started it," Drue volleys. "I mean, technically. With the pouting about the internet, and—"

"Do I look like I care who started it?" Raegan plants hands on her embroidered denim hips. "This trip is intended as an escape, especially for *this* one." She points the invisible laser beam on her finger between my eyes. "Missy, there's being passionate about your job, and there's *being* your job."

"And that's wrong . . . why?"

She tightens her scowl. "You've been eating, drinking, sleeping, and breathing high fashion since the beginning of the year."

"Again . . . your point?"

"Allie, it's nearly April."

"And I covered four Fashion Weeks in a row," I counter. "Along with all the insanity between them."

"Insanity." As soon as Drue murmurs it, she holds up both hands with palms out. "Annnd I rest my case."

"And once again, I second that emotion," Raegan quips.

"Are you two going to stop sometime soon?" I go ahead and snarl it. "Look; I have to keep up this pace—"

"Why?" Drue ripostes.

"*Because I have to.*" The reasons for my ambition, which they're both acutely aware of, are more suitable for reiterating over tequila shots at midnight, not in the middle of a French rose garden beneath a diamond-bright sun. "Besides, someone has to be the leading fashion industry advocate for girls with game like this."

I end it with enough sass to allow for a hips-and-ass combo shimmy, emphasizing the generous curves that have become my distinctive calling card to design houses across the world. I'm unashamed about the motion and undaunted about my achievement. Speaking up for women who'll never be a size two has been empowering for them *and* me.

"Hey. We get it, okay?" Drue pushes in for a sisterly side hug. "And we're proud as hell of you for all of it too—but dolly, all work and no play doesn't make you dull; it makes you dead. I'm serious, Allie. You've got to stop and smell the flowers sometimes."

"And the wine!" Raegan punctuates that by flagging down a liveried butler who's entered the garden bearing a gold tray with crystal wineglasses. I follow her motion, deciding I can definitely get on board with this part of the adventure. The conclusion isn't just about the booze. The hunk bringing the nectar, with his shoulders bulging under his black suit, is a nice additional perk.

"Oh." Drue drawls her approving vote. "Ohhh, yes. Lots and lots of wine."

As I accept the glass of lush mahogany liquid, I catch the server admiring my figure, clad in a Mac Duggal custom dress that catches my legs a few inches above the suede boots. He winks. I absolutely wink back.

Hmmm. Maybe this surprise trip will have its merits after all.

And I really owe it to this pair of wonderful wenches, who jumped through hoops I can't fathom to make it happen.

Shouldn't I give it all a try, if just for them?

The sun is a welcome bath of warmth on my face. The wine is a delicious buzz in my veins. And that butler is still glancing over like I'd be a nice replacement for his afternoon snack. I'd not normally take up a stranger on such a thing, but Paris Fashion Week barely gave me the chance to sleep, let alone rub one out in the shower. And there are a few special foil packets stowed in my luggage—for special occasions.

Maybe this is one of those occasions.

Maybe, in light of that, I can suck it up and survive on sketchy internet for a few days.

A thorough sigh leaves me. It's interrupted by my friends' stare down. They're peering like we've stepped into one of those DIY decorating shows and they repainted my apartment purple while I was out to dinner.

"Okay, okay." I finally throw my hands up. "I'll give it a go. Besides, I can probably spin this all into a bigger feature . . ." As I give in to some creative thoughts, I tap my chin with a finger. "Yeah. That'll totally work. I'll take lots of footage and then edit it into a longer piece. Something like *No Parlais Wi-Fi*, or—"

"Stop!" As Raegan stomps over, her features pinch tighter. "Are you still contemplating work? Even right now? Look around you! Alessandra Sophia Fine, you're the reigning mistress of all this!"

I tilt my head the same angle as hers. "Even monarchs have to work, Raegan."

She grimaces harder. "Uggghhh."

"Hey. I'm *trying*."

"Not very hard!"

"I'm twenty-five today, baby—not sixteen. And you're right. This is all lovely, but we're not at summer camp anymore. I can't just sneak away with you guys to knock back Fireball shots in the woods."

"Exceptional point." Drue lifts her glass, looking prepared to give a toast. "But the Paris shows wrapped three days ago, missy. Your vlog has been uploaded and all your print articles submitted. Don't think we didn't check."

I glower. "You guys suck."

She grins. "Only when we're asked nicely."

"I guess . . . I can send some basics to Dmitri and let him run point on emails for a few days." My business manager, in all his bustling glory, will actually be in control-freak heaven about this. Yet Drue's right; there's not a lot for him to control right now. Every major fashion hub on the planet is still in a post-Paris coma. If I check in a couple of times a day, there's nothing stopping me from taking my first five days off in—

When?

I ignore the chasm that opens in my mind as an answer.

"Shall I have Christophe take your bags up to your

chamber, milady?" says Henri De Leon. Hottie Butler apparently double-duties as the place's bellman.

"Ah—*oui*," I stammer. "Of course. My chamber." I throw another glance Christophe's way. If I'm going for this getaway thing, I'm jumping in with both feet and my whole libido. No time like right now to start.

After Christophe takes my luggage from the driveway, I tip and release the driver—longing to take back the words as soon as he fires up the car's engine. As he accelerates back toward the main road, the tires send gravel skittering. The churned dust lingers on the air like dystopian murk. The impression is intensified as soon as the De Leons follow Christophe back into the house.

For some reason, I laugh at my musing while casting a grin Raegan's way. "All right, Tigger." I purposely use the nickname now. Drue and I bestowed it on her in high school, when it was clear she was destined to become our squad's Type-A social planner. "What's first on the agenda?"

The woman starts her reply with a cute brow waggle. "I think the birthday wench just supplied the best answer for that."

Drue slides out a sneaky grin. "Everyone snap up. She totally did."

"I did?"

Rae grins with mischievous triumph. "Camp tradition, baby. It's time to sneak into the forest."

"With just one teeny-tiny upgrade." Drue smirks while lifting a flap on her satchel. I join Raegan in peering inside the compartment—and then cheering at the sight of three sizable bottles nestled inside. Their necks are wrapped with golden foil centered by ornate labels that match the crests carved into the mansion doors.

"It's Crémant," Drue states. "From the estate's private cellar. And Henri swears it's way better than Fireball."

"Gee. You think?" Raegan quips.

I laugh longer and harder than before. "Oh, hold the damn phone. Better than Fireball?"

"Seriously." Rae nods. "Because what says erase all your cares better than alcohol that tastes like cinnamon toast and gasoline?"

When Drue adds her giggle to ours, I know we already have a real memory book moment for the trip.

But it also confirms that I have to face an annoying truth.

That maybe, damn it, they're right.

Maybe it's time I *do* stop to sniff a few posies. Get lost in a forest. Get drunk beside a stream. Let a local hunk ravage me at midnight. What's working hard if I can't play hard too?

God, I hate them for being right.

But have never loved them more.

And with that thought, I turn and playfully smack both their asses. "Into the woods, girls."

"Into the woods, baby." Drue adds her droll grin.

"Into the woods, goddesses." Rae sing-songs her version. Of course.

Into the woods.

Where we're supposed to find stuff like enchanted apples and princes in disguise, right? Where true love's kiss and a fairy's wand will make the world perfect, right?

And sometimes there's just getting too damn carried away with things.

Because here's the deal.

I absolutely believe in searching for a better world—

just not in trusting that Prince Gallivant is going to help me find it. Real life and real relationships take a special brand of commitment—an element that isn't in my DNA if I'm looking to Angelo and Launette Fine as my proof of concept. And why count on a glittery godmother to create my magical ball gown, when I've got hundreds to be dazzled by every new fashion season? Best of all, I'm getting *paid* for the gig. The only spell that makes sense is the one I'm creating for myself.

The only enchantress I'm banking on is the one with curves and words and the drive to do something with them. The badass who looks back every morning from the mirror.

Or so I keep fighting to tell myself.

Hours later, that fight gets easier when I'm staring at my reflection in a sparkling forest pond.

The pool, fed by a small waterfall, is filled with jade and turquoise eddies that smear my reflection into dreamy layers. *Damn, I'm gorgeous.* Or is that the Crémant speaking? Okay, it's probably the Crémant.

Yaaay, Crémant.

Bolstered by that perfect rah-rah, I let Drue pour me a third glass of the fruity bubbles. Why not? The shit is beyond delicious. More importantly, life is too much of a beautiful buzz right now. No deadlines to meet. No video scripts to prep or rough footage to edit. No designers waiting to be interviewed. Right now, my world is just a canopy of emerald trees overhead, a carpet of lush grass underfoot, the cool waters flowing over my bare feet, and the freedom to speak whatever the hell springs to my mind.

"So I'm not saying that everyone on earth should burn every poncho in their closet, but..."

"Er, girlfriend?" Drue finishes with a frown, apparently

struggling with a knot in the daisy chain she's constructing. But I'm not spot-on sure about that, since the ripples make her fuzzy too. "That *is* essentially what you're saying."

"But what about rain ponchos?" Rae inserts from where she lounges in the grass a few feet away. "Like the souvenir ones they gave us on the Niagara Falls boat?"

Raegan giggles. I do too—but not for long. This is an important subject.

"The last person who made a poncho look good was Peggy Lipton." Since there's only silence from them both, I reward myself with my own laugh. "Okay, maybe Goldie Hawn. After the *Laugh-In* days but before the rom-coms. And Jacqueline Smith, who could make a sandwich bag look good . . ."

Before I can think of a classier act than Jackie Smith, Rae sits up and looks at her watch. "Well, at least you went an hour without talking shop this time."

Drue spills with a mock gasp. "Oh, that's got to be a new record."

I glower at both of them over the rim of my glass. "Didn't know you two were keeping track."

Drue lobs the expression back at me. "We're not and you know it."

"Let's keep track of something else!" Raegan reaches into the satchel and then hoists the third bottle high. "Like, let's say, a certain butler-bellhop hunk who was eyeing our birthday girl like his next scoop of crème brûlée?"

I lower my glass and raise a brow. "You have a strange obsession with dessert today, girlfriend."

"Stop evading."

"What? You don't want to talk about dessert?"

"And *you* don't want to talk about sneaking to Christophe's room and climbing him like a greedy little monkey?"

That's it. No way can I hold off my eye roll any longer. "First off, that 'tree' was probably just being nice and acts that way with all the birthday girls who come through the château. Second, even if that's not the case, he'll be the one doing the sneaking, not the other way around."

Drue does nothing for a moment but take a thoughtful sip from her own glass. Damn it, I hate it when she gets thoughtful.

"Sometimes you have to put in a little effort too, Allie. Believe it or not, it's worth it sometimes."

"Believe it or not, huh?"

Resulting in me having to smack back with sarcastic stabs like that.

"Well, it's clear which option you've set to default," Drue murmurs.

"What's that supposed to mean?"

"You already know that answer." She jogs up her chin. "You're playing judge and jury on every man who crosses your path, Allie. They're all automatically stamped guilty and then thrown into some theoretical dungeon..."

"Ohhh, dungeons can be fun sometimes. You think Christophe might have a kinky streak?"

And how are Drue and I supposed to ignore a Raegan zinger like that? Neither of us try, and I'm glad about it. As soon as our laughter subsides, we turn toward the wide walking trail back to the castle.

During the short walk, our argument points are left behind in the glade. I no longer rant about ponchos, and Drue ditches the effort to make me open up about my Prince Charming allergy. The quest is impossible, and we all know it. Talking about my past isn't going to change my issues about it.

Mom was doing the best she could with the emotional tools she had, which weren't many after Dad decided he couldn't "do the relationship thing." My head understands that now. In many ways, my heart gets it too.

Except when it comes to adding true love songs to my soundtrack.

Not going to happen, kids.

Even after we arrive back at the château, deciding to bypass dinner in favor of sweet wine and a platter of handmade desserts, I fling a glower at Raegan when she clicks to "Broadway Love Songs" on the sound system. With a snicker, Drue passes me the remote. "Yacht Rock" for all tonight.

Though an hour later, when all three of us are struggling to sing along to "Everybody Wants to Rule the World," another mutual consensus is reached. It's totally time for bed.

Beyond beat, I stagger into the castle's *grand chamber*. At once, a happy moan escapes me. The decadent four-poster bed is all mine for the next few days. After sleeping in a dozen hotels over the last four months, I'm ready to claim every thread of these luxurious linens as the best perk of my friends' grand surprise.

But an hour and a half later, I'm not even close to basking in the bedding goodness.

I'm still huffing, growling, and restlessly pacing the room—at the mercy of an adrenaline, wine, and sugar high.

And, at least for the last hour of that buzz, a sadistic surge of lust.

And heat. And need. And deprivation.

Oh, God. Definitely deprivation.

"Damn it," I growl and stab a toe at the floor. Where's a stud like Christophe when I need him? And how long has it been since I've relaxed enough to think about straddling a hunk like him? A French one, at that. Not that my life gives me time to be a hussy, but my one experience with a French lover was one to remember. Filthy words. Filthier moves. Worked for my multiple orgasms like an Eagle Scout going for a merit badge.

I laugh at that only because sobbing is the alternative. Which is stupid because the last year of my life has been one of its best. In the fashion-influencer arena, I'm no longer in the grandstands. While I'm not center stage yet, I'm headed toward it.

But sacrifices have been made for that.

Like being alone some nights. Hornier than hell. Ready to hump the bedpost for some relief.

But I'm not sorry about any decisions I've made to get here.

No. Not sorry.

Just maybe a little of something else.

"Damn it."

The echo feels justified. Perhaps even necessary. I don't allow myself to visit these feelings often. But right now, in this place and on this occasion, maybe the emotional expedition is necessary.

I cross to the window as if the decision itself draws me. I grab the window latch and twist, pushing the pane open.

It's a chilly but clear March night, with a light wind skittering small leaves across the gardens. Moonlight turns everything silver. The effect is heightened as the sprinklers come on, their spray turning into stars on the breeze before landing on the garden's Grecian statues. The water courses down all the inert, elegant faces. They're shedding the tears that I can't.

That I won't.

Displaying vulnerability won't change a thing. I'll still be standing at a window in the middle of the night, identifying with garden statues to distract from the shit that's really gnawing at me.

That sometimes, during the nights in which it's too quiet to ignore the thrum of my heart, I have to let it speak to the rest of me.

To tell me it's alone.

No. Not just alone.

Lonely.

My sugar rush vanishes. My head starts to throb. So does the triangle between my thighs.

What the hell is wrong with me?

"Buzzed," I mumble. "You're buzzed, honey. And tired. Ohhh, so tired." I swing my head around, focusing on the grand production that is my bed. "Yeah. Time for sleep, wenchie Allie."

With the hope that Christophe will stop by to fulfill a birthday fantasy, I decide to go commando under my long sleep tee. A blissful groan breaks free as I free my chest from my bra. *Nothing* beats that bliss.

Well . . . one thing might.

The recognition is only a few seconds old before I wrap one hand around a carved bedpost and let the other drift to the cleft between my thighs. A sigh spills out as my pussy comes alive. Ohhh, shit. This feels so damn good. When was the last time I did even this for myself? Weeks, at least.

Weeks.

No wonder my body all but screams at me to keep up the fun. No wonder I answer with higher gasps and quickening rubs.

I fall back onto the bed and let my legs dangle over the side of the plush mattress. I spread my thighs, exposing more for my fingers to touch . . . and arouse. I emit a longer moan while palming my breasts through my T-shirt. Squeezing them. Pinching them. Hardening them.

Vaguely, I realize that I actually remembered to pack my vibrator on this trip. But I'm too far gone to go looking for the thing. With tight, fast circles, I work my frantic fingertips over my tingling clit. Faster still. Faster. I sigh. I hum. I mewl.

Yes.

I'm almost there.

So close.

Almost . . . there.

Damn it. Yesssss . . .

Wait.

What the hell?

I sit up. Hold my breath. I'm not the only one generating sound in this room.

What on earth is going on?

Who's making all those strange, soft hums? And where are they making them?

I swallow hard, forcing myself to look at the towering wardrobe in the corner. The pachyderm of a cabinet is stunning but daunting. Its front panels are testaments to the craftsmen of centuries past, inlaid with mother-of-pearl pictures. Naked angels are dancing with moonbeams in different shades of the shiny nacre. But that's the extent of my observation about the handiwork of the thing for now. I'm mesmerized—hypnotized—by the wardrobe for a different reason.

Because . . .

"Holy. Shit."

Is the damn thing... calling to me? *Singing to me?*

The sound, a blend of electrical resonance and a harpsichord melody, is like no music I've ever heard. The song has no structure or rhythm but compels me like a symphony written solely for my cells, my soul, my spirit. No part of me can ignore it.

"What... the ..."

I can't finish because the chest starts to shake.

No more midnight roses.

My heart thunders with primal terror.

Still, I scoot to my feet and walk toward the damn thing.

Pulled by the golden light that glows from behind the eight-foot doors ...

Light?

"Oh, my God," I rasp. "Okay, Allie. You are either seriously drunk or damn deranged." I hope for the former but suspect the latter. With every step I take, the suspicion intensifies.

I reach for one of the wrought-iron handles. I'm dazzled by the sunlight still effusing from beyond, consuming the silhouettes of my fingers.

I pull the door open.

And at once am tackled by the sun.

All right, the human version of it.

But before I can scream, he grabs both sides of my face. He locks my stare with the amber force of his. I gasp as he holds me tight. Tighter. But I still don't scream. Why? Holy shit, why am I not shrieking like the horror-movie girl dumb enough to take a midnight swim in the lake?

He's two thoughts ahead. He stretches his thumbs in, pressing them over my mouth, trapping me from bursting with sound. Once more, he drenches me in his melted-sun gaze. There's a wild, desperate expression across his chiseled features. He doesn't relent the ferocity, as if he's been chained inside that armoire since the century it was made.

Beautiful.

The syllables are an aria in my mind, exquisite and unending.

He's so heart-stoppingly beautiful.

Thick, chestnut-colored hair tumbles around his bold but elegant face, some of it covering an inch-long scar over his left eye. But most of the mane is secured at his nape with a crafted leather thong. He's wearing a fitted brocade vest over a white linen shirt that has ties and ruffles instead of seams and buttons. His V-shaped torso and long, braced legs are as commanding as his linebacker-wide shoulders.

Wow.

No wonder I keep questioning the reality of all this.

Because with this reality, who the hell needs fantasy?

And isn't that the perfect tagline of the hour?

I even wonder if it was part of his agency's marketing materials. Drue and Raegan must have had a blast choosing this guy as my naughty birthday gift. I wouldn't think there'd be many male dancers around these parts, but I'm not asking questions or complaining. He makes Christophe look like a five or six to his solid ten on the Gods of Loire scale.

"Mon Dieu. Mon Dieu, c'est un miracle."

And holy *crap* . . . his *voice.*

If possible, his husk is sexier than its physical container. It's liquid velvet infused with the strength of the earth. It harmonizes perfectly with the soft song in my head.

Happy birthday to me . . .

Happy birthday to me . . .

"Okay." I smile to let him know screaming isn't on my immediate agenda. "I'll go with miracle if that's your jam, gorgeous."

When he tucks his eyebrows together, I notice other awesome things about his face. A couple of rugged nicks, besides the larger gouge, in his forehead. The luxurious length of his lashes. The stunning imbalance of his mouth, with the lower lip bigger than the top.

I wonder what his story is. He's probably some local kid working the family vineyard during the day and taking gigs like this for some extra cash at night. Who am I to fault him? Rough times call for strange measures.

Finally, he murmurs, "You . . . are British."

"Close." I play with his shirt ruffles, just to sneak my fingers against a little of the chest beneath. Chiseled. Hard. *Beautiful.* There's real power beneath his strength. "I'm American. Your people didn't tell you that?"

"No." He sounds like he's choking as I trail my fingers along his collarbones. "There was little time. My God, that feels magnificent."

He pushes closer, gliding his hands down my sides and over my hips. He caresses me with reverence, as if trying to memorize me.

Wow.

"That's what this is all about, right?" I slip my hands to the back of his neck, giving in to the moment with subtle sways of my hips. "Feeling good?" I jog my head toward the wardrobe. "Getting the hell out of there?" I refrain from asking why he took so long to pop out, since he's clearly been staged for this entrance since we finished dessert. Probably longer. But with that in mind, who am I to call the guy out for catching a catnap?

Now that he's rested, I don't have to worry about wearing him out.

"Hell." Shadows take over his face as he echoes the word. "An apt description." Just as quickly, he violently shakes his head. "But it no longer matters." His eyes are sunrise-gold again. "You are what matters."

Oh, damn. He's good. Did they give him the romance bestsellers' list as training material? It's working. His reverent touch makes me sizzle. His powerful presence brings my libido fully back online. If I'm not careful, I'll let this hunk do more than take off his clothes for me.

He cups my face again. "My miracle. You are real. You are here."

"Errrm... yeah." I'm tempted to leave it at that, especially when he dips his big gorgeous head and leans his brow against mine. But I manage to add, "Here is... definitely... where I'm at."

"I did not believe it." He lowers his long fingers to the sides of my neck. "When she told me it would be so. I did not believe."

"And that's why you stayed in there so long?"

"Too long." He presses his fingertips into my nape. Holy crap, does it feel good. His touch is so warm and strong and earnest. "I should have believed... so much sooner..."

"But you do now." I forced some casual cheer into it. "And I'd really love to get this show on the road. So shall we? Or should I say... shall you?"

I step back, but he catches me by the wrist, yanking me close again. "The road? Where are you going? And in the middle of the night? The moon is still high."

"Oh, my God. You're cute." I stop my giggle when he

doesn't break character, even given that permission. "All right, Marquis de Hunkville, we'll do this your way." I glance back into the wardrobe, despite the tick that goes off in his jaw as I do. "Did you bring music to get your groove on?"

"*Pardon moi?*"

"Where are your hot licks, hot stuff?" I reward myself for the wit by looking him over again. His historical culottes don't leave a lot of his lower physique to my imagination; an accurate-looking eighteenth-century fly conceals a breathtaking crotch and tree-trunk thighs. Handcrafted riding boots are filled by his massive calves. Holy hell, he's well-built. "Maybe you just play the music from your phone?" I venture. "Or maybe you don't dance at all. There's . . . a lot of you, after all."

"My . . . what? Foam?" He huffs. "What does a steed's spittle have to do with playing music? Though I can certainly play a few tunes if you would like some entertainment, my love." He steps back and extends an elbow. "Will you allow me to escort you to the conservatory?"

"I'd prefer to stay here." I mean, there's historically accurate, and then there's calling a client *my love*. Hell to the no. "If you need, I've got some curated lists saved to my laptop. Probably better than trying your mobile anyhow. The connectivity in this place is sketchy at best."

"You . . . are saving *what* atop your lap?"

"Never mind." I laugh again, trying to play off how nice it feels to have him gawking at my midsection. More than that, observing the fresh transition of his gaze. Sunrise to sunset in five seconds flat. "So no music. Good enough. Maybe . . . you'll just let me help, then."

"Help? With wh—" He erupts in a shocked snarl as I slide a finger along his waistband—and then lower. "My *God*. My love, what are you about?"

"Same thing you're about, Hunkville." I twist a couple of his buttons free. His hard flesh swells against my touch. "But knock it off with *my love*, okay? My name is Allie. There's two *Ls* right there to play with, if you want. And if foofy and formal's more your thing, Alessandra works too. So why don't you ponder a bunch of ways to say either of those while we get you naked, yeah?"

CHAPTER TWO

By every saint I know.

She is...

Magnificent.

She is...

Astounding.

She is...

Everything I have ever pleaded God to give me in a woman and never thought I would ever find. And it has taken me but three minutes to learn that. To feel that. To celebrate how she has called me out of my dark purgatory and into her beautiful light. To confirm that certainty across my soul and my mind, despite every astounding thing she does to my body.

My *God*, what she does to my body.

"*Ventrebleu.*" I groan as she opens my breeches with astounding swiftness. The woman's knowledge of masculine tailoring is thorough—and vexing. And what about her bold speech? Has destiny melted me alive only to fuse me with a gorgeous little bawd?

And what of it?

My family is gone. The honor of my name is gone. My world, as I know it, is gone. If the Almighty has seen fit to make me love a harlot for the rest of my days, then so be it.

There is but one hitch to the plan.

The woman has forbidden me from even using the word *love.*

Mayhap...because *she* wants to use it first? Does she already know about Kavia's proviso? If so, she is already aware of what she must proclaim to the world soon enough and wishes for this interlude to be ours alone. She desires to explore our devotion in the most perfect ways possible.

Well then... *oui.*

A thousand times... *oui.*

My cock does not argue with the vow. I am swollen, surging, and ready as she parts the fabric more, exposing more of my groin. But just as I think—and pray—she will free my erection, she works her sweet little fingers up to the closures of my vest. When she finishes, she shoves the garment from my shoulders. She prods me to rip off the shirt too.

Her delighted gasp is my immediate reward. "Holy... shit."

"I am not certain shit can be sanctified, my lo— *Alessandra.*"

She laughs. I savor its husky honesty. "Brilliant point, your marquis-ness."

A long moment passes. I shift as she twitches her lips, gazing upon me like a dessert croissant. Her brazen assessment is unusual but not unpleasant. "Do I...please you?"

The woman snorts. "You're a whole year's worth of Man Candy Mondays, babe."

"I am..." Lost. Literally. Thoroughly.

She lifts her eyebrows, guiding my attention back to her captivating gaze. "You're *très magnifique*, my friend."

"But I do not want to be your friend, Alessandra."

She splays the tips of her fingers across my ribs. "I don't want to be yours either, Hotness."

I watch, entranced, as she glides those fingers down.

Then down . . .

I groan, tight and low, as she dips them into my breeches. As she squeezes my raging flesh. I am stretched, my tip weeping, as she works my engorged length. Dear *God*, Kavia *did* conjure her from someplace dark and wicked and wanton. At the moment, I am beyond caring.

Almost.

"Alessandra." I seize her wrist. "Are you sure? I will not compromise your honor unless you are sure."

She becomes very still—before squeezing my balls again. My whole cock jerks in protest. "Oh wow," she mutters. "Now that's pretty hot."

I grasp the nuance of her tone, discerning *hot* is not open for literal translation. But it is achingly appropriate. It is nearly all I feel. "*Quoi?*" I finally manage to sputter. "Wh-What is your meaning, *mon amoureux*?"

"Your old-fashioned talky-talk." She smiles before pressing the lush bow of her mouth to the center of my chest. "All that honor and chivalry babble."

I grunt. "It is not just . . . babble."

"Even better."

With her free hand, she takes down my breeches. As she strokes my bare backside, I drop my head back. "Heavenly. *God.*"

"Not sure she's here right now. Will I do?"

I laugh. "Perhaps I should start lamenting *my* honor."

"No." She glides her magical mouth to my neck. "Tonight isn't for lamenting. It's for celebrating, remember? Birth.

Genesis. Creation. Mine. Damn, maybe yours too."

Perfect.

How does she know the perfect thing to say at just the right moment?

I seek out the answer by lifting my head. At the same moment, she does the same. Our mouths are now inches from each other. Our stares are pure, primal acknowledgments of one other. "What do you want, Alessandra?" I curl my fingers against her scalp and tug—and revel in how her gaze flares because of it. "What can I give you?" *Anything. Everything.*

She pushes up on her toes, closing the half-breath of space between us. "I want you to kiss me hard and deep—and then help me fuck our honor into oblivion."

ALLIE

As soon as the words are out of me, I'm nervous.

Beyond nervous.

Talk about an escalated encounter. Not more than a half hour ago, I lay here ready to rub one out with nothing but my warrior stud fantasies for company. Now, said Hunk of the Ages—the literal embodiment of my wet dreams—is taking his method acting super seriously. All his antiquated but arousing words. His stunning, convincing nobility. And his stare . . .

Holy crap, his stare.

Though right now, I'm not sure "holy" is a good descriptor for him.

Any of him.

A Lucifer-dark look takes over his face. A growl vibrates through his chest. He pushes the sound into me the second he dips his head and kisses me. His intent needs no interpretation, aided by his hungry groans. I part for him, letting him conquer my tongue with commanding sweeps. I answer with passion that's impossible to explain.

Impossible.

I seriously can't figure it out. This need pushes beyond desire. This heat is more than simple lust. This man really does remind me of a mythical beast brought to life. Every detail about him enforces the impression. The urgency of his energy. The golden fire in his stare. The ferocity of his every move.

He's unreal.

I can't breathe.

I can't deal.

Not that he's giving me a choice. When he's done with our kiss, he keeps staring as if I've turned into the center of the universe. Not just the hub of *his* world. To him, I've seemingly become the nexus of *the* world.

Which, to be honest, is freaking me out a little.

Okay, more than a little.

"Holy … shit." I drag a hand through my hair. My fingers hit tangles, painful reminders of how hard I partied tonight. I silently curse Rae and Drue. They must've been trading giggles over the birthday surprise they paid to have waiting in my wardrobe.

"What is it, *mon cœur*?" He stares harder—if that's possible. "Have I hurt you? Are you ill?"

A laugh spills out. "Oh, Hotness, it takes a much bigger effort to bring *me* down."

"A bigger effort." He tilts his head. "Do you mean like … this?"

I shriek as he seizes me by the waist and body-slams me onto the bed. Oh, wow. So much for thoughts of freaking out.

Allie really digs your marauder angle, Hotness.

So maybe I *can* let go ... for one night. Maybe it's even my duty—to Drue and Raegan, I mean. They've probably paid a small fortune for Marquis de Luscious to do this. Wouldn't it be like flushing their hard-earned money to toss him out on his backside? His *beautiful* backside. Yes, the same glorious glutes he engages while shucking his boots and pants.

It'd be so cruel of me to let their gift go to waste. Or right now, to let him go *anywhere*—

Except for the spot he does settle into.

Between my willing thighs.

"Ohhh ... wow," I greedily murmur. "Errrr ... yeah. Somewhat ... like this. *Exactly* like this."

Remarkably, my answer seems to mellow him. Not a lot. Enough to smooth the hewn edges of his face, even as he first strokes his erection along my clit.

"*Mon Dieu,*" he praises in a gentle growl. "My sweet Alessandra. You are ... sheer heaven."

Reflexively, I gasp. Then horrifically, I giggle.

His thick brows push together. Damn it, even his frowns are sexy. "What is humorous?"

"Oh, damn. I'm so sorry." Long ago, I learned to laugh when shit got too much. When feelings got too intense. But he doesn't need to know that. "I just laugh when things feel good."

A look of pure male arrogance settles over his beautiful features. "Then I must endeavor to make you do it again."

He slides back over my sweet spot, hitting more of the hypersensitive nerves, making me giggle longer and louder— until I notice his cocky composure disappearing in favor of a bewildered stare.

The stare he's directing down *there.*

A blush heats my whole face. "Uhhh...yikes. I guess I owe you another apology, buddy."

"Why?"

He barks the word like my contrition is an insult. I barely hold back from rolling my eyes. "Well, I didn't know I'd be having...company tonight. Not...down there. Is the jungle a deal breaker for you?"

"A...deal breaker?" He frowns while gliding a hand down, sweeping my untrimmed triangle. "But it is not broken."

Now I'm not sure whether to be frustrated or enchanted. As I work my lips together, silently debating the choice, he trails his touch lower.

"It is... *très jolie*." His whole arm bunches, veins standing out against the bulges as he moves his fingers to his cock, adding friction to my tender flesh. "Beautiful, my Alessandra. Every part of you is...beyond the realm of all my erotic fantasies. You are so much more than what I hoped or dreamed for."

His guttural sincerity makes it impossible to control my thick sigh. "Shit. You...are seriously good at the pretty talk, mister."

"Only because it comes from the center of my soul."

Damn. The man has no shortage of this stuff. But why do I keep resisting it? Because I know tonight's going to end with a cash-stuffed envelope? But if that's the case and we're both consenting adults, then why fight the poetry? It's a nice little touch. That and the whole body-of-a-god factor, of course.

And holy shit, his body.

He's sleek and hewn and poised perfectly over me. His jutting cock is slick from rubbing my wetness. His face, as intense as a storm yet ablaze like dawn, is framed by the dark waves that've fallen loose from the leather tie. I reach up, pulling the rest of his hair free. Touching it is better than fingering a bolt of the trendiest new winter fabrics—and everyone knows winter is my favorite fabric season.

He robs every breath from my body. Yeah, even inspiring me to hop on board with his costume-drama lingo.

"You...ermmm...touch my soul too." Swiftly I add, "*Mon cœur.*"

Those two little words, even in my crappy French accent, light up the man's gaze like the Rockefeller Square Christmas Tree. I bite my lower lip, seriously fighting the urge to answer with a laugh.

Except, to my shock, it's *not* a laugh.

I'm suddenly fighting...tears.

The big, embarrassing, spawned-from-the-bottom-of-your-gut kind.

"Thank Christ," he rasps before pressing a kiss into one of my palms. "I knew you felt it too, Alessandra. I *knew* it." He breathes the words into the center of my other hand. "We are destiny. Meant to be. Inked on the pages of fate itself."

Air hitches in my throat. "Jesus," I croak.

"He likely had a say in it too." There's not a hint of sarcasm in the man's voice, which means it should be Allie freak-out time again. But it's not—and now my brain has jumped into the holy-shit pit. "Though I did not believe it at the time," he goes on. "But I should have. By all the blood of all the saints, how I should have. And how I do now. So much..."

He sweeps his mouth down, taking my lips in a tender but deep kiss. Then he plunges even deeper, as if intending to make me feel the words. Not necessary. I've heard. I've *felt*. His pledge, as sincere as a prayer, has accomplished the impossible. Spoken to the soul I'd long surrendered to some permanent mute button.

Well, it's blaring now. In the middle of the most memorable one-night stand of my existence.

No.

Because of all this.

Because of this man.

I'm not even fully naked, but I've never been more exposed. Not like this. Not while *doing* this.

"Shit," I choke out. "*Shit.* Sorry. You didn't take this gig to get naked with a bawling mess."

"But your ... bawling ... is beautiful." He laughs his way over my slang before dropping kisses across my tears. "And your mess is mine. *You* are mine, *ma révélation.*"

Well, that does it. The rice paper sheet of reality I've been clinging to? Shredded. Replaced by the romance novella he's dedicated to selling me tonight. But if he's committing, so am I. All brain cells in. Time for this wild fiction. This crazy, sweet addiction.

"Yes," I whisper—before my world becomes nothing but the plane of this bed, the heat of this man, the strange peace in his passion. "Yes. Yours."

"*Mon cœur,*" he whispers, locking my waist with his hands. "*Ma belle.*" His whole form trembles as the hard, hot head of his sex nudges my folds.

"Oh, my God." My clit trembles, burning with my cream and his pre-come, ensuring my words are equal parts regret and arousal. "God," I stammer again. "That's ... unnnhhh ... so good ..."

Hotness flashes a cocky new grin. *Much* cockier. "Not as good as it *will* be."

"I totally believe you." And I mean it. "But hold that

thought." I reach for my toiletries bag, thanking myself for dropping it on the nightstand earlier. Ten seconds later, I'm pushing a foil square into his hand. "Better late than never, right?"

"Late for … what?"

I grind a layer of enamel off my teeth. "Give me a break, handsome. Method acting is awesome, but so is protection."

"Protection?" He practically barks it, whipping his sights toward the window. "Are we still under attack?"

"Ohhhh, honey." I reach up, tear the packet open, and wrap my hand around his length. His violent groan is a perfect payback for the effort. Feeling his flesh like this, erect and exposed, layers my lust with new anticipation. The impatience intensifies as I consider how his pulsing, hot length is going to feel inside me. Swelling and stretching and fucking me …

"*Ventre … bleu.*" His harsh breaths chop apart the syllables as I roll the rubber over his length. "What is this sorcery?"

His stunned gasp brings on my entranced smile. I drag my big toe down the muscled striations of his torso. "You have to be dressed for the party, Hotness. But now that you are …"

"What?"

I halt the toe. Really scrutinize him. His question rings sincere, but his gaze is that of a ruthless dictator. Crafty bastard. He's really going to make me say it. And holy shit, I'm really going to accommodate him. He's that damn good.

"Come to me, my lord." I raise a hand to his face, my lips trembling despite the sultry confidence of the words they form. "Come and … make love to me."

Suddenly, my nerves are pure heat. My skin is three sizes too small. My pulse sprints as he opens his knees, spreading mine farther. He notches his cockhead against my quivering slit—and I'm positive I've never been so aroused in my life.

"Oh, God!"

"Try again." He pushes away the hem of my tee and digs a merciless hand into my naked hip. "My name is Maximillian. Now say it."

"M-Max...Maximillian." The last letter clings to my tongue for a few seconds. It sounds so right. It feels so perfect. "M-Maximillian! You're making me...so damn wet...and—*ahhh!*"

I break into the cry as he cups my ass. He answers me with a new growl.

"*Sacré mort*," he grates. "You shall be the glorious death of me with that wicked mouth before any part of this hex comes to pass."

For a moment, maybe two, I really try to figure all that out. I finally go for an easier option: writing off his seduction as a product of the moment. "Oh, I'm only getting started."

He smiles against my lips. "So am I, *ma belle femme*. So am I."

CHAPTER THREE

MAX

I pray, with every fiber of my body and mind, that she has readied an adorable snippet to fling back at me. Her odd New World phrases are quite possibly the only reins on my raging lust. Before long, even they will not be enough to deter me. I need to claim her. I mean to have her. In every way I possibly can.

My head falls to one of her succulent breasts. I suckle her perfect nipple through her oddly pliant nightshift. Her answering sigh is like music through my veins.

"*Damn.*" She arches up toward me. "Do it again, Hotness. *Again.*" Her pleas are a sweet mix of supplication and direction as she twists a hand through my hair. She makes me so much harder. Hungrier. Lustier.

"Do what again, *ma belle*? Use those delicious American words of yours. Tell me."

"M-My nipples." She rasps it between heavy breaths. "Put your mouth . . . on my breasts again. Suck my tits, Max. Bite them."

"Mmmmm. As my lady bids." Following a savoring growl, I fulfill her wicked dictate. I deepen the sound as her erect tips stand out like crimson stains against her pure white shift.

"Oh . . . wow." She groans. "H-How are you so good at that

too? Walt. Don't answer that. I'm not sure I want to know."

"But I want you to know." I lift her shift higher. Higher still. I do not stop until her breasts are finally bared to my heated gaze—and worshiping mouth. "I want you to know everything. About all of me."

"G-Great," she blurts, though there is a new stiffness to her tone. Her body is taken over by the same tension. "Th-That's great. But m-maybe we can just stick to something basic right now? Middle names or something? Mine's Sophia."

"George Jean Valence."

"That's your *middle* name?"

"I was given George from my maternal grandfather. Jean was my father's name but has also been in the family since the Holy Crusades, when—"

"Okay, okay. Whoa, baby. I'm sure that's fascinating, but are you cool with tabling the PowerPoint for later?"

I kiss the spot directly over her heart. As the organ within answers with throbbing thunder, I spread my mouth into a new smile. "I believe it is too late to place my power on the table, *mon amoureux*—or anywhere but right here." I form a hand over that special place in her chest while raising my gaze back to her face. "My power belongs to you now, Alessandra. As does the rest of me."

I wait for the words to sink into her. Hopefully, to ease her disquiet. The care of my chivalry must be worth *something*, even if I barely have a worthy name to call my own anymore. But she hardly seems to care about it. So why the continuing furrows along her brow and the persisting strain through her body?

"Well, shit. Now I maybe *should* take notes."

And of course, the strange—but alluring—crudeness of her

words. No; not the words themselves. I am fascinated by how she speaks, not what comes out. Her renouncement of guile. Her embrace of honesty. Even now, when she is obviously insecure, she cares not about tucking her meaning from me. So I do not hide mine from her either.

"I do not understand, *ma belle*."

She averts her gaze. "It's...nothing," she returns. "Honestly..."

But her voice fades as I cup her cheek, tugging her sights back to me. I lean in, set on consuming them. "You are not nothing," I husk out. "So your feelings are not nothing."

She swallows once. Very hard. A new sheen appears in her mesmerizing greens. She lifts her slender fingers and braces my jaw in a mirror move to mine. "How are you even real?" she whispers.

Despite the spike of her scrutiny, I hitch up one side of my mouth. "Perhaps it does not matter."

At this moment, I mean it. If I am not real—if this is all only a chimera to relieve my darkness and I wake up in that endless void again—so be it. I shall change nothing about these moments—especially this one, as I roll my hips to embed my body deeper inside hers.

"Oh." She gasps. "Oh...*Max*. Damn...you're a master at that."

"I am the master of *you*."

"As *I* am the master of *you*?"

"You mean my mistress?" I savor the sting as she captures my lower lip between her demanding teeth.

"Mmmmm. Okay." She trills out a sweet laugh. "That works too."

"Always," I swear to her. "My sweet, saucy mistress."

I seal the vow by ensuring our bodies are fully one. Deeper and deeper I sink, plumbing the illicit recesses of her lush heat. I roam my fingertips down the valley of her chest and across the satin of her belly. I do not halt there. At last, my questing touch arrives atop the triangle of curls pointing to where my swollen flesh surges into her.

"Ohhhh," she exclaims. "That also works. Oh, fuck!"

She seizes my shoulders, scoring my flesh with her fingernails. We moan together. Surge together. Thrust together. Burn together.

"God's . . . balls."

"*His* don't interest me." She angles a leg higher. Digs her heel into the middle of my back. "Just bury yours deeper. *Please*, Max!"

Her breathy desperation is my final undoing. My cock throbs as I thrust harder. Faster. Deeper.

"Yes, Max. *Please!*"

My legs tense. My backside bunches. Bittersweet tension builds in my balls—and torments my mind. "I—I do not want to hurt you."

She drags her fingers across my mouth. Looks me straight in the eyes. "Hurt me, Maximillian."

My chest tightens. My cock swells. "Fuck." I can utter nothing else. Can *think* nothing else. I have been delivered to paradise by this woman. By her sweet, soft curves and her bold, bright sensuality.

And her unabashed, incredible honesty.

"Do it." She slides her hand down, surely leaving more marks with her brutal gouges in my chest. I am beyond caring. I rut into her harder, like the untamed animal I feel. I am overtaken by the urges to claim, to possess, to breed, to fuck, to own.

A sound escapes her. A whimper mixed with a cry. The sound weaves into my lust.

"Give it to me, Alessandra." I enforce the order by slamming a brief but brutal kiss to her lips. "Give it to me now, *mon miracle.* Let me feel that hot burst in every inch of your sweet, succulent cavern."

"Max!" she grates back. "Damn!"

"Do it, my beauty." I bite the curve of her jaw. "I want every sweet drop. Every perfect spasm."

The smacks of our bodies echo off the bedroom walls. I'm buried deep, delivering the pain—and the pleasure—for which she pleaded so prettily. I stare at every inch of her face, memorizing her. The aroused ridges in her forehead. The dark fans of her lashes against her cheeks. The glistening beads of sweat on her neck.

The climaxing cataclysm of her body.

"Oh, my God. Oh, holy shit!"

Her channel convulses around me. Tighter. Tighter still. I hear myself groan as if from a distance. Unsurprising. This dream goddess is ripping the thoughts from my mind, the morality from my soul, the control from my body—

The release from my loins.

"Blessed . . . fuck!" I am bursting. Shattering. Emptying. I am lightning and light, fire and fury, creation and damnation, completely lost but utterly found. I am so far gone with fulfillment, I barely care about my issue being wasted inside the bizarre sheepskin into which she has stuffed my manhood. For now, I cherish only this moment.

The miracle of finding her.

The completion of taking her.

The triumph of surviving the ordeal in that wardrobe,

which seems more viable by the second. Remarkably, I am still here. Still spilling the last of my heat inside her. Still claiming soft kisses from her lips. Still reveling in her heartbeat, thumping against mine. Still basking in the glory of her dewy nudity and her satisfied sighs.

Still forcing my mind to accept that this has happened.

Exactly as Kavia said it would.

Do you want to live, Maximillian? Then listen to me.

In your tomorrows, trust your heart.

She was right.

Every word of it.

Which means . . .

I cannot be careless about the second part of her decree.

One cycle of the moon. Before it is done, she must declare her love for you out loud, before witnesses, or the enchantment is broken.

Then you are broken.

Every part of me tenses. But I push aside the memory as swiftly as it has come.

There is naught to be done about that tonight. Alessandra has already given me the gift of her body, the prize of her passion. Dragging her—and the required witnesses—out to the vicar would be inviting unwanted attention.

There is also my selfish reason.

To extend *this* magic for as long as I can.

This moment, consisting only of her with me. This ineffable midnight. This enchanted forever. My body, tangled with hers. My senses, filled with her. The silver light suspending the air like winter's crystalline kiss.

I refuse to move, convinced that I can trick time by simply not moving. But soon, we are groaning together as my softened cock slips from her.

"Boo." She pushes an entrancing pout into the center of my chest.

"Greedy minx." I rub my lips along her temple. "Do not think yourself too settled there, hmmm?"

"No, *sir.*"

She giggles while lowering a hand to my penis. She starts to peel the covering from it. I stay her action with a growling grab.

"I said not to get too comfortable, woman. I meant it."

"And I believe you." Her adorable smirk fires my blood anew. "For the record, I'm all-in for that plan too—but let's throw away this bad boy and get you a freshie."

"A . . . freshie." I scowl. "You have *more* standing by?"

"As I'm sure you do." She bats at my hip. "But I still like the fact that you're blushing about it."

I grunt again, uncertain what is more troubling—her bald reference to my composure or her poise about removing the sheath herself. I continue the silent debate as she disappears around a corner, muttering something about "being back in a zip."

Instead of stabbing for her meaning, I instruct, "Just leave the skin near the washbasin for the chamber maid, *mon chou.*"

"Oh, ha-ha." The metallic *clonk* that finishes her quip is stranger than her wry tone. "She'd be really excited about that."

"The maid?"

I forget what I was going to add to that when the woman reenters the room. Still propped on my side, I take advantage of the view. The play of moonlight across her enticing hips. The curl of her ebony tresses against her high, full breasts. Best of all, the bright confidence in her stunning eyes.

"*Her* excitement does not interest me, *ma jolie chatte*."

"That so, my lord?" Her remark is witty, as if playing me like a courtesan, but I have doubts about that assessment. I cannot ignore her worldly ways, but nor can I disregard the additional evidence. Her white, straight smile. That pure, pox-free skin. Undoubtedly, she is either validated nobility or a kept woman—but I would have remembered a woman like her when visiting Versailles.

She is a complete mystery.

Which, to my combined delight and dismay, only makes her more alluring.

"So," she quips while sauntering back across the room, "whose excitement *does* matter to you, Marquis de Generosity?"

"Are you truly standing there and pretending innocence about the answer?"

"Pretending is pretty tiring." She tilts her head. "Wouldn't you agree?"

"Very much so." The words are rough on my tongue as her cat eyes work their sorcery on my blood.

"Besides." She slinks back onto the bed. "I can think of more interesting ways to . . . get tired."

My gaze drops to the stiff points of her breasts. From there, to the erotic rolls of her hips. A new growl forms in my chest but becomes a moan as she leans in and fully kisses me. With equal elegance, she pushes me to my back.

Paradise.

I can truly be nowhere else.

"*Merde.*" The word is a strained croak from my throat as she licks me from breastbone to pubic bone. But as she spreads that bliss lower, even basic words fail me.

"Alessandra!"

Except that word.

And, as she sucks my cock all the way into her throat, one more.

"*Fuck.*"

"That sounds like a great plan, my lord." She releases me in order to dart her tongue into the cleft between my balls and stalk. "But not yet. Not now."

"By every blessed saint." My legs shake. I tighten my buttocks. I am awakened. Once more transformed into a beast of rampaging lust. An animal I must give in to . . .

Right. Now.

In a ravenous rush, I reverse our positions. I crush her into the pillows, making her open for my crashing, commanding kiss. I moan, inhaling her every essence. She tastes like wine and cherries. She smells like spices and vanilla. She is an exotic world to me, yet my body craves her like everything familiar and beloved.

"I need to be inside you again, *ma femme*. Now."

She curls a small smile before reaching for her little bag again. From its magical depths, she produces another of the curiously shiny squares painted with a Roman soldier. Again with mesmerizing pluck, she slides the tight sheath over my cock. "I think I can get with that plan too, Hotness."

I add a wolfish smile to hers. It is a good mask for studying her more deeply. There are moments, like this, when I get glimpses into her mystery. To see that the woman may be all saucy smirks on the surface, but there's a challenge beneath her veneer, daring me for acknowledgment—and control.

"Go on," she finally prompts. "*Please*, Max."

"Are you certain?"

"Do you need proof?"

"Perhaps I do."

I fit my shoulders beneath her knees and lean in. She is now tucked in upon herself, angling her bottom half upward. Both of her intimate entrances are exposed for my heated gaze.

"Perhaps I will demand that demonstration by sampling your other sweet orifice."

Her breath catches again. *"Oh."*

"Do you savor that possibility, *mon miracle*?" I push my tip at the rosy ring between her lush buttocks. "Does your cunt drip when thinking of my cock plunging into you back here?"

She dips her head back into the pillows. She latches her hands around my neck, hanging on with brutal need. "Yes," she hisses. "Yes, damn it. Is that what you want to hear?"

I go still. Force my mind to find the answer she deserves, not the wickedness for which she pleads. "Not tonight, my sweet." I slide my cock back into the tunnel where we both know I fit perfectly. "Right now, I need to hear *other* things from you, Alessandra."

She scratches her fingers along my shoulders. "Other things. Such as what?"

"Such as how you love the way we fit. And the way we move. And the way we . . . make love."

Her lips twist. She cocks her head back, openly scrutinizing. "You sure you don't want to reconsider naughty option number one?" She flashes a breathtaking grin. "I mean, I'm game if you—*ohhh . . .*" She falters as I rebury my cock inside her perfect, hot glove. "Oh *hell . . .*"

"It is called making love," I assert. "And I *love* doing it with you, my sweet Alessandra."

Her mouth falls open. Her huge eyes follow suit, drenching

me in their emerald glory. "Then do it," she husks. "Now, Max. Deep. Hard. Yessss!"

I give her the full length of my shaft. The full force of my body.

And the full essence of my heart.

I do not stop until she knows the power of all three. Until they soar her to a star of orgasmic fulfillment.

As her cries vibrate in my ears and her body flutters around mine, I am catapulted to the same heaven. My cock burns brilliant as the sun, filled with white-gold fire from my pounding balls. It erupts, thick and wild. I mark her everywhere with it. I am the power inside her clenching core. The force through her throbbing sex.

As the climax overtakes my body, so does a deeper truth throughout my psyche. And my soul.

Kavia called my quest an enchantment. But now I see past that. I comprehend the term she really should have used.

It is a homecoming.

Alessandra.

It is good to know her name now, though it hardly matters. She could go by Lily Dragbottom and I would still know her. The contentment in her outcries confirms my hope that she feels the same—and will be ready to declare her love before witnesses as soon as the sun rises.

Right now, that simple truth is all I want. All I need.

We have all the time in the world to deal with the silliness of the rest.

CHAPTER FOUR

ALLIE

Time is not my friend this morning.

I groan and trudge across the château's frilly-to-the-point-of-gaudy breakfast room, hoping I don't trip over one of the ten thousand knick-knacky statues in my quest for more coffee from the sideboard. The service staff steps back, knowing better than to interfere in my quest for a caffeine IV drip after three hours of sleep. Raegan and Drue's not-so-little birthday gift is the reason I'm in this state.

Which, despite the coffee deprivation, is actually not such a bad one. Sometimes, sleep really is overrated—especially when a girl has given it up to be pounded into every inch of her chamber's mattress.

When I slipped out of bed this morning, he was sleeping like a dead man. I succumbed to the urge to steal another peek at that magnificent organ between his thighs—but had been proud of myself for letting better sense prevail and sneaking away. It'd been a clean and fair getaway—a perfect chance to stash the man away into the *Perfect One-Nighters* file.

All right, so maybe he's only one of three in the file, but at least I *have* a file. I'm not pathetic; I'm a workaholic. On top of that, I'm weird. On top of *that*, I'm built with curves. Lots of them. Most men don't know what the hell to do with my hips, my boobs, and my sarcasm, let alone the ultimate nail in my sex-appeal coffin. Just a teeny character flaw called *intensity*.

Honestly, the stuff does something strange to men. Yeah, even a few gay ones. I'm the girl nobody can handle. It's much easier and safer for everyone to watch from the friend zone.

So what if my rent-a-hunk from last night could actually deal with me?

So what if he made me do things . . . say things . . . *feel* things . . . no man has ever drawn out of me before?

So what if I let my mental defenses slip?

And I actually considered . . .

What if this guy is serious?

What if this connection is real?

"And what if you need to get the hell over yourself?"

I mumble it while grabbing a gorgeous croissant to go with my industrial-strength java. At the same time, I picture Max already sneaking down the mansion's back stairs, climbing into his Marquis de Sexy coupe, and enjoying the morning mist while laughing about how he shagged the horny American tourist.

All right, then. Fine by me. I can laugh about it too.

As soon as I dislodge the fist from my chest.

"*Bonjour, mes belles amies!*"

So much for the wallowing I planned to indulge before stuffing Max away into a permanent mental lockbox. Raegan's entrance is a center-stage affair, even without her I-Am-Gigi-Hear-Me-Roar singsong. Her sunflower-yellow boyfriend shirt, tucked into red and black cigarette capris and finished by rhinestone-studded flats, is as cute as it is loud.

I flash my amused glance toward Drue, who follows our Tigger from two cautious steps behind. "Well, who needs coffee now?" she drawls.

"Speak for yourself." I wrap a protective hand around my cup. Damn, do the French know how to make coffee that can peel paint. Just the way I like the stuff.

"Suppose I will." Drue settles in opposite me with movements as serene as her tone, which sets off my internal alarms at once. The resident Eeyore of our Hundred Acre Wood trio is usually more dismal than me before her morning caffeine. "Because it sure looks like someone needs it more than I do."

"You really going there? Because you two have only yourselves to blame." I narrow my gaze. "And with *that* out in the open, I'm officially issuing the birthday girl's mandate for a day of rest."

"A day of—" Raegan openly gawks. "No, no, and no. It's time for the castle tour. *Look*. It's on the itinerary." She yanks out her smart pad and jabs a finger at the screen. "Besides, Henri has already ordered the car."

I lift my head and narrow my gaze. "The . . . huh?"

"You heard me," she rejoins. "The limo is already on its way. The off-property attractions are included as part of the package I booked with the De Leons."

"And the *on*-property attractions?"

My snark instantly earns me a pair of confused stares.

"What?" I snip. "Come on, girls. The birthday wench has a right to know. Did Henri and Pasca throw in the Marquis de Multiple Orgasms to the package, or was he an extra amenity?" I take a big gulp from the cup in front of me. "Either way," I croak past the caffeinated motor oil sliding down my throat, "I sure as hell hope the plan for the day calls for several ibuprofen breaks. My head *and* vagina will need them."

The humor doesn't go over quite as I expected.

From Raegan, several wide-eyed blinks.

From Drue, the opposite—a hard crunch of a glower, a slow tilt of her head. "Okay, hold that hem right there," she orders. "Are you saying your kill-me-now look is a post-shag crash and not a creamed-by-the-Crémant hangover?"

I *clank* my cup down. "And are you saying you seriously don't know that answer?"

They fall into silence and then lean in, examining me like a pair of seamstresses actually eyeing the metaphoric hemline. I glare back, fighting to keep my face from heating.

Massive. Fail.

"King. Louis. Wept," Rae finally blurts. "You really *are* post-sex and not post-booze. Oh, my God!"

My blush feels like fire. Not that Drue and her saucy smirk even care. "Daaayyyum, wench. Who was it? *How* was it? Most importantly, is he coming back tonight? And can he bring a friend?"

A shrill laugh escapes as I surge to my feet. I flatten a hand over the space between the bottom of my bra and my belly button, hoping to calm the churning turmoil in that space.

Holy.

Crap.

"Okay," I say slowly, horrific comprehension finally dawning. "You two really didn't hire that guy to come to my room last night?"

Rae plummets into a chair. "Wait. There really *was* a guy? Honestly?"

I hike both brows. "You remember the part where I mentioned multiple orgasms? Mindless, mattress-ripping ones?"

"We drank a lot yesterday. Did you maybe just dream him?"

Drue dabs a finger on the air. "And how come you didn't lead with the 'mattress destruction' part?"

I push to my feet. "Can we get back to the subject here?"

Like how the hell Maximillian What's-His-Face got into my room? And why?

Because if they really didn't hire him, why was he there? And where did he come from?

My questions go abysmally unanswered.

Because they're interrupted by rhythmic booms across the foyer.

At first, my frazzled mind interprets the poundings as thunder. Too late, I realize they're footsteps.

Made by big feet.

Not just any big feet.

My system won't let me deny their source. The fevered sprint of my pulse. The explosions in my nerve endings. The aching pressure at the core of my sex, thrumming through every inch of my pussy...

As Maximillian, the effing prince of the most incredible sex I've ever had, all but marches into the room.

"Unnnh," Raegan mewls.

"Wahoo," Drue mumbles. She was probably going for *whoa*, but I sure as hell can't blame her for the misfire.

As Max swoops his stare toward the high-end tile floor, his hair flies out from its leather tie. The thick chestnut mane catches the light, ensuring every air molecule evacuates my lungs at once. He doesn't stay that way for long. My friends' new groans of appreciation have him snapping back up with spread arms.

"Gypsy witches." The words spill from him on snarls that are almost queries. His tone supports his baffled scrutiny of Drue's blue locks and Rae's sunshine pirate ensemble.

Drue surges to her feet, cocks a hand to her hip, and drawls, "If you say so, gorgeous."

"So. Hot." Raegan flushes and then flusters through a wave. "I—I mean hi. So . . . ummm . . . hi there!"

I take a few steps forward. "Maximillian?"

He stomps forward again. Straight toward me. He sidesteps all the gilded furniture in the room as if he doesn't see it. Or as if he's seen it too many times.

"Ohmigod." The three words combine into one hot rasp on my lips. It tumbles out as he steps closer. His gaze is the color of golden satin. His steps are focused and sure. Every hewn inch of him is visible beneath his historical finery.

He's utterly arrogant.

And totally breathtaking.

"Ummm . . ." It hums out of Raegan, lilting at the end. "Monsieur . . . Maximillian? Can I . . . errr . . . help you?"

"*Merci*, mademoiselle, but no."

He arrives at the edge of my personal space. He pushes all the way into it to cup my shoulders and then haul me in until our bodies are nearly touching. I suck in a huge breath. He still smells like midnight mist and secret sex. His gaze tightens, and his every pore oozes pure sensuality. "But she can."

"Oh?" Drue's tone drips with a smirk. "*Do* tell."

"Shut up," I tell her through tight teeth.

"Oy, Allie bear. I hope you weren't this much of a buzz kill last night."

"Shut *up*."

"Killing is not what this woman was created to do." His

words cling to the expectant air like raindrops on a window. Even Drue is speechless as he wraps a hand to the back of my neck, tugging me closer. "She is the exquisite opposite. She is beauty and nectar and passion. She has brought me back to life."

Raegan groans. "I just swallowed my tongue."

"Clearly that might not be the only swallowing happening around here."

I struggle for the strength to jab a middle finger at Drue. But like last night, my body isn't my own anymore. Not from the second Maximillian touches me. He's like dawn, spreading through a night in which I didn't even know I was living. As he pushes nearer, my core softens. Craving him . . .

Max, clearly reading this, flares his nostrils. "*Mon miracle*," he whispers against my lips before taking them in a torrid kiss. "Why did you leave me?"

For a moment, blissful and surreal, I forget the room exists. I forget *air* exists. Somehow, I'm able to stammer out, "Because . . . I thought we were all done?"

"Done?" He answers my attempt at sarcasm with a rough chuckle. "*Mon destin*, we are just getting started."

"Annnd I just swallowed my tongue again."

"Annnd I might have just joined you." But Drue isn't one to settle for a flirty wave and a dorky smile. "Who. On. Earth. Are. You?"

I angle back from Max a little. "All right, kids. It's true confessions time. For everyone."

Max tugs me back in, molding my torso to his. "You and I have already dispensed of such confessions—and such truths— *ma petite*."

Though my gaze is consumed by the ardent focus of the

man's eyes—and jaw and cheeks and lips and eyebrows—I'm just as conscious of the equally intense glance between my two best friends.

"Confessions? Truths?" Rae quips. "Do I need to keep growing tongues to swallow?"

"No." I push back from Max again, firmer about keeping the space I gain. "You just need a better memory."

Rae shakes her head. "Losing me here again, honey."

Drue raises her hand. "Times two."

"Oh, for crying out loud."

And so much for the extra personal space. Max splays a hand to the back of my head and tucks my face into his shoulder. "I am here, *ma belle*. There is no necessity to air your sobs aloud. Your dignity is safe with me. *You* are safe with me. Always."

Raegan bites her bottom lip. "Okay, yeah. I did need a new tongue."

Drue tilts her head over, making sure I can see her *holy shit* stare. "At the risk of redundancy, where have you come from, Master Maximillian?"

"At the risk of detonating both your brains, remember what I said the first time?" I charge. "About how he was waiting in my room last night? About how I didn't dream him? About how you two arranged for him to be waiting—"

"Full stop on the red carpet." Drue straightens and swoops her hands up like wings. "Cameras off, mics down, ears open— because what *we're* trying to say is that *this* is *not* us."

With every stressed word, she stares at Max with such convincing longing that I actually insert a territorial huff. I repeat the sound as soon as Raegan steps in, adding her own please-let-me-lick-him expression. "Honey, if we could claim credit for your...ermmm...good fortune...we'd absolutely be hopping on that apple cart."

But clearly, the last thing on the woman's mind is an actual apple cart. Drue is equally shameless about sneaking surreptitious glances at the prime produce comprising Maximillian's physique. At the same time, I come to a new realization. I can't even be irritated with them for it. Not really. I make my living describing beautiful things. Sometimes, art just needs to be appreciated. What better excuse to lay claim to the cantaloupes of his biceps?

I just wish the move worked for soothing the remaining tension in my brain. "Okay, so if you two really aren't responsible here, then who—"

The rest of my words are depleted by a sharp gasp. Because of the revelation they bring.

Rae echoes my eruption.

Drue's gasp isn't far behind. "Oh, holy guacamole."

"Guacamole?" Max, who's been silent but intense the last minute, underlines his echo with curiosity. "I am unfamiliar with this saint. Is he newly canonized?"

Rae and Drue pop him with confused stares—making me recognize how normal the costume-drama dialogue has become to me. "Never mind," I say—to him *and* them. "What matters right now is confirming this theory. Because if Dimitri freaking Thorne is responsible here—"

"You'll do what?" Though Rae's sarcasm is blatant, her nod toward Max is delicate. She doesn't need an overture to convey the meaning. Am I really threatening retaliation for the best damn birthday gift I've ever received?

"More exigently, who is Dmitri Freaking Thorne?" Max asks, pronouncing "Freaking" like it's Dimitri's middle name.

"My business manager," I mutter. "A term that should imply a few personal boundaries, right?"

"Unless someone is determined to turn 'all work and no play' into a new extreme sport?"

Clearly, Raegan is still having fun with her sarcasm too—which *is* reprisal worthy. At least to the degree of firming my lips and my stare at them both.

"You groovy gals think I can have a few minutes of one-on-one time with Monsieur Max here?" I ask through tight teeth. "You know . . . to wrap things up properly?"

"Properly?" Raegan hitches a hip to the table. Then doesn't move. "Where's the fun in that?"

"Or maybe we've just got a translation issue." Drue lifts a brow full of naughty intimation. "Maybe 'proper' means something totally different in French."

"And maybe you two could have that debate in another room?" I clench my smile too.

"Of course, sweetness." The dripping honey in Drue's tone matches the wicked enjoyment in her smile. She doesn't relent on either while gently jerking Raegan toward the door. "You want me to kill the lights on our way out?"

Max grunts. "*More* talk of killing?"

Drue grimaces. "Huh?"

"Reenactor," I inject. "He's a method guy."

"Ahhh." She reignites her devilish grin. "Well, he's slaying it."

A longer rumble vibrates from Max. "Your friend is very violent, for a female."

Drue laughs in full. "The *female* accepts that as high flattery."

Max pulls in a breath for a comeback—but the second

Drue hits the lighting dimmer on the wall, the air clutches in his throat. It precedes his wide gawk by just seconds.

I stand and watch his expression for a few stunned moments of my own. Drue's action has doused the glow from both the chandeliers, softening the light in the room. As Max drops his hands along with his jaw, I feel like I'm meeting him all over again. No longer is he my insatiable lover from last night or the smoldering and possessive hunk who came down here to find me a few minutes ago. Right now, he seems eons younger yet centuries older. His eyes are bright with innocence, but his scar, more brutal than I recall from last night, confirms he's lived a bit of life. His stance is still noble, but his gasp is thick with astonishment.

No. With utter awe.

"*Mon Dieu*," he rasps. "Did you see…?" He races to the switch plate, dragging me along with a painful handclasp. "What…beneath all the heavens…" As soon as he imitates Drue's motion in reverse, his stunned stare becomes a bewildered gape. "*Ventrebleu!*"

I smile. I can't help myself. His amazement is infectious. I lift my own regard to the chandeliers. This time, I really notice them. Their crystals are perfectly balanced. The romantic prisms they cast around the room seem to turn back time, transforming the space for my modern, judgmental eyes. Suddenly, I'm not looking at a chaotic memorial of an over-accessorized nobility. I'm beholding a testament to artistry, appreciation, reflection. To the wonder I feel while admiring the same light in Max's eyes. The amazement of watching his lothario-lover act crumble because of something like this.

It's kind of cool.

It's damn sexy.

"They're beautiful."

I'm only half-referring to the lights, but he glares like I've just divulged there's a hellmouth under the table. "Beautiful?" He cranks the dimmer again, taking the room from brilliance into shadows. "It is . . . *light*. Do you see this, *ma belle*? Look at this light!"

"Yeah, yeah." So I'm a little snappy about it. There's a fine line between stopping to smell the flowers—or gaze at the prisms—and pounding the character acting to a tired pulp. "I get it, all right? Wooo. *Electric lights*. You've never seen them before. Gasp!"

"Electric." He repeats the word while making the room look like a bad horror movie with the continuing light fluctuations. "Of course. Electric. If one could harness the power of the skies, they could generate light at will. I have read some papers about this."

He looks back at me with bright medallion eyes and a dopey smile. Well, damn it. How can I stay irritated with this big adorable hunk? Yeah, despite knowing the moves are calculated parts of his role play. Additionally, knowing that this encounter really has to be our goodbye. Neither fact dampens the new rise of my attraction to him.

The huge rise . . .

I don't think beyond that. I can't. Like last night, I kick my inhibitions to the curb and my insecurities into the ether. I use the clasp of our hands to swing Max back around, knocking him against the wall. Before speaking again, I work a little mental math. "You know, Hotness . . . depending on how much you charge for your extras, maybe we can talk about one more bite of dessert before you put me in your rearview."

"Extras? Dessert?" His voice has a tremor, but

he's confident as well. The man may be dedicated to his performance, but he's not stupid. He knows not to fight when a woman slams him against the wall and then plummets to her knees in front of him—like I do now. He also knows how to run his fingers through her hair with enough pressure to make her feel desired, needed, powerful . . .

Exactly like he does now.

"I know time is money and that Dimitri likely paid well for yours last night, but I've been working hard and have been saving up for a special birthday treat." I roll my gaze up his luscious form, making sure he watches as I run my tongue across the seam of my lips. "Could you be that treat, my lord?"

"*Jesu,*" he groans. His massive thighs tense beneath his culottes as I unbutton the flap covering his crotch. "*Ma belle . . .* what . . ."

"Sssshhh." I breathe him in, savoring the scent. There's still a hint of me mixed with his distinct musk. My senses ride the high into a cloud of erotic memories from last night. My sex tightens as I nudge his bulge with my nose. "I want to get my mouth on your cock, Max." I relish the taut buck of his hips. "I want to suck it until you come deep inside my throat."

"Alessandra . . ." He tenses again. The carved bricks of his abdomen take up the view between my face and his. "By every tooth in Christ's head. Please. *No.*"

Huh?

He reaches down, fumbling to cover himself. I struggle to understand despite my haze of sexual need. "No . . . what?"

He slides down the wall, parks his ass in front of me, and hauls me into his lap. "Come here."

"Ermmm . . . I thought that was the goal?"

"An endeavor that would make me the most fortunate

man on earth." His breath is warm in my hair as he presses my ear over his galloping heartbeat. "But we must talk about some things. With our clothes *on.*"

"Oh, my God." As good as his chest feels as a pillow, I push away. When I can maneuver a direct faceoff, I continue, "Max. Seriously. This isn't necessary. Not right now."

"This is very necessary, mademoiselle. And I will have your ear about it at once so that we dally no more time away wandering the paths of passion."

"Dally?" I hate how pathetic I sound, trying to speak past a suddenly tight throat. "Well, sorry about all the damn *dallying* I subjected you to, buddy. And you don't have to worry about wasting any more time with my 'paths,' either. You were sweet to come find me and all, but let's really not do this part, okay?"

This part. Yeah, I know it well. Some kids get chores lists and college advice. The lesson *I* received was the one about it being okay to believe in true love—for the two seconds the shit lasts. Like the sweep of a gown in a fashion week finale, love is the best high in the world—until it's last season's news. That makes this part a pointless exercise. Not worth the ten minutes of trouble. Whether it's said with sweetness or bitterness or anger or affection, goodbye brings the same result.

You're on your own, Allie. So get strong and deal.

But I'm only allowed two seconds in that mental mire before Max embraces my shoulders. "I'll have you for this part, woman," he growls, burning me deeper with his rich golden gaze. "And all the other parts."

I pull in a long breath. "And what the hell does that mean?"

He's ready—more than ready—to reply. But before the man can wrap his firm lips around a single syllable, the door to the foyer creaks back open. Raegan pops her cute face into the aperture. Her bottom lip is tucked beneath her teeth. "Are you two still . . . busy?"

"Christ on a cracker, Rae. It's been ten minutes. Of course they're still busy."

Drue ducks in but falters when eyeing Max's dishevelment. For a second, I indulge a silent preen of feminine pride. I've always wondered what it would feel like to be on the arm of the hottest guy in the room. Never mind that right now, Max is the *only* man in the room. Even at a Hollywood premiere, he'd still be the one turning the most heads.

"Sorry for the intrusion," she mutters.

"Speak for yourself." Raegan steps around, tossing her dazzling strawberry mane. "We have a lot of castle hopping to do today, and daylight's burning. If you two horndogs want to do the medieval mambo in every turret we tour, fine by me, but our wheels are here." She gives Max a onceover. "No time to change, big guy. The Heathcliff cosplay will have to do."

"Wait. Whoa." I lurch to my feet, readjusting my lacy plum V-neck top. "Who said anything about inviting him?"

Drue side-eyes me. "So you don't want to invite him?"

Huge huff. We haven't been at the château a full twenty-four hours, and plot twists are coming faster than underwear changes. Except now, the plot is my life and the twists are scary.

With the biggest twist of all right here in front of me.

Maximillian.

He complicates everything.

He's gorgeous. He's alluring. He's addicting. He's terrifying. He's a completely crazy enigma.

And I have no idea how to make all those impressions play nicely with each other.

"I'm sure he has other plans for the day, okay? He was—I

mean *we* were—just saying goodbye."

"*He* is right here." He rolls to his feet as smoothly as an action star preparing to fight. "He also has no other plans for the day and would be honored to escort *très belles* mademoiselles through our fair valley for the day."

Raegan bobs on the balls of her feet. "Hip, hip—as in hurray!"

The edge of Drue's mouth kicks up. Damn it, the man has charmed even her. "You hear that, Allie Sophie? We're beautiful mademoiselles."

"Damn straight we are." Raegan hooks elbows with Drue and me. "It's settled, then. Our carriage awaits. Let's be off." She guides us into flouncing steps out the door—

Only to halt along with me.

When I realize there are no booming leather bootsteps following us.

I pivot back around. What's the dude's holdup, especially when he was all but sucking the back of my neck a second ago? "You heard the mademoiselle, Sir Hotness. Let's go."

Max's gaze narrows. "You are going out?" he snaps. "Like that?"

"Like what?"

"In your pantaloons?"

I look down. Back up. "My 'pantaloons' are Lemaire. And they're both wearing Valentino." I swing a finger between Raegan and Drue. "Believe me, we're dressed just fine for this rodeo."

He answers with stillness. The unnatural kind, like what a guy reserves for the moments after hearing "I'm pregnant" or "I faked it." Since neither of those is true, I'm left wondering what's wrong—and landing back in a puddle of unnerved.

Trying, yet again, to define the element that can't be defined about the man. The strangeness I've felt ever since he popped out of that wardrobe ...

He sweeps a hand out. The gallant motion dips his shirt enough that one etched pectoral and rugged shoulder are exposed, showing off the flawless man beneath his lost-youth aura.

"Very well then, my lady. Let us depart to this ... ro-de-o." The last word is made of broken syllables, as if he's never spoken the term.

As soon as it's out, Drue and Raegan shoot me pointed glances and mouth out their feedback.

So cute, Rae says.

So hot, Drue says.

More of that feminine glow floods through me, though this time I fight a bizarre ache along with it.

Really bizarre.

I don't want him to leave the château. As if the moment he leaves, his beautiful, half-insane brain will remember he's really not some lost prince from hundreds of years ago.

A spell I'm not certain I want to break anymore.

A Maximillian I don't want to give up.

Which now makes me the insane one, right?

Not. Acceptable. I've got too much to do. Too many goals to reach. Blogs to post, people to impress, dreams to shoot for, magic of my own to make. No golden eyes, fantasy hair, prince-perfect bodies, or achy goodbyes allowed on that grid.

And no insanity either, damn it.

MAX

Insanity is not acceptable.

The thought first set in after I woke alone in bed, tangled in sheets smelling of spun sugar and dark fruits.

Sheets that smelled of Alessandra.

After reaching that recognition, and thanking all the powers of heaven that she *is* real, I dismissed the insanity explanation. I *did* imagine that she had somehow disappeared into the wardrobe with the same terrifying swiftness I had— fears given life by my dozens of theories about exactly what happened after I drowned in Kavia's hexed flames.

Kavia had simply put me to sleep and then convinced the mob I fled the castle.

There was a trap door in the wardrobe, and Kavia told Alessandra how to spring it.

Kavia truly possesses dark powers and had rendered me invisible.

Or Kavia has the knowledge of angels and can conjure love and beauty.

The reality of Alessandra confirms that theory most of all. She is a miracle. I will follow her wherever she goes, even if all she wants is to traverse the roads of the Loire, enjoying the sublime scenery.

Or so my naïve, misguided mind has led me to think—

Until I step out the front door.

And behold all of Kavia's dark enchantments for myself.

My home is still my home—I think.

There are the stables. Over there is the forest. The gardens, the fountain, the drive . . .

But it is all utterly strange to me.

Everything is physically here but also physically impossible. The lines are sharper. The colors brighter. The road is unnaturally smooth. The enhancements are more polished.

Alessandra pulls me toward a long, sleek carriage. The shiny black coach seems less a pleasure transport than a delivery conveyance ...

Or a prison wagon.

I freeze.

Very literally.

The visceral jolt turns my blood to ice, my mind to snow. I am unable to go another step.

"Wow. Nice car." I am warmed—just a little—by Alessandra's confidence. "Looks brand-new, actually."

I cloak another tremor beneath the guise of pulling her close and burying my face in her hair. The action affords a moment to study the coach further. The enameling has a depth beyond anything I have ever seen. But even that is not the most awestriking aspect of the vehicle.

"Where are the horses?"

"The ... horses?" She tilts a mirthful glance up at me. "Errrmmm ... beneath the front hood?"

I stare over at the sloped surface at the front of the carriage. It is embedded with two round glass orbs. They gleam like angel-powered chandeliers, their beams piercing the lingering fog.

"*Ma belle*," I finally chide, "there is not enough room under there for one horse, let alone an entire team."

Her lips quirk. "Come on, you gorgeous dork."

Once she tugs me into the conveyance, I succumb to a new scowl. The coach's exterior had me expecting equal opulence inside. While there are leather cushions and glass windows, even those seem utilitarian. But Alessandra and her friends do not seem put-out by the crudeness, so I keep the opinion private.

The more gregarious of the women, with her bright couture and uncoifed hair, leans forward from the seat across from us. "Soooo, do we finally get an introduction to Sir Sex on a Stick?"

I flinch. Alessandra's friends share her propensity for flagrant speech, though even the other man in the coach, scooting behind a driver's box that defies my imagination with its lights and numbers, does not seem to care.

What is this place?

Alessandra's light laugh stops me from further pondering the question. "All right," she drawls. "Down, Tigger." As she rolls her eyes, her friend giggles. "Maximillian, meet my tribe. This delicious creature is Raegan Tavish, and the goddess rocking the peacock tresses is Miss Drusilla Kidman. But call her Drue if you value your testicles."

"Mademoiselle Raegan." I pull her knuckles beneath my mouth. "And Mademoiselle Drue." Since she offers only a polite nod, I do the same. "It is an honor to make your acquaintance. Thank you for gracing our valley with your beauty."

"Oh, my," Raegan utters.

"Well, hell," Drue drawls.

I chuckle, sensing they have selected different ways of saying the same thing. No matter. Truthfully, I only care about what I read on Alessandra's face. Her tender smile and glowing gaze confirm how right it was to follow my heart to her. The love she clearly bears for these women is a testament to the truth of her spirit and integrity of her heart.

Drue and Raegan shall be ideal witnesses for the moment she pledges that heart to me.

I shall have that moment from her before this day is done. I swear it.

"This is Max," she offers, her voice suffused with new warmth. "Or if you prefer the fancy method-actor version, Maximillian."

Raegan clasps both hands beneath her impish grin. "It's epic to meet you, Maximillian."

"What she said." Drue begins braiding her long cobalt hair. "And is there a last name to go with that too?"

For a long moment, perplexity prevents my answer. They are staying in *my* home. Do they not know my last name?

In that interim, Alessandra interjects, "Oh, let's not wreck an awesome field trip with last names."

"Or blogger babe getting too emotionally attached?" Drue quips.

"Shut it," Alessandra says.

"Fine." Drue sighs heavily while producing an object from her reticule resembling a thin snuff box. The box is painted with enamel matching her hair, though instead of opening the lid, she starts tapping on the box's bottom. "I really just need social media handles, anyway. Out with it, mister."

"Out?" I blurt. "Uh, well . . . yes, of course. The . . . handles. Because they are important, and . . ."

"And this is the twenty-first century. The day and age where I'm not going to let some stranger keep doing the horizontal mambo with my friend without checking him out on every platform I can. You *comprende moi* now, dude?"

CHAPTER FIVE

ALLIE

Yeah, Drue can be a human sledgehammer with her candor—but never have I seen her verbally KO a man like she just has Maximillian, the new Prince of the Stunned Stare. And the Surreal Stillness. And the Pale Skin. Yeah, it's that discernible. Yeah, even through his thick morning stubble.

What about her words has gut-punched him so badly—and why are my nerves so dismantled about it? I don't do shit like this. Dismantling is what I've been through already, at least a thousand times in my life. That's what happens when one has to grow up before her parents do.

"Max?" I prod his shoulder. He barely flinches. "*Max?* Hey. Don't stress. Drue's not going to run you through the FBI database or anything."

Drue huffs. "Not yet."

I ignore her. I already know he is. All of us are still blank space to him. I frown as the weird dagger twists my stomach once more. The blade forged from the same instinct that struck me back at Château De Leon. The instinct that made me yearn to hold him back there.

And to stay there with him.

To have my brash, relentless marquis all to myself . . . for just a little while longer . . .

If I wasn't so close to tears, I'd laugh at that. Me, Allie Fine, broken of believing in romance before my sixteenth birthday, is obsessed with thoughts of being locked in an ivory tower with my own carnal prince.

If only I can get that prince to acknowledge I still exist.

"Max," I plead again. "Come on. Talk to me."

He finally lifts his head. But at once whips his red-rimmed gaze to Drue. "You . . . said . . ."

"That I wouldn't run an FBI background on you?" Drue sighs. "Yeah, yeah. In so many words, yes." She holds up two fingers. "And if you're legit, I won't. Scout's honor."

"No," Max intercedes. "What you said . . . before that. About it being . . ." He clenches his jaw. "The twenty-first century."

"What about it?" I use the chance to lower my hand to his shirt, attempting to close it fully. While seeing this man naked again has become a priority for the day, his exposed emotion stirs a protective streak I usually brandish for Rae or Drue only. Still, the action doesn't seem enough. Max is suddenly, noticeably . . . different. Pulled inside himself. Retreated to somewhere not of this time and place. And yes, I'm sure about that. I'm painfully familiar with the look. God knows how many times I've had to look at it on Mom's face.

And just like all those times I witnessed it on her, my nerves pang. My heart hurts. For him and with him.

"The twenty-first century," he croaks out at last. "By the blood of the saints. *Of course.*"

"Max." So now I'm silently freaking out. With Mom's trips to catatonia, I was always able to shut down and move on, but that feels pitifully impossible here. "What's wrong?"

"Kavia." There's a deep ache in his utterance. "*Kavia.* Did you know this? Did you see all this?"

"Did who see what? Max. Damn it. *Talk to me.*"

A heavy breath rushes from him. He dips his head, fitting his mouth into my palm. "All is well, *ma precieux cœur*. All *will* be well now. I promise."

I can't help a confused scowl. "And it wasn't before?"

"Not completely."

"What the hell does that mean?"

"That I just had to figure out the maze." He widens his lopsided smile. "Why did I expect to clear it when I couldn't even see what it was made of?"

I plant my face into my palm. "*What* are you talking about?"

He laughs. He does it rough and low, like I've leaned over and told a dirty joke. But in a language only he understands.

"The twenty-first century." He repeats it with a weird calm, gliding his finger down the window. "Yes. *Yes.*"

"He catches on fast," Drue quips—to which Max responds by slanting his smirk the other direction.

"Well, fast *is* one of my better traits," he says. "But I also know when slow is better."

Drue and Raegan break into laughter that fills the limo. Their peals are a perfect segue to the pop music station the driver has just cranked on. Though most of the songs don't match what we listen to at home, the three of us bounce to the beats in our seats as Max leans back, his gaze regaining its sexy sparkle.

Holy shit. That sparkle.

This man.

He's going to wreck me.

And I'm going to revel in every damn second of the

disaster.

I sneak him a secret smile of my own, hoping it conveys exactly that. When his takes on a curl of sultry promise, I wonder how much longer I can wait to maul him again. It might be a miracle if I last to our first stop.

Thank God Macklemore comes to my rescue. The first English song of the rotation makes me trade high-fives with my friends. As we sing along about the sunrise and euphoria and feeling glorious, I realize that for the first time in a very long time, they're not just song lyrics to me. Maybe this day can be a chance to start again. To know that I've been born for this moment and to be glad in it.

I sing it, and I believe it.

"We're heeeere!"

Raegan's shriek is perfectly timed to the end of the song. A dramatic French chanteuse takes Macklemore's place. Her achy ballad is ideal as we approach a castle that makes the De Leon estate seem like a crofter's cottage. The white stone structure has so many spires, its roofline resembles a cityscape. The main towers are as huge as grain silos. Trimmed gardens sprawl out from the structure on several sides, as spacious and pristine as Met Gala arrival carpets.

Because of all these factors and more, I can practically predict my friends' initial reactions.

"Paging grand and gaudy," Drue mutters.

"Paging amazing and awesome," Raegan answers.

"Come *on*. Overcompensation much? This was what those medieval dudes had to build to get laid?"

"Medieval *dude*," Raegan corrects. "His name was Francois the First, and he first commissioned Château de Chambord as his hunting lodge."

"Hunting what? Five-headed dragons and orcs who ate

babies?"

"Long-lost ideals." Max's expression changes again, twisting to match his wistful tone. "Francois was the last of the chevalier kings, and much of the castle's construction harkens back to a time when donjons and moats were used for practical chivalric purposes. Despite how he was no longer part of that time, he wanted to preserve a memory of it."

Raegan lifts a quixotic smile. "It's kind of cool that you know that."

Drue narrows a cynical smirk. "It's also kind of a bummer that those walls aren't dripping with the aftermath of bloody battles anymore."

Rae groans. I join her. "Max is right," I remark. "You have an impressive morbid streak."

Drue shrugs. "I blame moody France and all its ghosts."

"They do say parts of Chambord are haunted," Raegan interjects. "Ohhh!" She leans over and nudges Max. "Do *you* know where all the Chambord ghoulies hang out, Max?" As she straightens, she breaks out in rapid little claps. "Wouldn't it be epic if we saw a hunky prince or two?"

Max only answers with a dark growl. My own throat tightens, as I admit to a strange surge of empathy with the man.

What is going on with him?

No time for exploring that answer. As soon as the driver stops the limo in the visitor drop-off area, Raegan urges us out of the car. Her energy does nothing for mellowing Max out. Reading him is as impossible as nailing Wi-Fi in an electrical storm. His gaze gives me no further clues. A few times we pause and wait as he stops, taking everything in as if beholding it for the first time.

During one of those moments, I succumb to more of the

protectiveness that's becoming second nature regarding him. I'm still not sure if that's a good or bad thing. How can one man be like a nine-year-old *and* a ninety-year-old at once? But that's totally the case. I'm torn between yearning to shelter him and jump him at the same damn time.

I'm so confused . . .

And scared as hell.

Why didn't I just close things out with him when I had the chance?

Why didn't I know my bafflement—and fear—would just worsen if we spent more time together?

Why didn't I anticipate it would get worse in moments like these, as he slips his elegant fingers around mine? As he turns and angles his magnificent upper body down toward me?

"Hey." I use the moment of privacy we're given, courtesy of his tumbling hair. "You okay, mister?"

His eyes warm, giving away his pleasure at my concern. "*Oui, ma cœur.* This all merely requires some . . . adjusting."

"All of this?" I glance around, taking in the crowd's colors, textures, and ethnicities. "But aren't you from around here? You must be used to the chaos here by now."

"I have been away for a while."

"Like a few hundred years?"

I add a smirk to the tease.

He doesn't bite.

Not even a little.

"Hey. It was a joke, okay?" That's when horror punches me in the gut. "Oh, my God. *Ghosts.* Are you—does your family have history here, Max?"

"No." He pulls away, almost too fast. "Not directly. The place was empty for many years, so I—" He cuts himself off while gazing back up at Chambord's imposing white structure. "I...uhhh...hear that the children of my ancestors used to come and play here." He shakes his head, once more seeming to lapse into a daydream. "They would pretend they were warriors, tasked with protecting the keep from the monsters in the forests."

"Even the ones who ate orcs and babies?"

"Especially those." To my relief, he finishes it with a soft laugh. As he pulls me back against him, the gravel crunches beneath us. And just like that, all the modern conveniences around us are a blur, fading to a vision of what he'd look like if the surroundings matched his garb. The man would be just as hot during the times of Robespierre and Bonaparte as he is here and now. Perhaps hotter.

"Come on." I step back and tug on him, determined to end the weird moment with a return to tacky tourist mode. "We need to catch up. I'm sure Raegan has us prescheduled for a tour or ten."

"A...*tour*?" Max looks like I'm proposing a blow job in one of the *boudoirs* within. I have to admit, the idea is more appealing than the rote castle guide experience. But Rae's been especially excited about this château, having snagged us passes to the sole English-language tour of the day.

As we enter and approach Chambord's iconic double spiral staircase, Raegan and Drue wave from their spot at the edges of a bigger group. Everyone in the throng would stand out as Brits and Americans even without the stick-mounted sign saying *Visite en Anglais*. The placard is wielded by an Audrey Hepburn lookalike who'd obviously be happier corralling a group of two-year-olds.

"Bienvenue, ladies and gentlemen," the guide greets in a

clipped monotone. "Welcome to Château Chambord. We shall begin the English-speaking tour in a few moments, *oui*?"

Rae claps quietly. "This is going to be epic!"

As she and Drue shuffle forward with the crowd, I stop Maximillian by digging fingers into his elbow. "Hey. We don't have to do this rigmarole, okay? Not if you don't want to."

"Rig-ma-role." He tries out each syllable on their own, his strong lips twisting into their sexiest angles, before letting out a gruff laugh. "Rigmarole?"

"It means we're going to tromp through a bunch of boring rooms and stand behind some velvet ropes." I wrap my hands around his forearms. "And even if it's been a while for you, the history spiels are probably going to be the same."

"The … spiels?" He states the words with the same curious care he gave rigmarole. I don't mind. Not everyone on the planet walks around with the latest vernacular flowing from their phone.

"I just think it might be more fun if you and I just … go on a tour … of our—Max?"

My seduction falls prey to puzzlement as his gaze darkens and narrows.

"*Max?*"

I shout it as he makes a beeline into the next room.

As soon as I follow him in, my blood is consumed by a weird chill. The shivers can't be wholly blamed on the graveyard temperature of the portrait hall, but the dank air isn't helping. And it's not just permeating my skin. Something about the vibe is invading my spirit too.

I take a long look around. The massive space has stone floors and stark walls. On those walls are old paintings ranging from baroque to neoclassic. I join Max in gazing at them. At once, I'm astounded by the glorious silks, satins, and brocades from past eras—but am freaked by the trends into which they were fashioned.

When Max stops and peers harder at a portrait of a perfect eighteenth-century noblewoman, with a wig to make hairspray companies giddy and a waistline that isn't humanly possible, I loop a hand beneath his elbow and press my cheek to his bicep. It's like cuddling with a bowling ball but in all the good ways. I enjoy the sensation nearly as much as the new connection to him—a mental proximity that's as satisfying as the physical part we've already gotten so right.

"I cannot . . . believe it."

"Right?" I murmur. "There's going for a great look, and then there's just stupid. I wonder how many birds were sacrificed for the feathers on top of that hair tower. You think the guide might know?" At once, I whip out my phone, turn off the flash, and snap a few shots.

He snorts, but the sound isn't infused with the mirth I expected. Instead, he rolls the levels of his jaw against each other before muttering, "I am quite certain she did not care."

"You think?" I peer a little closer at the painting. "Hmmm. I wonder if the divas of yesteryear would actually get along with the fashionistas of tod—and oh, holy crap."

As soon as the inspiration hits, I swipe to one of my favorite screens for notes: Future Blogging Goodness. At once, I form a new sub-tab. Just as feverishly, I type in the ideas that keep coming.

- *Time After Time: Fashion Forward or the Same Game?*
- *Let Them Eat Gluten-Free Cake*
- *A High Heel by Any Other Century*

- *What Does a Girl Wear to a Beheading?*

- *Do Panniers Require Panties?*

"I'm a freaking genius," I mutter. "What do you think of these, Max? I'm a genius, right?"

But there's nothing but silence from him. The soup-thick, semi-scary kind. He's lost to the same eerie energy he's displayed since walking in here. But the interwebs don't call me the queen of persistent humor for nothing—and I'm not giving up on Hotness's mood. Not yet.

"So tell me . . . you think she actually did the whole rib removal thing too?"

Well, that sure as hell gets his attention. To the point that he slices me with such a hard stare, the scar over his eye looks like a vein. "The *what* thing?"

I squeeze his arm, indicating I'm kidding. It's also nice to have an excuse to paw him. "Relax, Hot Stuff. It's mostly urban myth, you know." But it occurs to me that maybe he doesn't. "They say that certain women of privilege had their bottom ribs removed in order to have tinier waists. Of course, that buzz wasn't widely spread until the nineteenth century, and this portrait looks more like it's from the eighteenth—"

"Yet that befits Lettie like silk around a stone."

"It befits her? Lettie?" I struggle to make my expression more baffled than jealous as I dart a glance between him and the portrait. Because I have every right to that mix of reaction . . . why? Because he's referred to the woman in the portrait, one Vicomtesse Violetta Caron, born 1775 and died 1793, by a casual nickname? Because I actually feel the vehemence beneath his words like a whoosh of heat from an opened furnace?

Damn it. This is seriously messed up. I should be running as fast as I can while the man glares even harder at his friend Lettie. As he flares his nostrils, pulls in harsher breaths, and twists a hand around one of the ropes until his knuckles are taut and white.

Running.

Now.

But my heart and spirit order me otherwise. Loudly.

"Max? *Max*." I grip him tighter. He stays as immobile as one of the ornate suits of armor flanking the doorway. "Hey. You okay?"

He doesn't answer. But he doesn't have to. I already see the tension plowing across his forehead, tightening the corners of his eyes. I already feel it in the tautening muscles beneath my touch. I have no idea what to do. What to say.

"Max."

I try again anyway.

"Is this a trigger or something? Do...do you—" But I clench the words into silence. They make no sense.

Do you know this woman?

I need to get a huge grip. And stop entertaining ideas that are more stupid than surgical rib removal for an ideal dress fit.

As I wage that inner war, Drue moves over and bounces a probing stare between Max and me. "What's going on? Why do you both look like Satan's suddenly ripping out your spleens?"

"I—I don't know," I whisper.

She jumps her brows. "What the hell is up with him and the paintings?"

I barely hear her—though every word she speaks is like a scream.

Because she's right.

Max has wandered—okay, stumbled—over to the next portrait on the wall. The painting triggers equal tension up and down his tall form. That means I'm throttled by the same reaction from my own senses. The feeling that he's peering at somebody he actually knows ...

This is crazy.

Beyond insane.

I shake my head. Desperately fight to clear it of this chaos.

"M-Maybe it's all tied into his reenacting thing." I don't sound convinced, but I'm a big fan of fake-it-till-you-make-it. "I said he was really a method guy, right?"

"Is he going to melt down?" Drue doesn't buy my explanation either. Not one bit. "Shit. We didn't check the cutlery at the breakfast table, did we?"

"The cutlery?" I snap around to face her. "Hold on. You *are* worried about the bats in his belfry, aren't you? Like, really and truly?"

"And you didn't believe me until now?"

"Which means?"

"Honey, the dude's got bats, all right. As long as they stay cute and funny, we're good. But if his shit starts going goth rock video or—"

She's prevented from taking that any further by the tour guide's new spiel. "Chambord is the largest castle in the Loire Valley and one of the most famous in the world. It has four hundred twenty-six rooms, two hundred eighty-two fireplaces, and over eighty staircases, including the famous double spiral staircase, rumored to be designed by Leonardo Da Vinci. Remarkably, the longest the château was ever occupied was a period of twelve years, though it had its fair share of regal guests and visitors. You see many of them in the paintings along these walls. Sadly, Chambord's golden era ended with the French Revolution, during which the castle was stripped of its furniture, artwork, and flooring. Though you shall see many recreated chambers on our tour, the glory that was Chambord will never be as it was when these nobles roamed its halls and gardens..."

The girl keeps droning, as engaged as a fifth grader giving a book report. But I'm not listening from the second Max bolts the opposite direction, pushing back through the crowd.

"Shit." I match his urgency to escape. I need to get to him. Need him to know that no matter how freakish his behavior, I know the emotions beneath it are real. The aloneness. The sensation that nobody in the world gets the weirdness—and the need to flee it as fast as possible.

"What the hell is going on?" Raegan charges. In her book, skipping out on a guided tour is on par with a hit-and-run. "Allie? Where's Max—"

"I'll handle it." Because my heart will allow me no other choice.

"That's not an answer."

"I'll *handle* it." I regret the snip. Sort of. Raegan planned our day with a lot of love and care. But she's also the one who insisted on inviting Max, and this is the fallout. "You two go ahead. I'll figure this out. We'll catch up. It won't take long."

I don't stick around to make sure they're okay with the call. I only know what my gut is telling me. That this is about way more than simply bats in Max's belfry—and that whatever caused his stress back in the portrait gallery, it was visceral. And real. And I hope he won't continue to bury it.

While I'm not exactly into kumbaya circles and sharing-is-caring time, I'm sure that beneath the man's sinfully hot exterior and carnal sexual skills, there's a core of bewildering but captivating purity.

I all but throw people aside so I don't lose the hunk in the crowd.

But that's exactly what happens.

I burst back out in the foyer, combing the masses, but I see no familiar head of thick hair or shoulders that could toss a caber like a matchstick.

Damn it.

After a minute of the desperate search, I slump against the wall and finally face the truth. My one-night fling with the sexiest but oddest man I've ever met might truly be over. Whoever he really is and whatever he was really up to, my marquis of mystery wants to remain that way.

A squeal slices the air from somewhere above. The sound is high-pitched, happy, and female—the kind of shriek a woman would have from running into a six-foot-plus, hotter-than-hell male dressed like a reincarnated lord of the realm.

Pure intuition guides me to sprint up the circular stairway. Halfway up, I'm seized by a violent instinct to retreat. Doesn't this epitomize every lame, half-whacked chase that Mom gave to her string of pitiful princes after Dad? Isn't it stupid to go after a guy who doesn't have all his mental nuts, just because of what his *other* nuts did for me last night? By following him, aren't I kicking fate in the crotch?

But I climb every damn step.

Following him.

At the third-floor landing, I hear another happy shriek.

There are a couple of girls standing there, dressed in bedazzled T-shirts, colorfully printed leggings, and bright-pink Chucks. They've got to be the sources of the squeals from a minute ago. I fake interest in the balustrade as they continue their animated conversation.

"What the hell was that?" the first one poses.

The second girl, a tiny blonde with fishtail braids, pops her gum. "Don't you mean *who* the hell? But I didn't see a name badge anywhere."

"Doesn't matter," volleys the first, clicking her nails. "He's still got to work here. That historical cosplay stuff isn't, like, normal everyday attire around here, right?"

"Don't think so." Another gum snap. "And he went into that restricted area like he owns the place."

"Should we wait around and see if he comes back out?"

"Ew. Stalker."

"Yeah, you're right . . ."

Their chattering fades as they hurry away, wanting to get the jump on the crowds for the craft fair being set up in the garden. As soon as they're gone, I hurry toward a sign across the landing that reads *Limité* in bold letters. I swear the universe's neon translation of it goes something like *He Went This Way, Allie.*

The certainty slams me. But as I approach the sign and the dark hallway beyond it, that conviction is joined by another.

Buh-bye-Maxie isn't going to cut it. Not for me. Not this time, with this guy. Not before I can at least tell him—

What?

That last night might have been more than just a roleplaying shag for me? That in those God-awful moments of mush we exchanged, a bunch of my cynical emotional boxes popped their lids? That it had felt good—so damn good—to toss aside the stress about what I said, how wittily I said it, and what sound bites could be pulled from it, for a few beautiful hours? To forget about how many followers I've gained, deadlines I've met, and people I've pleased? To be simply pleasured, worshiped, adored for everything I already *am*?

But I don't really have to say any of that, right? I can just make sure he's okay. Just be a good person. Just heed the strange voice that keeps calling me to care for that exposed wound in him. Making sure he gets first aid doesn't mean I have to stay for his whole rehab, right?

"Right," I mumble as the passageway narrows, twists, and then ends at a scuffed wooden door with a wrought-iron handle. "You're just being a decent human being, Allie. You should be proud of yourself. That's all this is. You're just checking up on a friend who's having a bad day." I lay my fingertips across the top of the handle and ignore the fact that they're quivering a little. "A friend who's escaped behind a weird dark door in a creepy, moldy tower . . ."

I shove determinedly at the door. The hinges let out a long creak that echoes off the stark stone walls.

"Max?"

Silence.

I close the door behind me but find myself alone in a small storage closet. What the hell?

"Max? Are you in here?"

His harsh exhalation knifes the air. I can feel him in here, his presence a welcome weight across all my senses, but all I can see are brooms and mops and old-world wooden shelves stocked with New World cleaning stuff. The high slit windows are hardly any help, their streams so bright that more shadows seem to be created than illuminated.

"*Alessandra.*"

My next step is practically mandated by the desolation in

his voice. "Where are you?"

"Go away," he orders.

"The hell I will."

"Dear *Jesu.*" Back to his misery, his grate rougher than the whole box of scouring pads at my eye level. "Damn it, woman. Just go away."

"Screw you," I retort. "Just tell me where you . . ."

The words fall away as my attention latches on a vertical divide in one of the shelves. Not such a strange thing—except that the shelf below *and* the shelf above have the same gap, in the same location. In the stone floor, there's a gap between the supply boxes—and it corresponds to the same divide. It's as if someone's recently pushed back all of that shit and then walked straight through the wall at the back of the storage closet.

Like I do right now. But the action makes my toe collide with a tiny pedal embedded in the back wall. I depress the lever, and a new squeak of hinges marauds the tower—from the fastenings of a hidden panel in the closet's wall.

I push harder on the portal.

It gives. I gasp.

"Holy. Shit."

There's a secret passage beyond the hidden door.

With my inner Nancy Drew on apeshit overdrive, I step onto the bottom landing of a bell tower about five feet square on all sides. I gaze up—to the narrow, winding stairway that leads to the top. I have to squeeze around to the tower's other side in order to access the stairs, their bottom aligning with the more obvious entrance to the space. Clearly not a lot of people know about the trap door through which I've just sneaked.

Following a man whom I hope is still sane. And safe.

There's only one way to find out for certain.

I have to follow my heart.

CHAPTER SIX

MAX

I hear the woman's impatient huffs as she ascends the bell tower. She is now just a few feet away, ready to emerge onto the small landing with me.

I'm stupefied by her tenacity—until I recognize my own idiocy. Did I expect she would give up looking for me now, when I survived centuries to get to her?

Centuries.

Once more, the concept of it—the reality of it—bursts my mind apart like a gust through summer dust.

Is it truly possible? The scholar in me fights the idea, but that same logic confirms its viability. I think about all the wonders that came to pass in the short decades I was first on this earth. All those inventions and ideas would seem fantastical to even my closest ancestors. Hot-air balloons. Circular saws. Bifocal eyeglasses. Threshing machines. Iron bridges.

And iron killing machines.

Such as the newest, demonstrated the last time I was at court, by that Dr. Guillotine . . .

As I clutch at the base of my throat, a shuddering sough escapes from it. And then a name, drenched in pure gratitude.

"Kavia."

I repeat it, this time as an apology.

"I doubted you," I rasp. "I even attempted to fight you."

I remember everything—*everything*—as if that moment were two days ago. The bloodthirsty mob. My throat-clutching fear. Kavia and Carl arguing in the hall. Her revelation of my birthright and his calling out the woman as a witch. I was ready to give up then. To simply surrender to the horde. If they were ready to take my life, at least I knew where my eternal soul would go.

But Kavia wouldn't relent.

She knew of bigger things.

She knew.

But had she known . . . of all *this*?

Had she known her sorcery possessed the power to suspend the very fabric of my life—my body, my mind, my soul, my consciousness—for over two hundred years? Because of what? The force of . . . true love?

I clutch the back of my neck. Grip myself with punishing force. "True love," I mutter—but finish with a caustic grunt. Am I truly expected to believe *that* is my salvation? To think Alessandra will?

You easily believed it all last night. You were confident of that poetry when it came time to get your cock inside her, oui? It was not any trouble to believe in that magic when the situation suited you most.

And where did all that wizardry finally get me?

I am still racing for my life.

Chasing time itself.

In a world I know nothing about.

Depending on a woman who likely thinks my mind is barely my own. And would she be wrong, after my insane flight from the gallery?

A room that, the last time I was in it, was lined with opulence and filled with chamber music . . .

Gone now.

Everything I know . . . is gone.

Lost to the mists of history.

I have as little control over this reality as the bizarrely colored bird I watch defy the wind with its giant *thwopping* wings. The creature grows louder as it flies closer. It suspends midair, hovering over the land, its wings spinning so fast. Their sound is deafening.

Only as it rises and departs do I see the colorful creature is not a bird but a flying machine. My jaw slackens. I gape as the apparatus roars overhead. I am awed, afraid, and anxious. Will this be my state of mind for the rest of my time here? The rest of my living days?

The rest of my life.

Which is now . . . how long?

How many days remain for me to savor this existence, whatever it will be like at this point, in this time? If men are now creating flying contraptions like that, have they learned how to alter the cycles of the moon as well? If so, how long do I truly have left? A month? A week? An hour?

It does not matter.

Because it will not be enough.

I will not be able to simply sit Alessandra down, recount what happened with the mob and the wardrobe and Kavia's spell, and expect her to believe a word. As for her supplying what I need to fulfill the hex and ensure my survival . . .

Her own heart?

Never.

She belongs to *this* time. An era in which mortals do

not have to wait on God for miracles. Men—and apparently, women—have already seized them. Humans now exist in a dazzling whirl of light, color, speed, and motion—all of it self-made.

In a world pulsed by all this power, where does the power of *love* belong?

Or can it belong at all?

My soul does not like what my head returns as an answer.

As if fate needs to pound that defeat into me, Alessandra appears at the top of the stairs. She joins me on the platform beneath the tower's domed cap. At once, the wind whips the hair back from her face. Her frown, centered by those stunning cat eyes, matches how she looked last night after freeing me from the wardrobe. It is a look of both irritation and fascination, though she acquiesces to neither.

So gorgeously stubborn. So decidedly pragmatic. I know both of these traits about her already but not why they are there. She is a woman of stunning inner strength, and I sense it is because of great personal trials. But what kind?

I yearn to know that—and so much more. Things are so different in this time, yet I have already seen sad similarities to the past. There are so many new marvels and modern machines, yet the people still seem filled with fear, frustration, worry, and misgiving.

All the elements that define Alessandra's steps toward me. "Hey."

"Hello." I abhor my moody mutter but selfishly hope it brings out more of her breathy but determined tone. Even now, as I struggle to accept my days with her are likely limited, she soothes my rioting senses but fires my lusting blood.

And always, *always*, fills my world with her illumination.

Especially as she plants both elbows atop the high stone ledge and then pops up on tiptoe to peer over. "Okay, wow to the tenth," she declares. "Look at this view!"

"I prefer mine better."

She sneaks a glance over to see I am captivated only with the curves of her profile. As I expect, a cynical laugh twists her lips. As I do not expect, a rosy blush sneaks over her cheeks. "You should be smacked for using one of the most tired lines in the book, mister."

I grin. Her vernacular is not difficult to sift through. "But you are not tired."

The blush intensifies. "No."

"And you have not smacked me."

"No." A gentle laugh this time. She tilts her head, causing sable tendrils to whip back across her face. Her gaze is lush velvet green in the lingering morning mist. "Maybe I'm feeling merciful, since your own mind isn't cutting you any breaks."

Her meaning is tougher to digest this time. "My mind is not your concern, *ma chérie*."

"What if I want it to be?" When I issue naught but a measured breath in response, she loops her hand beneath my elbow. "You going to spill with the deets, buster, or do I really have to crack open your skull and pry it all out?"

I step back and raise my eyebrows. "Has this century made *every* woman bloodthirsty?"

"You got other centuries in your pocket to compare it to?" She bumps her hip to mine, underlining the jest. "Was that how you knew about that trap door in the closet? And this incredible view?"

As she speaks, minstrels start to play on the lawn below. The vendors for the artisan faire greet one another. A new breeze fills the air, replacing the morning's damp with the scents of fresh grass and newly baked pastries. For one moment, a perfect suspension in time, I close my eyes ... and am in a different France. A peaceful era. Two hundred years ago.

Nearly my yesterday.

"I have been up here before." The confession tells her everything and nothing. I am content with that. "To think."

Strangely, I am not stunned when she throws her head back and laughs. "To *think*, huh?"

"You find it surprising that I think?"

"I find it surprising that you think up *here*."

"Why?" My curiosity is sincere.

"Oh, come on." She sweeps a hand around. "This isn't a place meant for thinking."

Now I get the chance to laugh. "Then what is it a place for?" I turn but at once acknowledge the miracle—and mistake—of the action. With my body fitted more intimately to hers, the erotic implications of her gaze are not so simple to chuckle away as mischief.

Alessandra intensifies the impression with a defined shift forward. Her lips purse. Her breathing quickens. She is, even in her modern pantaloons and unbound hair, the epitome of feminine perfection. A stunning, sensual contrast with the pastoral scene below.

"It's a place for ... escape." She pushes in tighter, stealing my breath with her opulent curves, her decadent gaze, her spice-and-fruit scent. She intoxicates me. Captivates me. Utterly and wholly beguiles me. Is it any wonder that she was the force that pulled me through time? Is it also any wonder that I care not if witchcraft made it happen?

"An escape." My repetition is a taut croak, but I care not. "From . . . what?"

"Not *from*." Her emphasis is also throaty. "It's an escape *into*."

I swallow hard. She captures the motion beneath her nipping lips, trailing them up the column of my neck. "An escape into . . . what?"

"Into freedom." She suckles the underside of my jaw. "Into fire." Adds a pair of defined kisses. "Into exposure."

I am a mass of awakening and thrills, of wanting and waiting, of freedom and fire. "Ex . . . posure," I repeat, though can hardly hear myself. The carnal hum in my senses is like a thousand singing cicadas.

"Do you want me to expose you, Maximillian? And let you expose me too?"

Good Christ. How she knows exactly what to say to me. Where to ignite me. And precisely how to look at me after she does. Desire is a conflagration in her eyes. Lust is a rosy sheen on her pursed lips.

My blood roars. My cock jerks. I kick up one side of my mouth. When Alessandra emulates the look, I thank every saint I can remember.

She knows what I am going to do to her.

And how I follow through, seizing her close and smashing my mouth to hers.

Hard.

Deeply.

Thoroughly.

To the point that she grips me desperately. Surrenders her melting body to me. And then groans with beautiful abandon as I stab my tongue even farther. She widens her mouth for me—the only invitation I need to make my invasion ruthless. I crush her lips without softness, needing to fuse her to me. To get inside every inch of her fascinating, captivating beauty.

She pants as I greedily stroke her beguiling swells. All of them. The fullness of her breasts. The lushness of her waist. The roundness of her hips. Perfection. This woman is sheer luxury and sensuality and perfection . . .

"Max," she breathes.

"*Ma revelation.*"

She returns a sweet, high hum as I grip harder, better aligning her heated core against the ridge of my cock. As strange as this era is, I am supremely thankful for its effortless clothing and thin materials.

"You feel as good as I remember," she whispers into my chest. She hitches her hips, clearly seeking more friction between our bodies.

"*Jesu,*" I finally husk. "Do not stop. *Do not stop.*"

As she obeys the mandate to the last syllable, my blood heats like liquid gold. My thighs lock. My buttocks clench. Air pumps in and out of my nose. I sound like a damn bull while struggling for a semblance of romance with a gentler kiss. Alessandra accepts my tenderness for all of three seconds. On the fourth, she tangles her fingers into my hair and pulls me down for a brutal embrace.

Our lips mash. Our moans mesh. Our mouths battle and bruise each other.

And I am done.

Consumed.

Torched by fires I have not experienced since Kavia first cast her bizarre spell on me. Sending me to my fated gateway. The destiny for which I was ultimately created.

To be with this woman. To take her body and soul to the stars, over and over and over again. With Alessandra, even the illicit seems possible. Yes, even in this high spire. Perhaps especially here, wrapped in wind and embraced by the sky, where the world stretches out as a modern tapestry and giant machines defy gravity...

Where maybe—yes here and yes now—we can dare to make time stand still.

With our connection. Our passion. Our consummation.

Alessandra also believes it is possible. I know it as soon as she cleaves fiercely to me when I pin her against the tower's cold stone ledge.

By sighing in ecstasy when I lock my hands around her wrists.

By sighing sublimely as I pin them to the top of the rampart. Her breath climbs to a groan as I roll my hips, grinding harder between her legs. She grabs at my neck and parts her thighs. My cock is cushioned by the hot evidence of her desire. Even through our clothes, I start to feel every desirous drop that has beaded on her slit. I rejoice in every perfect quiver of her lust.

When our mouths finally break apart, my anticipation grows bestial. The same primal need takes over her features. Her stare is hooded and primal. Her lips are swollen and parted. Her skin is flushed and dewy.

She is exquisite. Incredible.

"I need you," she rasps. "Damn it, Max." She twists open the buttons of my breeches. "I need this beautiful dick inside me."

I suck back a groan, taking her breath in with mine. *Yes.* I will take the very air from her lungs. The beats of her heart. Anything and everything that gives her life, if only to brand myself on them for the few moments fate has allowed me.

Moments may be all I have left.

I rage against the thought with a snarl. She answers with her own savage vibration. I cut it short by plunging my mouth to the base of her throat. She tips her head back, offering more of herself to me. I accept the invitation, sliding my lips toward the cleavage exposed by her pretty plum garment. I push aside its lacy edges, savoring how the fabric stretches across her breast, before reaching in to caress the perfect mound beneath.

She tightens her hold around my pounding stalk. I growl hard with the heavenly way she strokes me. Her fingers are strings of divination, knowing the most sensitive parts of my balls and cock. Or perhaps all of me is like that now, burst open under her touch like a seed brought to life by spring's first warmth. Now I need to grow, to push, to explode with that life.

To give that life to her . . .

But I am dealt a sobering blow—by the most ridiculous of foes. Why, at a moment like this, must I remember a gentleman's code that has not meant anything for hundreds of years? Yet I cannot deny it. My decorum yanks me back. This time, it must.

"Max?" The wind turns her hair into flowing ink strokes on the air. "What the hell?"

"Hell is indeed what this feels like, *ma cœur*." I attempt a steadying breath. "But I cannot, in good conscience, press myself on you like this, and—"

"You mean the same way you pressed on me last night— and rocked my damn world?"

I punch my own brows together. What rocks have to do with this is beyond my understanding but bears not on what I must declare. "Last night . . . was different."

"Uh?" She wastes no time on the retort. "Is that so?"

"Yes." I stiffen more. Her waves of irritation are confusing. Is she angry about me prioritizing her honor? "I was . . . in a different position then." *Such as being freed from a bottomless black cage and having you naked in my arms.* "Though even that should not have happened. I should be properly apologizing for it now but cannot. Every word would be a falsity. I do not regret a moment of it."

"Well, of course you don't." Her words are mild but her expression remains rankled. "Don't worry, my lord. I get it, okay? Last night was a paying gig, and you don't want to set a precedent by giving out freebies." She juts out her chin. Her gaze glints like a tigress in wait. "You tried to tell me that this morning in the dining room, but I wasn't listening. But I hear you now, and I understand."

And that demolishes my proud glower. "You . . . do?" My perplexity nearly chops it into four syllables instead of two.

"Well, sure." The tigress doesn't waver. "You're just being a good businessman. Nobody can fault you for that."

And now, suddenly, I comprehend as well.

With furious force.

Once more, I trap her against the ledge. This time, I am not gentle about breeching the juncture of her thighs. Or ramming my hardness against the cleft where I belong.

"A 'freebie'?" I do not soften a note of the growl—and take an equally stern interest in its impact on her. The flare of her nostrils. The undulation in her neck. The quivers down her body. In response, my body swells and throbs and stiffens. I should be ashamed, but being branded a lothario brings a unique and powerful rage to a man. "Is that your challenge about this, *ma petite*? That you are not paying for this now?"

I bite the corners of her lips with deliberate purpose. "Then have not a care. There is plenty of payment I can demand of you."

New shivers take over her body. I revel in every one of them. "Th-That depends."

I lower my stare. "On what?"

"If I can afford it."

"Oh, you can afford it." I shift over to bite her bottom lip. My voice is husky with arousal. "But do you truly want to pay?"

"You think I can't handle this, Hotness?"

I stroke her cheek with the pad of my thumb. "I think you are stalling, *ma belle.*"

She stuns me, just a little, by grabbing me by the hair again. Fusing our mouths together again. Her tongue finds mine and starts a hot, frenzied dance. For a few moments, I let her take that control. It is good to just succumb to the passionate wonder of her. My maddening minx. My magnificent miracle. The woman who, from the moment we crashed together last night, has always seen the man in me. Not the *noble*man. Not the heir of De Leon. Not the secret dauphin of France. No one but her "Hotness." The lover who can give her anything, *everything*, she has always dreamed and fantasized about.

She has only misjudged one aspect of me so far. An error I plan on correcting right now.

Until there is no doubt left in her mind.

"Oh, my God." She gasps the exclamation as I bend down, yanking her breeches as I go. Their curious fabric allows her legs to stay parted. *Perfect.* I step back over and stand in the opening. *Better than perfect.* She is bared for me now, and my mouth all but waters with the anticipation of seeing her sex in the full light of day.

"Max. Holy shit. What—"

"Lift this." I flick at the hem of her long, knitted shroud. "Lift it and show yourself to me, Alessandra."

She sighs. "Do you know what you do to me when you say my name like—"

"Do it." I enforce it by digging a hand against her waist. "Bare your sweet center to me."

She pouts—but then slowly, sweetly obeys my command. *Completely perfect.*

The trimmed hair on her mound takes on a burgundy tint in the sunlight, reminding me of rich dinner wine. I lower my hand from her waist to brush at the dots of liquid already collecting below.

"Lift your hips. I need to see more."

She complies with barely a sound, though whimpers as soon as I spread her. With excruciating care, I explore her soft, wet layers. *Mon Dieu.* She is texture and color and cushion and heat, opening for me like the heart of a flower.

And at last, I arrive at the pulsing pistol at her center.

It stiffens as soon as I spread back its hood. Beckons me to stroke its quivering length . . .

"Max!"

I stretch a finger down, plunging inside her perfect, tight tunnel. She moans. I cut off the sound by kissing her deeply. When I am finished ravaging her mouth, I slide a second finger into the depths of her sublime, silken pussy.

"Ohhhh!" She trembles, grabbing me around both shoulders. I stab in my fingers with more brutal force. "It . . . it aches. *Please*, Max!"

"Please what, *chérie*?" I close my teeth around her upper lip. She is ambrosia, tasting like desire and wind and woman.

She gasps, pushing her body up at mine.

"You . . . you seriously want me to beg?"

"Hmmm." I kiss my way across her face but use the tip of my tongue to tease at the shell of her ear. "Perhaps I do. Yes, I believe I do."

Her feminine growl is beyond alluring. "Most men wouldn't dare this shit with me, mister."

"Well, I am not like most men, am I?"

"Bite me, Hotness."

"Beg me, Alessandra."

As soon as I add a third finger to my erotic thrusts, her magical litany hits the air. "Please, Max!" she cries. "P-P-Please . . . get inside me. We—we don't even need a raincoat, okay? Tell me you're clean, and I'll believe it. Holy shit. I *shouldn't* believe it, but . . ."

"I am clean." I am sincere, though newly perplexed. "But why is it important that I bathed this morning?"

She bursts with a throaty giggle. "Why, indeed." As she nuzzles the front of my neck, she adds in a whisper, "Me too. I've been working seventy-hour weeks since last summer and haven't had time to even look sideways at any guys—unless you count gangly boy toys passing me on the way to a catwalk. But I take the pill for cramps, so we're good to launch rockets." She moans as I remove my fingers—in order to line up my cock with her weeping entrance. "And dear God, how I need rockets right now."

Bewilderment jumps in with my perplexity. Boys as toys? Cats walking? And why must she propel rockets and take medicines to do so?

Under other circumstances, I might attempt to unravel all those riddles, but right now, her pussy beckons my cock like star glow. With equal fire, whether she knows it or not, her soul calls to mine. The cosmic blaze that belongs solely to her. Always, *only*, to her.

"Max." Her moan, thick with need, fills my ears—as her body, slick with lust, clutches my shaft.

The moment I sink into her, I am lost.

"*Ventrebleu*." I suck at the curve where her neck meets her shoulder. Lose myself in the dazzling, dizzying dream of her. "I cannot . . . fight it . . ." *Not now. Not ever*.

"Then don't." Her response comes on a shuddering sigh. "Please, Max. Don't stop."

"Never." My pledge resounds through my head as heat runs through my body. I stab her over and over, fucking deeper but not deep enough, chasing the elusive star of fulfillment for us both.

"Wrap your legs around me." I issue the growl into her ear. "Now higher." I drag my lips across her mouth, in a deep, hard kiss. As soon as we pull apart, I dictate, "Higher, *ma femme*. I need more. Your filthy speech . . . It enflames me like the cream from your naughty pussy. It makes me want to fuck the color from your eyes. The very thoughts from your mind."

"Then do it." She flings her words with bared teeth, scoring my shoulders with the same vicious need. "Screw me like your little tower bang toy. Take me like the trollop who couldn't wait to get up here and set your perfect penis free. Like the woman who's been dreaming about your cock since the second I woke up this morning . . ."

"*A l'aide mon Dieu*."

"Uh-uh." She lowers a hand to claw at my backside with the command of a goddess. "God needs to help *me* first. You see, he's tormenting me with a beautiful man who knows entirely too much about how to touch me. How to fuck me." The velvet depths of her eyes thicken with lust. "And how to move me."

I lower a kiss to her silken forehead. "Because that man was made for you. Because you were made for him." As our chests press and our heartbeats tangle, I swallow back the urge to spill more. Right now, she is poised for fulfillment and fire, not a barely believable truth. These moments are for magic. The wind on our bodies. The music on the air. The climaxes, ready to take us both.

"Ohhhh, my God," she rasps, as if cued to confirm my point. "Max. *Max*."

"Alessandra," I breathe into her hair.

She cups my backside with more force. "I'm ... I'm going to ..."

"Tell me." I snarl it, giving her exactly what she craves. Exactly what her pussy needs for its last notch of surrender.

"I'm going to come."

"*Ce moment, ma belle*. Do it right now."

Her body, tight and hot, keeps milking me. Her scent, aroused and potent, swirls around me. "Need you ... with me."

Her priority on my pleasure is a new layer of heaven— sending my self-control to utter hell. I have become naught but need. My cock craves more of her tunnel's merciless grip. My mouth is thirsty for more of her sweet, suckling kisses. My whole being demands to fuck her deeper. Then deeper still ...

"Good Christ." I grate it into her ear, savoring how her hair tangles against my face. I am relentless with my lunges now, driving into her tight, slick sleeve. She is the willing chamber for my dominion. The fiery hell of my damnation.

The delivering heaven for my salvation.

I slam into the hilt and then stop. I am a beam of white-gold heat, blazing and pouring and coming. Alessandra is welcoming softness and primeval light, panting beautifully through her own pinnacle. I study her. Memorize her. Pray my seed will never stop so I can spend forever filling her like this. But already, I grieve the moment my body will give out before my heart ever will.

My heart.

Jesu. That is why this all feels so different than last night.

Ten hours ago, I was drawn to her. Excited by her. Desired her as I never have another. But now, I recognize how much further I have fallen for her.

How much more terrified I am of leaving her.

I understand so much more now.

But not everything. Not yet.

But enough to know, as our bodies rock more gently and our heartbeats start to slow, that I can speak my next words and know they are the truth.

"I see you, Alessandra." The affirmation unlocks a new part of my soul, like a window flung open to the morning after a storm. "I see . . . you."

She is quiet for a long moment, as if that post-storm light has stunned her too. "You . . . you really do."

I narrow my gaze. "Why are you afraid of that?"

She swallows. Gazes up at the small bird's nest in the rafters of the tower. "Because it means that eventually you'll see everything." When she turns her head back, every troubled gleam in her eyes is exposed. "Even . . . the ugly parts."

"*Oui,*" I finally reply. "But is that not the way of things for life? Accepting the ugly parts with the good? That is the balance of who we are as humans, *n'est-ce pas?*"

Heavy air rushes from her. The sound is not a laugh, though I cannot decipher the truth of it, either. "Well, damn it, Hotness," she finally mutters. "You trying to turn me into weepy YouTube fodder?"

I clench my jaw. "Only if this Hugh Two, whoever he is, sees the Alessandra that *I* do." I lower my head and take her lips in a reverent kiss. "*Ma belle crème. Ma surprise miraculeuse.*"

After ending the kiss, I circle an arm around her waist to keep her secured as tight as possible. To my shock, she does not fight the hold.

A new laugh spills from her. "This is . . . nice," she finally declares.

I release a low hum as her fingers thread through my hair. "Hmmm. *Oui.* Nice."

"No." She wets her bottom lip. "Better than nice." She spreads her fingers along the side of my face. "Who *are* you, Max? *Maximillian.*" The question is edged with sardonic wit. "It's beautiful. Does it come with a last name? And do you think I finally might get to learn it? Or maybe more about where you came from before popping from the furniture in my suite last night? Or anything else except your extraordinary ability to make me scream for your junk like a porn star?"

Once more, she seems tempted toward a laugh. I use the moment as an excuse for dodging her queries. What would she do with the complete truth? I only have my twisted gut to serve as my advisor.

"I was born here, in the Loire," I start softly. "My father was an entrepreneur, inventor, and landowner."

"Oh, wow. Impressive. And what about your mother?"

I feel my smile give way to a swallow. "Well, she loved life and everything in it. She gave herself to everything and everyone with passion, whether she was knitting blankets for the poor, puttering in her herb garden, or playing with my brother and me . . ."

I grit my teeth against the sudden ache in my heart. The pain is relieved only when the woman in my arms rubs her comforting hand there. "You're talking in the past tense," she observes quietly. "About them both."

I mold my hand over hers. "*Oui.*"

"So your parents have passed?"

"*Oui.*"

"How long ago?"

"A long time." *Ventrebleu*; too long to fathom. And yet not long enough. I can still remember every second of Kavia's weeping when she came to tell me the fate that had befallen them.

"I'm sorry," Alessandra whispers. "But your brother—"

"He is gone as well."

She stops rubbing. "Damn. I'm sorry, Max."

"I know." I lower a reverent kiss to her lips. "*Merci,*" I whisper. "For the bravery and depth of your heart, *ma femme.*" I hope she hears what I cannot verbalize. That her forthright comfort is just what I need in the midst of fate's ineffable storm. Empathy and respect, not pity and simpering.

Because she sees me too.

"You've known a lot of sadness in your life, haven't you, Hotness?"

I give her only a quizzical glance. How do I properly answer that? Only half the query is tripping me up, however. Defining sadness is not the challenge. It is the other word that stops my thoughts.

Life.

"That is an interesting question, *ma chérie*."

"You're an interesting man, Maximillian of the Missing Last Name."

"Not as interesting as the woman who just let me … do what I did to her … atop a castle spire."

"Oh, 'interesting' is just where that started, buddy. But as long as we're back on the subject of interesting…"

I grunt hard. And tense harder. She ignores both.

"Come on, Max. I have to go there, and you know why."

"Mmmph." The protest is useless, and I know it. At least the effort makes me feel better.

"You tore out of that gallery like real ghosts jumped out of those paintings at you," she asserts. "Care to share why?"

I yearn, so ardently, to do just that. To bare my truth just as I have most of my body and soul. But I listen to her voice and the sardonicism that stands for cynicism. For all I know, time travel has already been discovered in this century—but it also could be reason for imprisoning or executing a man. In the time from which I just jumped, mobs were doing the same for flimsier reasons.

"Max?" she persists. "You can tell me, all right? None of this goes past our little salt circle." But as soon as I avert my gaze, her breath snags. "Were some of those portraits … of your ancestors?"

"No."

Not my ancestors.

My friends.

Intimates I never had the chance to bid farewell…

"Okay, then. So … what? Throw me a bone here, Hotness." She shoves away, turning her back on me, her shoulders hunching. "For the love of Christ, Max. Don't make me start calling the local loony bins, asking if a beautiful man in pirate gear has just escaped and—" She yelps as I grip her waist and yank her backward against me. "Damn it," she blurts. "What the hell are you—"

"You think I am beautiful?" I growl it into the back of her silken neck. Indulge my senses in a long breath filled with her sweet scent.

"Is that a rhetorical question?"

"Answer me."

She gasps as I add a gentle bite to the force of my affection. "Holy. Shit."

"That is not an answer."

"You...you turn my knees weak." She sags against me, as if needing to prove it true. I clench my arm to hold her up, relishing the press of her ass on my cock, already throbbing for her again. "Is that what you want to hear, Hotness? You want to know how I've never had this crazy kind of connection with anyone else? How you turned me to goo from the second you appeared last night? How you liquefied me again when you walked into the breakfast room this morning? How I've wanted to bite the head off every woman you've melted today—which, by the way, is nearly every female in this place?" She throws an arm back, again seizing my hair. I groan into her neck, stroking my free hand over her arm. "How I wanted to do exactly this with you?"

I release a rough rumble. "Because you think I am beautiful."

"Y-Yes."

"Because you feel connected to me."

"*Yes*."

For a moment, I do not say anything more. The moment in which I weigh the need in her words, the heat through her body . . .

But most of all, the gift of her spirit.

The bond she has just avowed to me.

I hold her closer before whispering a surrender of my own into her ear. I recognize the extraordinary power I'm about to give her with three terrifying words.

"Then marry me."

CHAPTER SEVEN

ALLIE

I push away from him.

And this time vow to maintain that distance.

Holy. Shit.

One look at the determined angles of his face confirms my stunned suspicion.

He really did just say . . . what I thought he did.

I press a hand against the roil in my stomach—until a bubble of laughter replaces it. "Okay. Hold on." I wag a finger his way. "I get it now."

Max's brows jump. "You do?"

"Of course." I nod, laughing again. "Nice zinger, pal. I dove in too deep on the personal grill-fest, so you lobbed back some briquettes with a prank proposal."

He gives me half of a brusque shake. "The . . . prank?" With the other half of the shake, he's scowling with double the tension.

"Yeah. And very well-played, I might add. For a second, I thought you were actually serious."

"I *am* serious."

"Uh-huh." I windshield-wipe my index fingers in the air. "That's okay. It doesn't matter now."

He pushes back in on me. His posture is total *I'm going*

to strangle you. The glimmering gold lights in his eyes say something else. Something that definitely involves robbing my breath but in different ways. Not the multiple orgasm kind, either.

"It. Matters."

I don't need his bulldog impression to get the point. I show him so by stepping back with more defined purpose. The motion exposes me to more of the wind, gusting uninhibited over the fields surrounding the castle. I claw my hair off my face before lifting my gaze again.

"Come on, Max," I finally chide. "Let's slow the roll. We just met last night. Granted, it was the most epic first date I've ever been on, but..."

My words are taken over by my grimace. I already hear how I sound and confirm how I feel. Like a Class-A jerk. While the guy lives in the country, he's not a bumpkin. Still, he's got to be reading the same page as me, right? Any second, he'll bust into a laugh that lights up his face, confessing to the cute diversion he tried to get over on me.

Any.

Second.

Now...

But there's still no laugh from his side of the conversation. Instead, I get a few new glints in his stare, soft yet sorrowful as single candle glows. The little kicks at the edges of his lips convey the same attempt at new cheer. A lame and uncomfortable quest, even from where I'm standing.

Which is way too close.

Because damn it, how I yearn to do nothing but rush over, wrap my arms around him, and comfort him.

And maybe even say yes to his wild proposition...

No.

No!

"Alessandra?"

"Yeah?" And who's the one sounding desperate and doleful now?

He reaches for my hand. Encourages me to step closer with heart-halting tenderness in his gaze. "Please, *ma revelation*. Have not a care now. As you said, I was just… lobbing a zinger."

I release the tightness in my shoulders.

The rest of me … not so much.

Why don't I believe a word he's just said? How the hell do I figure this all out? Figure *him* out?

I was never the girl who wanted to play damsel in a tower, mostly because I knew nobody was coming to rescue me. But this man is so different. Makes me feel so differently. Not just about him. About everything. I hate having made him this sad. I'm ready to do anything to make him happy again.

What the hell has he done to me?

As we make our way back out to Chambord's entrance area, neither my head nor heart are ready with an answer to that. And Max stays so mysteriously silent, I wonder when the emo rock soundtrack is about to start up.

"Allie! Max! *There* they are!"

Saved from the emo rock by my happy-dance best friend.

Raegan bounds the last few steps to us, literally bringing the beats with her. A fast-paced club track blares from her ear buds before she stashes them into a pocket. "Got in some steps on that crazy-ass staircase," she explains. "Did you know the king used to have his mistress take one flight and his queen take the other because the two spirals never meet?"

"Proving again that sin is the true mother of invention." Drue completes her drawl by giving both Max and me a onceover. "On that note, what have you two been up to?" Since it's one of her don't-talk-because-I already-know-the-answer questions, she goes on. "And next time, can I watch?"

"No." I verbally stomp on the word for a couple of reasons. One, to ease the stunned stare on Max's face. Next, to impart a bigger concept.

There isn't going to be a next time.

Thankfully, Drue picks up on the nuance with twice her usual speed. I'm grateful for the incisive look she flashes as Raegan links an elbow with Max. As our strawberry-haired friend yanks him back toward the limo with her trademark bounce, Drue slows her pace to match mine.

"Okay, missy," she orders beneath her breath, making sure we maintain a safe distance as the rear sweep squad. "You're going to fill Auntie D in on all the deets, or I really will watch next time."

I want to roll my eyes, but that would mean losing sight of Max's beautiful backside. *Damn*. His ass may be the perfect justification for reviving breeches as a fashion trend. I store the thought away while teasing my friend back. "You'll have to be a little more specific, nosebody."

"Ah," Drue croons. "Specifics. That it? All right. How about the fact that Max is strutting with freshly fucked glory but scowling like someone farted on his brie?" Shoulder nudge. "What happened, lover? You turn him down for anal?"

"Nope." I force my eyes to stay straight ahead. "I turned him down for marriage."

Drue halts. She does it so hard, I almost check for scuffs on the toes of her treasured Tory Burch booties. "Before or after you granted him anal?"

I choke. "Jesus, D."

"You think I'm kidding?" After we start walking again, she presses, "But *he* was kidding, right? Like, a postcoital funny to ease the tension while you two were getting dressed?"

I wince. "Yeah." Chew the inside of my lip.

She coils a dark-blue strand of hair around her matching accent nail. The other four fingers are coated in an iridescent hue, so they become prisms in the sunlight. "So what are you *not* telling me here?"

"Huh?" Hiding my trepidation is impossible, but Drue doesn't seem shocked by that, either. "What on earth are you—"

"Allie." She folds her arms. "Come on. It's *me*."

I resort to a full scowl. "Which means . . . what?"

"That it's time to call this one like we see it." She taps one of her Tory'ed toes. "Your knight in tight breeches may have the bod of a bronze statue and an accent made for a race car commercial, but sometimes crazy is just crazy."

I copy her folded arms. "Gee, don't sugarcoat things on my account."

"How I see them doesn't matter." And of course, she decides clasping hands is a better move. She uses the grip to pull me to the side of the path. "Are you seeing things clearly?"

"Well, I didn't accept his proposal, if that's what the hell you're getting at."

"Hey." She twists her grip a little tighter. "I'm on your side."

"I know." I sigh while gathering her into a hug. "I do, okay? It's just that . . ."

"That what?"

I sweep my stare once more up the path. Raegan and Max have stopped too. Despite the mini-mob of women hovering nearby, clearly debating which one of them gets the privilege of moving in on him, the Marquis de Hotness is still riveted on me. It's exhilarating but unsettling. I can't shirk the sense that he really was serious about the proposal. And if that was the case, what I just killed off inside him with my rejection.

"Girls!"

Raegan saves me with the burst of her shout and a wild wave of her hand. "Tick tock. Hustle, hustle! Château de Cheverny is expecting us in five!"

It's certainly not the last time the woman has to hurry me along throughout a day at the speed of tourists-on-crack. But maybe that's a blessing in disguise. I *think*. I'm definitely going for the group's straggler award, despite how every locale is more interesting and breathtaking than the last. Still, I can't seem to pick up the pace. My steps drag, no doubt galvanized by my psyche's deep mire of confusion. All that muck is centered around one particular member of our party. And despite their usual back-and-forths, I know Rae and Drue notice. I also know their thoughts must be trailing the same direction as mine. Back to Drue's claims in Chambord's portrait gallery.

Maybe they're more accurate than we gave her credit for.

A lot more.

Maybe crazy *can* come disguised in the form of a ripped, rugged pseudo-knight who can talk like a poet, kiss like a fantasy, and screw like he's galloping off for the Holy Wars tomorrow. Maybe Max's act isn't one at all. Maybe his wide-eyed wonder through every second of the day is a genuine display of his disconnect from reality. It's hard to believe otherwise, watching as even the basic stuff, like cash registers and coffee makers and ear buds, cause him to stop as if watching an alien give birth.

And then there are the times his reaction is . . . intense.

After four more hours of castle touring—meaning two hundred and forty more minutes of his strange behavior and my increasing confusion—we're back at Château De Leon. Everyone's ready for some rest, food, and afternoon tea to dispel the chill that never really left the day. I'm dying to kick up my toes in front of the expansive fireplace in the big sitting room on the third floor, so I don't hold back my groan of delight when spying the elevator doors once we step into the château's main foyer.

"Thank God for the forward-thinking De Leon who ponied up to have that installed."

Raegan joins her weary chuckle to mine. "I've hit triple my normal step count today in stairs alone." She darts a glance at Max. "So make me feel better, big guy. Tell me you're a little sore too."

"A little." He kicks up one side of his full mouth. "But in all the best ways. It has been a while since I enjoyed a day of fresh air and walking."

"You don't say." Drue returns to hardcore sarcasm as we all enter the lift.

All of us except Max.

At once, he skitters away from the doors like a lion refusing to enter a cage.

"Hey, Hotness." I motion for Raegan to keep the door open while I step out. I wrap a hand around the stiff fist at his side. "You all right?"

Max's chest rises and falls with violent heaves. It's like he's never seen an elevator before. "Why is there a *dungeon* inside this place?"

I should be laughing at that. I'm not. His trepidation—his terror—is real. "A what?" I say as gently as I can.

"You heard me," he grates. "Why is there a dungeon in the middle of the grand vestibule? And why are you all freely entering it?"

"It's okay." I circle my hand around, coaxing his fingers to open. "It's just an elevator. We're only going three floors." After caressing his palm with gentle circles, I twine our fingertips. "And I'm right here."

He swallows, dips a reluctant nod, and, with steps resembling a man trudging to the gallows, follows me into the elevator. He's low-key about the death grip he has around me—until the gears whir to life. As we rise, I try not to wince from his stress-ball squeeze.

"Okay," I finally rasp into the base of his neck. "We're here. It's all over."

He doesn't relent his hold. Part of me is just as reluctant as him to let go. The man's sculpted chest isn't a bad place to be face planted.

He stumbles out of the lift. Stops for one second. Then another. He peers around as if we're a *Star Trek* crew who just beamed onto a new planet. "*Mère de Jesu.* How . . . how did we . . ."

A deafening clatter cuts him short.

Rae and Drue rush over to the doorway between the landing and the sitting room. Beneath the ornately carved arch, Pascaline De Leon is standing as if the whole opening itself has frozen over. Her pallor is that pale. Her eyes are that wide. Her mouth has dropped into a stunned O.

She's been the epitome of French style and etiquette since

we got here—until now.

She remains as motionless as a zombie, oblivious to the full tea tray she's just dropped.

"Shit," Drue blurts. "Pasca? Ça va?"

"Oh, my goodness." Raegan kneels, rights the big platter, and starts reloading its contents. "Madame? Can you move your toes?"

Drue snorts. "Her *toes*?"

"This is all sterling silver."

"Oh, yikes. You're right." Drue grabs the woman by the shoulders. "*Pasca*. Talk to us. Are you in pain?"

The woman doesn't acknowledge them. At all. Instead, with hands still raised and splayed, she continues gawking at the sight that caused her freak-out in the first place.

Max.

"*Mon Dieu,*" she finally chokes out. "*Mon Dieu. Ça ne peut pas être.*"

"What cannot be?" I state it with as much authority as I can, now that Max's expression has become a weirder dichotomy. He looks like the emperor with no clothes but is just fine with everyone in the kingdom eyeballing his junk. The aura isn't *totally* off. The man has impressive junk.

But before I can press Pasca—or anyone—for a tangible answer, there's a new disruption, courtesy of the small pony now bounding up the main staircase. Okay, so the wolfhound isn't a pony—but could play one on TV. Effectively. Holy shit, the dog is huge.

I'm about to exclaim that aloud, but Max cuts me off with his own eruption. His shout is part sob, part victory cry.

"Chevalier?" He grabs the post at the top of the stairs, whipping around it to propel himself forward. "Chev! *Mon cher ami!"*

When they meet in the middle, he falls to his knees to accept the dog's affection. The heartiest laugh I've ever heard from the man spills out, along with more French endearments.

"Whoa." It's all I can think to blurt, especially when noticing the reunion's effect on Pascaline. She's noticeably agitated, literally wringing her hands.

Rae, attempting to thin out the tension, lifts a game smile. "Ah, well, look at that. Someone certainly loves his dog?"

"Though who came up with the name?" Drue comments. "Chevalier? Is it a classic movie reference, maybe? A shout-out to Maurice? But that's seriously going way back—"

"That is not the dog's name."

Before any of us can seek clarification about Pascaline's meaning, she's done an about-face and started beelining across the sitting room behind her. The move is like catnip for Raegan. She gives instant chase, her hair a blazing cloud behind her, leaving Drue and me to pick up the rest of the tea service mess—as well as the blown fragments of our comprehensions.

"You thinking what I'm thinking?" Drue mutters.

"That you brought all this on with the *crazy is as crazy does* bullshit?"

"Or that *you* brought it all on by bonking the lord of the manner?"

"You asking for details, wench?"

"You offering them?"

Our soft giggles are interrupted by Raegan's reappearance. Correction: Raegan's stressed-out, bug-eyed, NASA-worthy splashdown of a reentry. "You guys need to come here. *Right now.*"

At the far end of the sitting room, there's another door.

It was closed last night, and we were too eyeballs-deep in chocolate and Crémant to go exploring. Now, we rush to follow Rae through the open portal. We step foot into an impressive portrait gallery.

"Oh, yaaay," Drue deadpans. "Because we haven't seen enough paintings of dead guys today."

"Hush." Rae's rebuke is a new piece of strange. She's never the chastiser of our trio. As soon as Drue and I trade nonplussed glances, we hook elbows and walk deeper in. This display isn't as extensive as the hall at Chambord, but fewer paintings doesn't mean the works are less opulent. Not that I care, once my stare takes in the painting Pasca and Rae are standing in front of.

It's . . . Max.

Every beautiful, throat-drying, crotch-soaking detail of him. His shoulders, broad and masculine, filling out his cobalt satin jacket. His jawline, jutting and defined, pushing at his frilled white stock. His stance, fierce and noble, with one hand resting atop the head of his pony-dog. His hair, the exact same shade of sun-kissed cinnamon, tumbling into his opulent golden eyes.

But most of all . . .

His scar.

The exact same length. The exact same angle. The exact same place on his temple . . . directly over his left eye.

"*Ooo la la.*" I say it with a grin but wonder why Raegan and Pasca don't reciprocate. They stand shoulder-to-shoulder, gazing as if the painting depicts the Apocalypse's fourth horseman instead of my gorgeous Loire lover.

"Wow." Drue disconnects from me to stand back, folding her arms. "*There's* a candidate for hottest historical cosplay."

"It's a stunning painting." I transfer my regard to Pasca. "It's Maximillian, yes?"

She notches a regal nod. "Maximillian George Jean Valence De Leon."

"And he actually has a last name." Though my triumph about that is eclipsed by the wonder of the recognition. "De Leon. Which means . . . he actually lives here?"

"*Mon Dieu.*"

Pasca crosses herself. It's not exactly the answer I was looking for.

"What the hell?" I mumble. "Does he live here or not?"

"Honey." Raegan scoots a little closer. "Right question, wrong tense."

"Huh?"

Raegan tugs me toward the right edge of the portrait. Along the way, a strange weight bears down on my chest. I don't have a chance to interpret the sensation as my friend guides me to an identification plate mounted against the brocade wallpaper. As if she already knows I'm having trouble comprehending the words, Rae translates out loud. "Maximillian George Jean Valence De Leon, Fourth Comte of Leon, born seventeen sixty . . . and died seventeen eighty-nine."

The pressure on my chest gets heavier.

The ends of my nerves are pricks of ice.

The neurons in my brain struggle to fuse back together.

"Okay, seriously?" I charge. "Still not grabbing the melodrama, kids. What does this mean, except that Max comes from a hearty gene pool?"

"Same page." Drue adds her puzzled scrutiny. "The guy resembles his great-great-great-great-somebody-or-other. What's the biggie?"

"*Resembles?*" Raegan jabs a determined finger back at the painting. "Come *on*. That's a little more than a resemblance. Tell me I'm not the only one who sees it. The eyes. That posture. That *scar*."

Drue rolls her eyes. Rae doesn't surrender. I'm compelled to study the portrait again. My stare is drawn to the strong, steady goldens of the painting's boldly handsome subject. And once again, I'm unable to blink. I'm unable to feel.

"I ... I don't get it," I finally stammer.

"*Stop*," Drue says. "Of course you do." She hooks a hand to my elbow, pulling me back to our original position, a few feet behind Rae and Pasca. "This is a freakish genetic coincidence. Nothing more."

Raegan spins around. "This isn't just freakish, damn it. This is ..."

"Coincidence," I supply. "The *other* possibility on the table here, yes? And that has to be the case. Because Rae ... honey bunch ... I love you, but—"

"But what?" she snaps.

"Okay, park it and chill. I'm just trying to figure this all out. And I'll admit, there are a lot of similarities. But Fancypants Max here doesn't have the ... brawn ... that I'm used to. And my Max has lighter hair."

"*Your* Max?" Drue doesn't give up the opening for a jibe.

"For the sake of the argument," I rebut.

"Not hating, baby." She raises her hands. "About time you had a *my* anything other than work."

"He was probably painted at a younger age. And the pigments in the portrait have likely darkened over time." Rae's explanation earns her a nod from Pasca but new huffs from Drue and me. But the girl is ready to give back as good as she gets. "Holy crap." Her scorn hits the air with the force of ours combined. "Why are you two ignoring a truth that's right in front of your face?" she demands. "Even after watching the man gawk all day about everything from debit cards to central air, while wearing threads from a casting call for the next Jack Sparrow, you're buying that he's just an eccentric local boy who loves cosplay?"

"All right, all right," Drue relents. "I'll nibble on your crazy a little, girl. But only a *little*."

Rae tilts her head. "Because you recognize I might be right."

"But about what?" Drue counters. "I mean, I'll give you the *Twilight Zone* type stuff. There's been a lot of wide-eyed puppy in our hunky historical hound dog." She flicks a glance at me. "Sorry, Al, but it's true."

My turn to go for the placating pose. "No sorries necessary. I'll concede at least that point. But you guys, he's an *actor*. We all know about them." I tick a nod toward Drue. "Hell, you even dated one."

She chuffs. "For about two seconds."

I pounce on her perfect leg-up for my explanation. "Because they're crazy with feet!"

A new smirk comes from Raegan. "At least you got that much from attending every Fashion Week on the globe."

As Drue snort-laughs at that, I pivot toward Pasca. The woman is still as pale as the ghost she claims to have seen.

"Madame," I murmur, "I mean no disrespect, but what you and Raegan are suggesting here is—"

My breath snags the second she spears me with a glare.

A new approach is needed. Right now.

"Okay, so can you just tell me if *that* Max"—I point

the direction of the foyer—"has ever had an interest in the performing arts? Even if he hasn't openly pursued the instinct until now—"

"I have never, in my life, seen that man in the flesh before."

Her declaration is so determined, a long moment passes before I can respond.

"Fine. So what's your explanation, then?"

Pascaline's stare is a careful assessment, her scarf flowing over one shoulder. "What your friend said... that the man came out of the wardrobe in your chamber... This is true?"

I fold my arms. "Yes. Why?"

And just like that, the woman is back to her pensive hand wringing. "It... it cannot be," she whispers, now sounding outright creepy. "*C'est impossible.*"

"Madame?" Drue queries. "*What* cannot be?"

An eternity of silence. More of the woman's uncertain fidgeting. "It... is perhaps best that I do not say," Pasca finally states. "It is..." She palms her forehead. "You say it as... crazy?"

"*Now* you're worried about crazy?" I'm tempted to finish it with a laugh. While a part of me resists fanning all these delusional flames, I'm eager to hear why she believes the unbelievable. That the hunk who helped me burn up the sheets last night is the same nobleman who posed for that painting over two hundred years ago.

Pascaline lowers onto a velvet settee. Her shoulders are stiff as she braces her hands on the edge of the seat. "Public records declare that Maximillian De Leon was killed by a murderous mob during the early days of the Revolution. His mother, father, and brother—Christophe, Ysabeau, and Bastien—were publicly beheaded not long before."

"Damn," Raegan whispers.

"That's rough," Drue adds.

Rough. My heart repeats it while my mind's eye fills with Max's face from the tower at Chambord this morning. I remember the pain—the *grief*—on his noble features while telling me his whole family was gone. As if his sorrow was still fresh . . .

"Hold up. I'm confused."

Sometimes, I'm morbidly grateful for Drue and her droll outlook on things. This is definitely one of those times. As she drops onto another settee, she's already emphasizing the point with a narrowed scowl.

"If that's really the case and the whole family was executed and eradicated, why does this place still carry the De Leon name?"

Raegan shifts her weight and bites her lower lip. "Okay, that's a damn good question."

Pasca nods, not just agreeing with the assertion. Clearly she's already anticipated it. "Christophe had a sister, Fiona," she explains, "who, remarkably, kept her head during the uprisings. The deed to the land was signed over to her by Napoleon himself in eighteen oh-one."

"To a woman? Who wasn't his spouse?" I glance over. My bafflement is mirrored by Rae and Drue. "That wasn't exactly usual back then, was it? Even under the Napoleonic Codes?"

"You are correct." Pasca pushes to her feet, though still doesn't look too sure about her movements—or much of anything around her. "But nothing about the situation with Lord Maximillian De Leon was 'usual.'"

"Meaning what?" Rae is now more openly fascinated than freaked out.

"Meaning that Napoleon had a good reason to remain in good favor with the family. A new government does not negate the value of good politics, especially when one has plans to crown themselves emperor."

Drue rocks her head back. "And the De Leons were going to stand in his way?"

"Perhaps." Pasca's expression is threaded with as much ambiguity as her tone. "If what was rumored about the family was true."

"A secret?" Rae, now like a kid entranced by a fairy tale, follows the woman. "What kind? Were they spies or something, working with the resistance the whole time? Were they like the Scarlet Pimpernel? Did they send coded messages about the king?"

Pasca halts. Squares her shoulders. "Many thought… Maximillian himself should have had the throne."

"Huh?" Rae gasps.

"Ditto," Drue says. "How is that possible?"

"Holy shit." I plunk down to the couch next to Drue, clutching a fist across the anxiety parfait I once called my guts.

"Ysabeau De Leon was a favored consort of King Louis and was often invited to his chambers," the woman discloses. "It was rumored she became pregnant with his child during the court's Yuletide festivities in seventeen fifty-nine."

"She wasn't yet married then?" Drue queries.

Pasca frowns. "Of course she was."

My friend jolts away from her perch on the couch arm. "What the hell? So this guy—Christophe, right?—was *fine* with his woman sneaking off to consort with the king?"

"Most certainly." The women is koi-garden calm about the pronouncement. "The king's favor was like being touched by the sun. It meant monetary gain and prosperity for the entire De Leon family. And since Christophe was unable to bear a child with Ysabeau himself, he was joyous about her fertility with King Louis. Before she even began to show, Maximillian had the man's unconditional love."

Drue shakes her head. "In short, he was a saint."

"But what about the second son?" Raegan inserts as her eyebrows nearly mesh together. "Was he also one of Louis's bastards?"

"Bastien was legitimately of Christophe's seed," Pasca answers. "It happened very easily after Maximillian arrived."

Drue nods. "The performance pressure was off, so the rockets started firing."

If we were having a normal conversation after a day of adventures, my mind would be off and running down that tawdry subject path with Drue—but there's nothing normal about this exchange. Not one damn thing. Not even if Pasca's historical snippets are true—and that's all before the outrageous claim still being considered here. The enormous possibility I still haven't completely dismissed.

But to do that, I must forge on.

I haul in a deep breath and force my next question to spill out. "So what did the peasant mob do . . . to Lord Maximillian?"

Pascaline looks over, clearly sharing my blatant discomfort about the subject. But she nods, indicating she won't insult me with a candy-coated truth. "The public accounts simply state he was executed," she offers.

Drue frowns. "But not exactly how?"

"For the love of . . ." I glower. "Are specifics necessary?"

"Don't," Drue retaliates. "Executions were the YouTube of the eighteenth century."

Rae sends over an apologetic wince. "She's telling the truth, honey."

"Can we stick to the subject?" I can't help my prickly retort. We're talking about how a person died. A *real* person. A man who feels more real than I want to admit.

Thank God Pasca seems to recognize that. I gratefully accept her empathetic look before she steels herself and goes on.

"Of course, there is an alternative version of what happened that day . . . when the mob stormed this place. Tales are passed along through the château staff and in lore told at the local taverns." She stops, clearly debating whether to say more. "The tale is scoffed at by most," she asserts. "It is . . . wild fiction. Insanity."

Raegan lays a gentle hand on Pascaline's shoulder. "And it's what you think too?"

"What I *thought*," Pascaline rasps, and swings her head back and forth with resignation. "Until ten minutes ago."

I say it for her. "When you saw Maximillian."

She stills her head. Swallows hard. I can feel a little of her conviction waning, as if she expects to be waking from a dream any second. To be honest, I'm grateful for her hesitation, despite how I rise and join Rae at her side. After a couple of seconds, I let my long sigh guide her gaze back in my direction. I make sure she sees the message of my regard. *I know exactly how you feel.*

"Go on," Raegan finally encourages her.

Pasca looks up at the portrait of the first Maximillian. "At first, when you all came out of the elevator, I simply thought it was a strange coincidence." She works her hands against each other again. "He seemed so similar to the painting . . . but living

144

in a castle that is centuries old, one learns to accept bizarre occurrences at times, *oui*?" She drops her hands but purses her lips. "But when he called to the dog . . ."

"Chevalier," I supply.

"Still a weird name," Drue grumbles.

"And not that dog's name," Raegan asserts.

"No." Pasca points a determined finger at the portrait. At the animal lying at the man's feet. "It is *that* dog's name."

"Oh, hell," Drue mutters.

"I *knew* it," Rae pronounces.

I don't say a damn thing.

I can't.

I'm only able to force down a painful gulp. My throat is nothing but a pinhole, shut down like a dam after a massive rainstorm.

A storm in which I've been dancing, oblivious and delirious, with the most perfect lover I've ever known. A man who hasn't just penetrated my body over and over again. A human who has climbed into my psyche too . . .

Who has seen into my soul.

Who has understood it all.

Who has adored and valued and treasured it all.

As nobody else has.

Because he's a lunatic who fancies himself a reincarnated prince from two centuries ago?

Or because . . . he really *is* that prince?

I can't fathom either one of those answers.

Not yet.

I only know there's one way to start getting there. I have to hear the whole truth. About all of this. "All right, Pasca. Tell us, then. What really happened to Lord Maximillian De Leon?"

CHAPTER EIGHT

MAX

Of all the astounding things I have experienced today, this is one of the best.

"These are called ... sweatpants?"

Henri De Leon shrugs. "*Oui.*"

"But they do not make me sweat." In truth, they are the most sumptuous garment in which I have ever been clothed. The cloth is fine and soft, molding itself to the body in the sweetest of ways. I am baffled as to why the people of this era, with their progressive ideas about clothing, are wearing anything other than this finery.

"The idea, I believe, is that you would eventually do so." Though Henri's tone is casual, his frown tightens. Given the bizarre manner in which he met me an hour ago, I would have a similar composure. It is another reason why I keep the conversation on simpler subjects, such as getting into the short black frock—he called this part a T-shirt—that is an equal godsend of comfort to my skin.

As I stretch the garment over my torso, I surrender to a groan of complete pleasure.

Henri tautens again, clearly misreading my sound as disapproval. "I apologize, monsieur, that I do not have more suitable attire to offer you." He gestures to my ensemble. "I only have these because of coincidence. A guest left them two weeks ago and told us not to bother with the return shipping."

"Why?" I do not hide my incredulity.

He shrugs. "I imagine they purchased others."

"That quickly?" I lift the bottom of the shirt and again examine its hem. "But stitchery like this must take weeks, if not months!"

"Yes. Well…" He looks me over from head to toe, appearing relieved for the chance to openly scrutinize me another time. "Perhaps we should simply be grateful he was built more like you than I am."

"Very grateful." I chuckle, hoping he feels invited to join me. When he remains as stoic as a priest, I risk reaching and clapping him on the shoulder. "Monsieur, please be not troubled any longer. I am profoundly thankful for your kindness. You found a stranger in your library, rolling around on the floor with your dog, and have now nearly given that man the clothes off your back." The tension in his shoulder slackens. I attempt a new smile. "That stranger is deeply in your debt."

"Stranger." His grunt strips away the word's credence. "Look me in the eyes and tell me you believe that, Maximillian." He nods as I stiffen my stance. "Ah. So that *is* your name, then."

I look back up but only get as far as the end of his bold, straight nose. A nose uncannily similar to mine. "I think we both know the answer to that, Henri."

"My God," he says. With his long De Leon fingers, he scrubs one side of his jaw. "It cannot be—and yet it truly is."

"So…you do know?" My spine is now as stiff as the steel pieces of his hanging coat rods. "The whole story?"

He nods in shaky spurts. "I—I am sorry."

"Why?" I counter. "I would not believe it if I were you

either. I certainly did not when Kavia first chanted that terrifying spell, and—"

"Oh, my God."

"Pardon me?"

He sinks to the bed, dropping his hands and gripping his knees. "Kavia," he utters. "You . . . you actually know her name." He looks back up, unabashed about his stare now. "Like the whole story about the spell, it was not a detail made public, especially during the months after that wretched day."

Now I do not mask my curiosity. "Apologies for the necessity of repeating myself, monsieur—but why?"

He compresses his lips. "The staff, Kavia included, felt it best that his lordship's disappearance remain shrouded by mystery."

"Like his true identity." I do not distill a note of my bitterness. I never knew about being the unacknowledged *dauphin* to the throne, so it was never a personal hardship—until now. I shall never truly know if the secret was the radicals' motivation for targeting our family, especially after our generosity to all of them—so the sting of their hatred will always burn doubly deep.

There is naught to be done about it now. The new tenderness in Henri's gaze demonstrates he knows that too.

"It cannot be easy to hear that," he murmurs. "Good God. None of this can be easy for you, my boy."

I turn around, bracing hands to my waist. "I believe 'easy' is now over two hundred years in the past, my friend. But I cannot even be certain of that, considering all I have heard today . . . about the Revolution."

Henri's nod is solemn. "Ten years that changed our land— in good ways and in bad." The crush of his scowl intensifies the

impression. "But none of it forged without spilled blood...
and rolled heads."

My throat is fire as I swallow hard. "So that day... when
Kavia evoked the spell... was just the start of the madness."

The man nods. "Ten years' worth."

"Christ."

I raise a hand and pound the wall. But while my memories
are the instigators of my rage, it is those same recollections I
draw on for new strength—and much-needed focus.

"Kavia," I grit out. "Wh-What about her? And Carl? And
the others on staff?"

Henri moves close and forms a hand over one of my
shoulders. His mien is openly paternal. My gratitude for it is
deep. "There is no account of them remaining at the château
after the mob invaded that day," he says. "Nor are there any
records of their deaths."

"At all?" I swing up my head. Narrow my scrutiny. "Even
after the Revolution?"

"Even then." He ends it with a regretful exhalation.
"Which could mean a number of things. They could have fled
the country, resettled in Germany or England. Or they could
have remained and changed their names to keep their heads.
Or..."

"Or what?" I demand when he purposely stalls.

Henri steps away. He visibly fortifies himself before
issuing his answer. "Or they could have taken hope from what
Kavia's dark arts did for you and tried the same thing for
themselves."

"Dark arts." I all but spit the words. While I understand his
reasoning behind the term, it sears like an insult nonetheless.
"So mayhap she was called out as a witch for them and then

murdered without the honor of keeping her name."

Henri is still, stiff, and silent. His agreement with my words is inherent in every inch of his stance.

"She saved my life," I finally snarl and drag a hand through my hair. "*She saved my life*. And I swear to you, Henri, on every drop of blood in my body, there was nothing *dark* about her noble deed. She sent me here, even knowing I might have limited time to get things right but *knowing* that it was *light* that called me, not darkness."

The man remains quiet and contemplative. "Limited time," he finally echoes, his syllables equally cautious. "What does that mean?"

"Exactly what it implies." I pause, needing the strength of a new inhalation to speak the rest. "Less than a month, if what she said was true. But everything she did to get me here was right, so I have no reason not to believe her."

"And what all was that?" There's genuine interest in Henri's new query. He is a true De Leon, his mind open and inquisitive. "What she did . . . to get you here?"

I pull in another breath. "She told me it was nothing *she* did," I relay, shaking my head with bemusement. "She said that it was the power inside of me. That it was the force of soul-matched love."

And there it is.

My own admission, out loud, of what has happened to me. Of the mighty force that has brought me here.

A confession that will likely halt Henri's trust in my testament. He is a man in and of this cynical century. To pledge his figurative sword to me now would mean a renunciation of the world he knows and believes in.

Yet Henri rises from the bed with a full, proud smile on his lips. I smile too, obeying the surge of warmth through my chest. Perhaps humankind *is* desperate for magic again. Maybe that is what Henri wants to tell me.

But he does not get his chance.

"Holy mother of all the bullshit in the world."

Because suddenly, cynicism is back—in the form of the woman now standing in the doorway. A frustrated frown enflames her stunning face. She is tapping one lovely, lush, bare foot. Merely glancing at her bright-pink toenails sends a rush of heat to the hardness between my thighs.

That is *before* I fully absorb the magnificence of the new ensemble into which she has changed.

Dear. Sweet. *Jesu*.

In her tight black breeches and dark-red shift, she convulses my breath. Jolts my cock. Enraptures my spirit. Every inch of her is radiant with the energy that originally brought me to her, whether she chooses to believe it or not.

And at this moment, Alessandra clearly does *not*.

ALLIE

Henri De Leon isn't the smooth boss of socializing anymore. Not that I expected him to be once Pasca told me how he returned from the hardware store to find Max and the pony-dog rolling around together on the library floor. Apparently Henri had reacted just like she had, except instead of toppling a tea tray, he'd spilled a toolbox.

The guy's face still looks stunned, though he's managed to get Max into some normal clothes at last. *Yessss*. Good old-fashioned sweats and a tee.

But it hasn't toned down his hotness factor one bit. Honest

to God, since when can a man turn a Belgian beer T-shirt and a pair of sweats into a sight that belongs on the *Hunks in Unexpected Places* Instagram page?

And just like that, my libido's doing the thinking for me again. I've allowed that slip too damn often the last twenty-four hours, but it's happening all over again. Like it always does when I step foot into the same room as Maximillian De Leon.

Maximillian De Leon.

Dear God.

After everything that went down with Pascaline in the gallery, I can't deny that's likely his name, but I'm still grappling about the century in which he received it. The conviction bolsters my determined look at Henri. "Monsieur, may I speak to your . . . guest . . . alone, please?"

Henri glances to Max as if seeking royal permission. "This is acceptable for you?" And then, God help me, actually asking for it.

"Not just acceptable, my friend. Necessary."

Henri's jaw tightens. "The time . . . is *that* limited?"

Max nods. Yes, like freaking Henry the Eighth. The hunky pre-joust-stab one. "Right now, every moment counts."

"Of course." Henri dips a nod. "Whatever you need."

As the man backs out of the room, I dig my fingernails into my palms to keep my composure. The man needs a padded room and intense psychotherapy, not deference and awe. The resolve helps with maintaining my determined stance from the second Max swivels his attention back to me.

Thoroughly on me.

To the degree that he's my new human microwave. And my nervous system is his melted cheese.

I raise my chin higher. Refortify my posture. Like that

helps with anything—especially because he takes instant note of it. I see that much in the newest arrogance across his face.

With that same steady confidence, he steps over. He doesn't stop until he's deep inside my personal space. He reaches to grasp me by the shoulders.

"Don't," I grit out.

I'm peeved as hell at you.

I freaking crave you.

His serenity just grates harder on my ire—and teases my sex like a physical stroke. "*Ma chérie.* What is wrong?"

I release a rickety breath. "What the hell *isn't* wrong?"

"I do not understand."

With a push of physical *and* mental effort, I step back. It's only a step, but it's a start. "While you were off with Chevalier, I was in the De Leon portrait gallery."

"Oh?"

"Yeah. *Oh.* There are some interesting pieces in there. But you already know that, don't you?"

Something dark forms in his gaze. He reaches for me again. This time, my fortitude isn't so strong. Just like that, I'm a steel shaving in front of a mega-magnet. I'm quickly being outpowered, and that makes me even more pissed.

"Alessandra. I know this must be vexing for you."

"I'm not vexed. But plenty of others around here are, and that's why I came to find you." I raise my head and search his stunning face. "You want to really honor me, Max? Then give me some honesty. What's your game here?"

"My . . . game?" He drops his head and shakes it slowly. "*Mon Dieu*, Alessandra. Is that really what you think?"

"Damn it." I toss my head with an angry flinch. "I'm not going to rain the police down on you, okay? Not if you promise me that this fuckery ends now."

He flares his nostrils. "Exactly what fuckery would that be, mademoiselle?"

"Are you really going to make me spell it out?" I toss my head the other way, realizing I'm fast entering dangerous diva territory. "Fine, then. You want exact? Even though you know how much you look like the guy in the portrait upstairs? And how you likely also know about the crazy gypsy curse that made him disappear, giving him a chance to escape execution if only he followed his heart?"

When his features remain disturbingly steady, my lungs expel a harsh breath. I inhale with the same force. Why is he so accepting of this? So not stunned or confused?

"So what's your play on this, buddy?" I'm finally able to level. "How are you spinning this? Are you just out to make a euro or two doing the swashbuckling cosplay thing, or is this something else? I mean, you're not saying…" I have to stop and focus on pulling in air now. "Oh hell, Max. Are you actually saying that guy's been reincarnated through you?"

At first, I get only silence as reply. And stillness. Utter, creepy stillness.

"No," he finally says. "Not reincarnated."

"So… what, then?" I charge. "Channeled? Resurrected?"

He steps closer. "Try… transported."

I get down a dry gulp. Then another. "Excuse me?"

When he answers with nothing but his intense wildcat stare, I charge, "Are you seriously telling me… the wardrobe in my bedroom… is a… time machine?"

He shoves out a hard breath. "I only know that when Kavia hid me inside it, the year was seventeen eighty-nine and a mob was storming my home. When I reemerged—"

"Stop." I whirl away.

My thoughts are reeling. My logic is battered. "Pasca was right," I laugh out. "This . . . this is insanity. It has to be."

"I have told myself the same thing at least a hundred times in the last twenty-four hours."

"You don't say."

I wheel back around, trying to distance myself from the man who's still too damn close, dominating the air in the room and the sense in my head. But holy hell, he looks sincere. And now, seems so . . . sensical. So calm.

Too. Damn. Calm.

"Oh, God." I drop my head into my hands. "Why am I taking any of this seriously?"

The air shifts again. He edges closer again. I steeple my fingertips across my nose, fighting to breathe normally. Too late. The air is inundated with his pine-and-sea-salt scent, and my whole system reacts. Whether the man's a first-rate shyster or a first-rate nutcase, my body doesn't care. My chemistry craves him. My senses stretch out to him.

God help me.

"You already know why." His voice runs warm vibrations down the side of my neck.

I spin away from him, reach for the bedpost, and clutch it.

Because this is only chemistry.

You're only a science experiment to me, Max De Leon. Or whatever the hell your name is.

Atoms and electrons. Cells and reactions. Mixtures and explosions.

Only. Chemistry.

I repeat it, over and over again, as he pushes in at me from behind. The chiseled striations of his torso mold against my back. He slides his big hands down my arms. He keeps going, meshing his fingers with mine. My mind battles back. Orders me not to dwell on how wonderful his hands feel against mine or the decadence of his ripped body as he pulses and rolls against me.

"Th-This . . . can't be happening," I manage in a gasp.

"Why?" His murmur surges me with waves of silver and gold arousal. "Because it is easier to believe you bedded a scoundrel instead of a man who crossed two hundred years for you?"

"No." But it pours out of me as a moan instead of a protest as he reaches around and cups my breasts. "I . . . I can't do this." I hardly recognize my own voice now. It's low and lusty and needy—and dips even more into that sin as he captures my nipples between each thumb and forefinger. Primitive heat becomes arrows of arousal to the trembling tissues between my legs. "I can't do this. I *won't*. Not until . . ."

"Until what?"

His demand makes me whip around in his arms. "Until I know who you really are," I charge. "Please . . ." I latch a hand into his hair. "If you adore me as you say you do, stop insulting me with this fairy tale about the magic wardrobe. Just tell me what your real name is—and why you're really here."

I tighten my grip on his thick waves. They're warm and mesmerizing between my fingers. The same effect takes hold of his gorgeous features. He no longer evokes a nobleman lost in time. He looks like a god born to command it.

He makes sure I know it too . . .

By hauling me back to him in a scathing sweep of motion.

By plunging his head and kissing me with the same whoosh of passionate violence.

At once, all the reason in my head is destroyed. All the resistance in my body is dissolved. My blood erupts into a forest fire as he molds his hands around my ass. My careful boundaries with him are nonexistent. Or maybe they never existed at all.

I want to—I need to—be pissed, but I'm not. Damn it, this man has spiraled me too high. If this feeling could be bottled, it'd be the only drug in demand across the globe. I don't ever want to come down . . .

Even as a greater realization strikes me.

Was this what Dad did for Mom?

Was this the feeling she tried to recreate, with such hideous failure, with all the men who came after him?

Was this the feeling she kept chasing . . . instead of raising me?

So much for never coming down.

At once, buckets of tears brim in my head. Yeah, the kind that start as a throat vise and then make their way up, already causing a throbbing headache. I hate them. I hate the thoughts that have caused them, at a time like *this*. And I really hate the pain they cause on Max's face, as he dips his forehead against mine and hauls in a bunch of fierce breaths.

"My name is Maximillian George Jean Valence De Leon," he whispers. "I swear it to you, Alessandra, on the graves of my parents. On the very hand of the Almighty who brought me to you. On my *own* life, which is just a pittance now, but . . ."

I stop him by smashing three fingers across his mouth. But attaching words to the action is impossible. How do I tell him that I'm one synaptic connection away from believing him now? Or that it doesn't even matter? That he could be King freaking Tut, yanked right out of his pyramid and transported here, and it wouldn't make a difference?

That I'll never be able to give him what he so clearly wants. What I now see he clearly craves. A woman without a messed-up mind and scarred heart. Who has no idea how to give him the passion and devotion he deserves. The affection and joy he so freely gives from his own heart.

Damn it.

Fast train. Short track. This situation. In blazing spades.

How have we gotten here? This was all supposed to be fun. A seductive game. A rush for the moment. A commitment of the only body parts I *could* give him.

Which, of course, are firing on every cylinder once more.

As this man takes my lips—and kidnaps my breath—with another kiss.

A *kiss*?

Horridly wrong description of the year.

This is an obliteration. A carnal, sexual takeover. A full-throttle tongue tango. After three seconds, my psyche has melted in the same blaze as my body. There's no turning down the heat now.

I slide my hands down from his hair and dig them into the thick cords of his nape. I pull on him with needy demand. A rough sound bursts up Max's throat. He forces his tongue past the seam of my lips and lunges in, stretching me with brutal desire and invasive heat. We stab at each other with our tongues. Bite at each other with our teeth. We suck and roll and lick and crash like lovers who really *have* been apart for hundreds of years.

Holy *shit*, what he does to me.

Will it ever be any different? Do I want it to be?

The answers don't really matter.

All there is, all there can be between us, is this potent arc of attraction, this unstoppable torrent of lust. And though it's only temporary, it's perfect. Potent. Powerful. There's nothing to do now but concede to beautiful force. To let it drag me under and knock me senseless. To surrender until all that's left to breathe, to feel, to swim in, is the fierce, wild flood of Maximillian.

His hands, moving under my shirt to spread across my bare waist.

His thighs, sinewy and sure, spreading mine out by important inches.

His torso, pressing and mashing against mine...

Until his cock, thick and throbbing, pushes at the middle of my stomach.

My sighs become high-pitched whimpers. I grab his hair again. I'm not gentle. But Max is so intent on bending over me, biting my breasts through my T-shirt, that he barely grunts in return.

"Ohhhh!" I moan. He's really going at them, like a kid with an ice cream cone who doesn't know any better. I seize him around the shoulders with both hands, certain I'll fall backward to the bed otherwise. "Oh, Jesus!"

He relents. But only by a little. He arches one sexy-as-hell brow and drawls, "Do you want *that* to be my name?"

I'm only capable of responding with another long groan. But I give it to him with a blissful smile. I'm helpless, floating on the silken river of his voice and the feral joy of his bites. I damn him and thank him at once, already onto his cunning game. The man clearly knows how thoroughly he's conquered so much of me.

And is about to claim more.

"I can be your Jesus, Alessandra." He descends his hands, sliding under my leggings. "At least for now." He molds those long, graceful fingers around my bare ass before claiming my skin in bold strokes of heat.

I moan as he pulls harder . . . grinding our bodies tighter against each other. "F-For now?"

He nods. The movement makes his stubble abrade my neck. "I will be your god before we are done, Alessandra. And we will not stop until that is your full, screaming truth."

CHAPTER NINE

MAX

Before we are done.

The moment the words leave my lips, Alessandra stiffens beneath me. "Damn," she gasps as I begin my invasion, suckling hard at her neck. "The things your mind comes up with, Hotness."

"And that is just my mind." I smile against her skin but punctuate the promise with a gentle bite. "Other parts of me have better plans for you, woman."

"Oh." She breathes in and out, pushing her chest against mine in all the finest ways, before dragging her hand over my engorged cock. Her eyes widen. She looks down to where my borrowed sweatpants are soaked straight through. "Oh...all right. M-Maybe that'll be...all right."

"*Maybe* it will be?" I cock my head as she raises hers. "And why would it not be?"

"You know why not." She lifts one of her fingers to trace my lips. "We can't just keep doing this, Max."

"Doing what?"

"You know that answer too."

"Perhaps." I breathe the word into her forehead. "But it changes nothing." As I pull in more air, it is filled with her fulfilling warmth and fascinating scent. "If you want me to stop, then you need to direct me. With specifics."

She attempts to shove me back—more or less. "Fine. Stop . . . stop doing that shit to my neck . . . w-with your m-mouth. Oh. Hmmm . . ."

"Shit." I cannot keep the teasing tone from my voice. "Like this?"

"Yes, damn it." Her shaky little huff is like a physical caress of its own. "Exactly l-like that."

"Mmmhmm." I flow the sounds into each other, reveling in the tremors they cause through her. As the shivers cascade down her belly and across her thighs. I do not cease my lusty obsession over her full, firm, enchantress curves. They make me drunk with desire. *Two hundred thirty years.* I have paid a boggling price for the sight of all this perfect skin. I would willingly pay it again.

But right now, it is time to collect my reward.

I need no other permission than that.

I drag her breeches down with a swift, forceful plunge. At once, the most perfect valley of her body is exposed to my gaze.

"And . . . things like this?" I ask while kissing the topmost edge of her soaked cleft.

"Damn it. *Max.*" A yelp escapes her as I push down harder. With dedicated effort, I finally work the clingy garment around her knees. "Yes! *Unnnhh.*"

We fall together to the bed. As soon as we are down, primal heat invades my senses. With her sweet curves pinned beneath me and her glower a dagger, I struggle to remember the theme of her argument, but the woman looks ready to recall it for both of us.

"Okay, and definitely stuff like this. Damn it, Max. I'm serious. Let me up!"

"Why?"

"Because this can't continue. We can't just keep making this a thing. You got it?"

She jerks at me once more. Yet this time, the effort is merely a show. In the writhes of her body, the curls of her fingers, and the thrust of her chest, there is a sweet, savage tension. She needs more—but she is afraid of more.

"A thing." I nearly touch my lips to hers with the deliberate growl. "That you do not want anymore?"

"Wanting has nothing to do with it. I just don't need it in my life right now, Max." Her temple furrows. "Not ever."

"Then...you do not feel this anymore? All of this, between us?"

Deeper grooves take over her forehead. "Feelings don't count anymore, okay?"

"Then leave them out."

The air in her throat snags. "Uh...huh?"

"You heard me." I force her into stillness by sliding my crotch along hers. "Forget the feelings, Alessandra," I snarl softly. "I am not asking for those right now."

"I...I don't get..."

"Only think of the need."

"The—the wha—" Her moan is thick and achy as soon as I thrust forward again. With twice my purpose as before. "Oh, God. Oh...*wow*."

"And the craving."

"*Stop it.*"

"And the calling." I raise my hands to her face, drilling past the confused glare she fights to form. There, in the deeper realms of her entrancing greens, I confront her deeper truth. "You know what I am talking about now, *oui*?" I husk. "You feel it—you *know* it—as completely as I do. But has your mind already killed that certainty in your heart, Alessandra? Has your confusion destroyed your belief before it even had the chance to grow?" She squirms again. I wedge my body tighter between hers. "Am I now simply insane and not the lover who has seen through to your soul? Has given that soul every drop of my passion and desire?"

I push my hands into her hair. Is it strange that I relish the moment she winces? But I would rather have a few seconds of her honest pain than the perpetual wash of her lies. I lift a satisfied smile...

Before the woman grabs again at *my* hair.

"Oh, Maximillian," she whispers. "It's not *your* sanity I'm worried about."

Against my scalp, her fingertips turn into tiny trembles. They are not necessary. I know, I *see*, what she longs to reveal but is terrified to expose. I have met no other person more conflicted. Craving to be seen. Fearing the exact same thing. Even now, she's still running. Battling to be strong when what she needs is to shatter.

With a god to help her get there.

I succumb to a new smile.

I happen to know just the god for the job.

I start by lowering a new kiss to her mouth. It is tender this time but also solid. Just commanding enough to keep her mind spinning as I push her shift up. Then some more. Then the last few precious inches, until her glorious nudity is revealed to me in full.

Then I stop.

And simply stare.

And utterly worship.

By every saint who ever lived, she is the most stunning woman I have ever seen. In *any* century. I am pitifully lost, craving to lunge back and fit myself between her thighs—and then to stay there a good long while. To bury myself, heart and soul and cock, into her mesmerizing heat.

But she is lost too—in a vastly different way. She is far from me now, flying in a void of bewilderment and doubt. Silently, I vow to repaint that sky for her. Every damn inch.

"Worrying about your sanity is a fruitless quest, Alessandra Sophia."

Her gaze flares but quickly narrows. "That so, Maximillian George Jean Valence What's-Your-Face?"

I fight the craving to laugh. "That matter is one best left to your God."

Her eyes widen once more. She slides her thighs together. Braces her elbows back so her breasts rise toward me, her erect nipples draped by the bunches of her crimson shift.

She is *mine*.

She always will be.

If only she would see it too.

I cannot give up trying to prove it—even if that means keeping the woman naked and sexually satisfied for the next month.

I am sure I can talk myself into that sacrifice . . .

"Ah," she murmurs. "My God. Who's going to do what? Hear my confession? Absolve my sins?"

I jerk up one side of my mouth. "Right now, he shall simply demand your obedience."

I move back in, parting her knees with my own, clear about my intent.

"Strip your shift all the way off, Alessandra."

I am not surprised when she sits up with an easy smile. I am also not surprised when she eagerly removes the garment. I let her watch as I generously wet my lips.

Suddenly, being her god is my very, *very* fine fortune.

"Pinch them," I direct, barely hearing the words above the roar of my blood.

She obeys at once. She bites her bottom lip while tugging at her succulent tips.

"Harder."

She moans high in her throat. I growl from deep in mine. Her nipples are hard berry buds, centered in puckered flowers from which I cannot rip my stare.

"Lie back down." There's a growl in my tone, and I let it serve as her sole compliment. I am too enflamed to indulge more poetry right now. Too consumed by the illicit thrill of having her naked and supine for me here in this bed. The pillows and sheets for the master of the manor. Where I would have taken my rightful place, two hundred years ago . . .

It never would have been right.

Now it is right.

"*Mon Dieu*. Yes. So very, very right."

I obey the call of my soul to speak it aloud and revel in Alessandra's answering stare. Her smile is knowing and adoring. Her gaze flows with satin sensuality. Her skin is a tapestry of dewy arousal.

"Now put your hands back on your breasts," I charge. "Squeeze them, *ma cœur*. Harder than before. Worship them as you know I would. Until they hurt."

As she obeys me to the syllable, I snarl, "You are my perfect, filthy girl, *oui*?"

"Yes." The sound spills as if she has kept it leashed for a

long while. "Oh, Max. Yes . . . I am."

"You make me want to do dirty things too, *ma belle*. Right here. Right now. In a stranger's bed. Because I cannot wait." I demonstrate that by ripping off my clothes as if their soft folds have caught fire. Not a wild comparison, since much of my body feels the same way. "Like this," I say, kneeling back so she can watch as I stroke my erection and pinch my balls. "And this."

The pain produces pre-come. I shake the hot pearls into the valley between her breasts. At once, Alessandra's nipples darken to the shade of currants. "Oh, God," she whimpers. "Oh . . . *God*."

"You are right." I use my cockhead to spread my milk along her skin. "And now it is time for absolution."

Her thick lashes lift. "Yes, my lord."

I take a huge breath, but it is impossible to gather enough air for the pride in my chest, the celebration in my soul. The trust in her eyes, the readiness of her obedience . . . They are a consummation I never dreamed of before, a completion I shall never know with another. Yes, I am that certain—to the point that I do not doubt a note of my next command to her.

"Push your breasts together."

"Yes, my lord."

I shift into place, moving up to straddle her torso, my cock nudging the tight, perfect groove she has created for me with her beautiful swells.

"Angle your head up, against that pillow, and open your mouth."

"Yes, my lord."

And then she is silent because she has complied with eager actions and lust-filled eyes—the same perfect depths that watch me now, brilliant and expectant and aroused. And waiting...

"I shall command your body with mine, Alessandra—right here, in the vale closest to your heart, so every beat of your blood will feel every throb of my desire. With each thrust, your mouth will accept my cock... and then my come."

I correspond every description with its action so that my penis is couched by her lips and her tongue vibrates along my underside. Until the day my sorry life ends, I will not forget the sight of her glorious mouth sucking me in like this.

"*Ventrebleu*," I grate. "You are *magnifique, ma petite bouche*." I pull out, sliding my saliva-covered length back through her generous, hot swells. "Open again. Accept your absolution."

I ram her harder.

"Again."

Deeper.

"Again."

Every time, the sluice is slicker. Her moans are harsher. Her mouth is better. Her nipples are harder.

My cock swells bigger. My balls pull in tighter. "Spread your legs, Alessandra." I almost chuckle as she retorts with a growl, sending waves of pleasure through the erection I still have buried in her mouth. "I will not forsake you, *ma femme*. I promise. You shall have your redemption."

I fulfill that vow right away. I steady my legs in between hers and test her tight cleft with my pulsing cockhead, ensuring she is truly ready for me. As my tip slides an inch without resistance, I angle my head up to take her mouth in a brutal kiss. Our moans join in complete hunger and clanging desire.

She is... my completion.

Of my journey. Of my life. Of my purpose.

Follow your heart, Maximillian . . .

She sighs for me. Shudders and moans and clings until she is fighting for air, just as I am. We finally force ourselves to drag apart and gasp for air in heaving breaths.

"*Jesu.*" I hide none of my wonderment, meshing my stare with hers while continuing savoring nips along her lush lips. "You taste . . . like heaven."

Alessandra laughs softly. "I taste like *you.*"

She releases her breasts and slides her hands up to my shoulders. "I need more than your taste, Max."

At the fervency in her voice, I roll my hips forward. As my cock settles deeper inside her, we release contented hums.

"And I need more of you."

So much more.

She will never know how much.

Her grip tightens. Her eyes plead. Her lips part. "Fuck me again, Max. *Please.*"

But right here, right now, I shall attempt to show her . . .

All of it.

CHAPTER TEN

ALLIE

I'm an explosion. An implosion.

A flood. A famine.

Pure fulfillment. Desperate need.

It's all there, pushing at my spirit the same way his cock challenges every corner of my body. Everything is set ablaze, painful and wonderful and full. He thrusts so deep, I can feel him in my teeth. Every penetration turns my body into a rave dance club at midnight on a Saturday. I pulse. Pound. Tremble. Burn. Crave.

Spinning higher.

Soaring farther.

And still, needing more. Not just in my pussy. In my blood. In my senses.

All of him . . .

Hunger coils my muscles, turning my fingers into talons.

"*Unnnhh*," Max groans. The sound becomes a growl, prefacing his heated bite into the base of my neck. The jolt turns my breath feral. I need to give back as good as I've gotten from my beast of a lover, but even twisting my body in ways I never imagined isn't enough.

I need to make him hurt too.

I lunge up at him, teeth bared. His pectoral is the most

succulent cut of meat I've ever tasted. His skin is a perfect mix of salt and musk and man.

"Fuck. *Ma femme. Ma petite tigresse.*"

He retaliates by twisting his head down and sucking at my aching nipple until I shriek in delicious agony. The entire time, he drives into me with punishing force. Every time his cock hits full hilt, another dark moan punches up his throat. That thunder grows louder and louder, inciting us to grab and grope and seize each other.

Soon, we've screwed our way across the bed and my head dangles over the edge. Max grunts his approval, since the new position angles my breasts even better for his appetite. He leans over and digs in, biting my other breast like a lion devouring its kill.

"Ohhhh!" I cry out, hating him and cherishing him for the resulting shudders of pain and pleasure. I clutch at him harder, clawing his biceps just to stay on the damn bed. The whole time, he doesn't falter a stroke of his deep, hard invasion into my core. "Oh . . . my God." It's never felt this good. Or hurt this bad. "You are such a bastard."

He laughs with dark intent—but still doesn't miss a single thrust. "My beauty." He scrapes both hands down to my waist. Uses the hold to keep me fixed on the bed—and impaled on his cock. "Spread your legs wider, *mon étoile.* I need to fuck you deeper."

My heartbeat doubles. Triples. "Yep," I get out between gasps. "Arrogant." But my volume spikes to a pair of shrieks as he delivers sharp smacks to the insides of my thighs.

"*Wider,*" he snarls—and with that single command, alters me yet again. My head falls back. The world spins. My nerve endings shatter. My inhibitions are blown apart.

"Yes," I hiss. "Yes . . . yes. *Je t'appartiens. Chaque pouce de moi.*"

I am yours. Every inch of me.

I'm lost in him. The way he moves. The way he speaks. Even the way he breathes, as if my skin alone has become his oxygen. I pity every other woman on this planet. None of them will know the perfect, pulsing bliss of being wrapped around him tonight.

But he only gives me a second to indulge the thought— before replacing it with a better one.

The need to obey his new dictate.

"*Now*, Alessandra. Make it all come for me . . . now!"

"Max! Oh. My . . ." But I can no longer form words. Or thoughts. Or breath. I can't comprehend anything beyond the blinding existence of now, as the dirt of his promises is spun into the sand of his desire, then the glass of his violation, and then the slice of his ultimate dominion.

"Yes. *Yes. Oui, mon cœur.* Give it all to me."

That's what I give him. All of me, open for his fucking. All of me, climaxing around him. All of me, taking his scalding come as he lunges and then holds himself deep inside me.

For many minutes afterward, we remain like that, entwined and sweaty, his cock still seated deep inside me. I settle my ankles against his taut ass and my arms around his rippled shoulders. A sigh leaves me, filled with enough of a sated hum that it belongs in a damn movie. Max replies with a soft snarl. When I shiver from the reverberations, he presses his lips to my neck and does it again. I twist a hand into his thick waves and giggle.

"I'm getting real chills from that, mister."

"And they are making me hard again, mademoiselle."

"You know what? You're a really impressive machine."

"Hmmm. Does that mean I get to fuck you again?"

I laugh while lifting my legs higher. I pull his head down toward mine. "That's exactly what that means, Hotness."

♦ ♦ ♦ ♦

An hour later, we're sated with pleasure and spooning without shame—though my bewilderment hasn't waned. Max is caressing me with a combination of his fingertips and knuckles, savoring every inch like I'm a decadent dessert. Something melted, since that's how I feel by this point. He glides those graceful digits over and over, quiet and sensual and sure, responding to my shameless sighs with his soft but arrogant snarls.

There goes my theory about him being some local hunk getting by between gigs at the family's vineyard. The man has serious postcoital game. He didn't learn this erotic elegance in a barn. But it's also impossible to think of him as some displaced ghost. No way is the man curled around me, warm and hard and ripped, some lost and cold spirit.

Another breath of bliss spills out as he scoops the hair off my neck. He tucks his lips in, nuzzling heated attention along my tingling skin.

"Alessandra," he whispers into my ear. "Alessandra Sophia..."

"Hmmm." My core temperature climbs again. "Yesssss?"

"You are a goddess."

More tremors. Yet another sigh. "Well," I murmur. "I'm fun if you love curves." A laugh swirls out as he thumbs one of my nipples. "Which you clearly do."

He growls into my nape. "There are those who don't?"

Wry huff. "There are plenty of those who don't, and you're fully aware of that, monsieur."

"*Quoi?*"

For a long second, all I do is gawk. Is he for real with all the incredulity?

"Come on, Max," I finally chide. "I work in the fashion industry, remember? In the world I run in, a twenty-five-inch waist is heifer status and five slices of lettuce with a cherry tomato are a full meal."

He rocks his head back. The shock in his stare intensifies. "People . . . *choose* to live like this? To behold stick figures as beauty?"

And now I'm officially mute. Either the guys in Loire really don't get out that much, or he actually *is* the time-traveling lord who nearly made Pascaline pass out. Either way, he's clearly not going to accept my answer alone on this.

I crawl around until locating my clothes and then yank my phone out of the built-in pocket in my leggings. After swiping through Raegan's half-dozen texts to remind me about tonight's plan—pajamas, fine wine, and an eighties music video bingefest—I tap at the buttons leading me to the New York Fashion Week photo file. The entire time, I'm aware of Max watching me like an infant captivated by a prism.

Finally finding the shot I'm after, displaying one of the industry's hottest models strutting the catwalk in an Alexander Wang catsuit, I turn the screen toward him. "There. In my world, *that's* a goddess."

His stare bugs but instantly narrows. "But that is a boy. Or a walking twig. Or a breadstick. Or a—"

"Point taken." I laugh out the words. "You're a boobs and

hips dude."

"I am a . . . *dude* . . . who likes to feel the flesh I am sinking into."

"Oh, hell." I giggle it out. "You know, you're adorable—even if you *are* insane."

"You call *me* insane, when you belong to a vocation that venerates walking twigs?"

"Well, I'm trying my damnedest to change that." I glance over, making sure I haven't lost him. At this point, I'm usually dealing with a glazed stare and some noncommittal hums from a lover, but Max's attention is still cranked at full power. *Wow.* "When I first started in the business, nobody would give me or my blog the time of day."

He jerks up a little, making me stop. "Pretend I am still crazy and do not know what a blog is."

Because he doesn't?

"It's like a newspaper, but it only exists on the internet." I pause again, unable to ignore the perplexity in his eyes. "We good now? You know the internet, right?" I turn to my side and brush my fingers along his shoulders, unable to resist soothing the new tension there.

"Just go on," he finally says, leaving me hanging on the answer. But maybe that's a good thing.

"Anyhow, I can't remember a time when I didn't want to be involved in the fashion world."

I pause for a long moment. Then another. Well, there's another first. I've never said those words out loud to anyone, even Drue and Raegan. I skim my hand down Max's arm and take his hand, hoping he can sense that. Relief warms my chest when I see his gaze tighten as if he does.

"It's not just the clothes themselves. It's the attitude. The

MISADVENTURES WITH A TIME TRAVELER

fantasy. The idea of these artworks being created but not just stuck in a gallery or on a wall. Clothing is walking, moving art . . . and it changes all the time. That's been exciting to me since I was little. I guess it was always my favorite way of escaping, you know?"

"Escaping?" His echo is a genuine curiosity. I see that much in his narrowed gaze. "Escaping . . . what?"

At once, my insides twist.

Well, crap.

I've painted myself into this little figurative corner, haven't I?

But right away, another observation hits.

Maybe this corner is exactly where I want to be. At least with him.

Especially with him.

It feels right to tell him this. It feels *good* to tell him this.

"I was raised by a single mom. She had me young, and though she and my dad tried to make things work, he skipped out before I was three. Things were hard. I think Mom had a list of stuff that made him run—and a lot of times, I was at the top of that list."

Max twists his lips. Shoves out heavy air from his nostrils. Mutters a lot of pissed-off stuff in French.

"Stop it." I smack a hand to his chest. "It's fine, okay? *I'm* fine—and fashion was a big part of why that's the truth. It saved me. Took me to lots of beautiful places, even when I wasn't allowed to leave our apartment. Some little girls watch princess movies and dream of getting the prince. I watched them and drooled over the costume design."

Despite my wry laugh, my confession seems to weigh the air. With his shoulders dipping as if sharing that burden, Max pulls up my hand and turns it over. He presses a patient kiss on the back.

Just like the prince I never wanted. Who's crimping my heart like a damn accordion pleat.

Focus. Just get the rest of it out.

"When I grew up and started chasing my dream, I learned it wasn't going to be as easy as saying I wanted in—especially because of my zaftig silhouette. But I was damned and determined to fit in. At first, I starved myself to that goal. I was proud of the size six I finally whittled down to, despite being too dizzy to even pick up the hair I was losing." I pause long enough for him to inject a rough exhalation. "And the shittiest thing about it? Nobody in New York even cared. To them, a six was still outside the magic circle of perfection. So I came up with a new goal."

A gentle smile returns to his generous lips. "Which was?"

"To widen the circle."

"And you did."

"And I did." I flick a finger back over the phone, closing the image of the catsuit goddess. "And I still *am*." With another tap, I open the *InStyle* app and click the link to the article I filed for them three days ago. "In addition to my *Fine Things* blog, the big hitters in the industry are listening to my feedback about how their designs need to be changed and refined for the girls that have *flesh to sink into*." I tuck a fast kiss to the bottom of his jaw. "You know I might have to borrow that line, don't you?" I murmur. "Want to negotiate a byline?"

"Of . . . course . . ."

But this time, I know I've lost him. While I'm sure he's listened to everything I said, he's fixed on my phone like I just yanked a star out of the sky. "Uhhh, mister? If you're looking for the pizza delivery apps, I'm pretty sure Sottocasa doesn't deliver here from Brooklyn."

He hardly blinks. "Brook . . . lyn?"

"Where I live. Well, at least for now. I've submitted some test reels to the Hemline streaming fashion channel. If they respond positively, it could mean a reporter job—and in a few years, maybe my own show." I sigh with meaning. "The big-time. It would change everything." I tilt my head, amused at how he peers between the phone and me like a puppy figuring out a new pull toy. "Want to see some pictures of my apartment and neighborhood?"

His face brightens. I don't hold back on my answering smile, though I'm flirting with disaster and know it. What is my problem? I came up here to confront the man about being either an overboard cosplayer or a deceptive freak, not to end up offering him a virtual tour of Brooklyn in the nude.

But what the hell do I do about that revelation now? Totally join the crazy, of course. "Okay, settle in." Crap, I'm even giddy about it, rolling to my stomach and using the rumpled covers to prop up my phone. Max slides close, lazing his massive thigh across my ass while leaning his cheek on his opposite hand. With his other hand, he restarts his magical caresses along my spine.

For a second, I forget what I'm doing. "*Unnhhh*. That feels . . . like heaven."

"*Oui*," he murmurs. "It does. *You* do."

Another sigh. "Can I just bottle you up and take you home with me?"

"I will go even without the bottle, *mon miracle*."

Shit.

I'm in such serious trouble with this god.

"Okay, what was I saying again?" I laugh, but the sarcasm hits a blank wall with Max—until the second my phone lights up with a familiar face and phone number. Too damn familiar.

Rae's timing is impeccable, as usual. But while I groan, Max's smile could light up the sky clear to Paris. "Ah! It is Mademoiselle Raegan!"

"Oh, yes," I deadpan. "Just look at that."

"Such a brilliant likeness." My quip has shot right past him. I wish I could claim a shred of shock about it. "Who is the painter? I see no signature on the portrait..."

"*Aggghhh*. Don't touch—"

But my yelp is too late. He's already reached over and swiped the screen.

"*Ventrebleu*. What kind of paint is this? It is smoother than glass!"

"Can't answer, darling. *Somebody* answered my phone." After a short huff, I grit into the device, "*What?*"

Rae huffs right back. "Hey. Where are you?"

"Busy."

"Well, get *un*busy."

Her tone carries more meaning than just ignoring my implication. As in major-emergency meaning.

"Why?" I sit straight up while demanding it. Max rises with me, though his stare is riveted to the phone. "Are you guys okay?"

"We're okay," Raegan fills in. "But there's been a new... development...down here."

Before I can ask what she's talking about, Max snatches the phone out of my hand and places it flat in his own. In the process, he inadvertently activates the speaker feature.

"What the *hell*, Max?"

My censure goes ignored as he gapes at the thing as if it's a brick of gold covered in fairy poop. Under normal circumstances—if there's such a thing as *normal* with this man—I'd lose myself in his adorable allure all over again. But Rae's urgency dictates my focus.

"Can you just get your cute little ass down to the foyer?" she charges in a tone that's too sticky sweet, even for her. "Preferably clothed. And preferably *now*."

"Damn it, Rae," I bite out.

"Not going to work this time, Allie Bear."

"Okay, then. I'm pulling birthday girl privilege. You have to fill me in just a little. What the hell is it?"

"You mean *who* the hell is it? As in, who else besides Drue and me has the ability to track you down in the middle of the French countryside?"

I expel rough air from my nose. Well, I did ask—and have certainly received. But now a more urgent perplexity has replaced its predecessor.

What ignited such a hot flame under Dmitri Thorne's ass that he hauled himself all the way from New York to here?

MAX

He is, without a doubt, the most fascinating fop I have ever met.

My reaction to the new arrival in the château's foyer is immediate and absolute, even weighted against the Versailles dandies who used to press me into vapid bocce matches. Though other aspects of those summer days are fond to recall, I rapidly dismiss all the memories while beholding the tension that takes over Alessandra's face.

Because of the fop?

Why?

There is nothing daunting about the man. Though he is as tall as a river reed, he seems equally as bendable. He poses with more airs than a court rake with bejeweled buttons, but his manners are far from court-worthy. I am disturbed and defensive by how he scrutinizes my home, one velvet-clad arm pulled in as if to grab for his smelling salts any moment.

"Dmitri." Alessandra's voice is as stilted as her posture. "What the living hell? Did somebody die?" She is so adamant, I wonder if more truth than humor drives the quip.

The man pulls her in for a double air kiss. "So nice to see you too, darling." He steps back and dabs at his hair, affording me the chance to stare at it without repercussions. The coif is unlike anything I have seen, including on courtesans with pompadours styled around everything from bird houses to birthday cakes. It resembles a giant spiked flower—that expired a year ago.

"You know I'm always happy to see you, sugar," Alessandra tells him, lifting a genuine smile. "But right now, I'm wondering why."

"Can't say the same didn't cross my mind, pooky." He releases a delicate grunt. "What's the next town over called? *Le Nowhere?*"

A sniff dices the air from our left. Pascaline stands in the entry to the darkened breakfast room. "The Loire Valley is one of the most visited places in France, monsieur," she snips. "Many of your presidents have had their photos taken on those steps just outside."

"Oh! Well in *that* case . . ." The fop makes a wide arc with one hand. "Wait. No. Still don't care."

I erupt in a growl while stepping over to grab this peacock by the satin lapels of his ridiculous costume. "Who taught you respect, *enculé*?"

"Oh, *my*," Pasca utters.

"It's all right, madame." The fop tosses back his head to rid his face of the hair this time. "I like a man who knows his way around insightful insults." He curls his hand back in while sweeping his keen gaze over me from top to bottom. "Which part do you like better about me, gorgeous? The cock part or the sucker part?"

"Neither." Alessandra stomps over, wrenching my hand away. At the same time, she pushes at the man, her hand disappearing into the lacy cascade across his chest. "Obnoxious needs to take a break," she dictates. "*Now*."

"Not the word I would have used," I say, jabbing my chin. "But sufficient enough, given the—"

"And arrogance needs to take the same hike." She jabs the same hand into the center of my chest. "And now that we've settled that"—she relaxes into a diplomatic pose—"Max, may I introduce you to my manager, PR guy, walking appointment calendar, and aspiring pain-in-the-ass, Mr. Dmitri Thorne. And Dmitri, please say hello to my new...errrmm...friend here in the Loire, Maximillian De Leon."

I am forced to stow more grumblings as the man waltzes forward and dips a respectful bow. I begrudgingly return the deference. Thank God Mother forced so many etiquette lessons upon me. "*Un plaisir.*"

The man arches his well-plucked brows. "I'd love to be more than just one pleasure for you, gorgeous."

"No." Alessandra jerks him back. "You would *not*."

"But darling." He looks me over with a defined pout. "He's

so very *yums*."

"He's also very *mine*." Her glance back at me is rife with so much possession, my blood rushes with an answering call of desire. "At least until we're out of here." She shakes her head as if to rid herself of the thought. "Which isn't for a few more days still, so—"

"Hmmm. About that." Dmitri whisks around, brandishing a thick sheaf of papers. "I'm sorry to burst your wine-flavored bubble . . . but actually, I'm not."

Alessandra frowns. "What do you mean?"

"Well . . . a few days just became tomorrow."

My chest fills with bricks.

Alessandra's face fills with confusion. "Huh?"

"Can we just get to the point here?" Raegan pins Thorne with a scowl, continuing the look even as she adds, "Please."

"Agreed." Drue emerges from the shadowed room behind Pascaline. "What's going on, pretty boy? Can't the fashion world deal for a few days without her?"

Thorne openly preens. "First of all, flattery will get you everywhere. And next, the answer to your bleary query is *no*."

"Screw that," Drue volleys. "Allie needs a break, damn it. Some rest . . ."

"And, apparently, a few other things," he quips.

I raise my brows. "More than a few."

"Oh, I don't doubt *that*," Dmitri drawls. "But this has nothing to do with anyone's lasting power and everything to do with our Allie-rific's rising—or shall I say *shooting*—star."

As his announcement sinks into Alessandra, my heart is halved by her reaction. One side of me beholds her tentative smile of surprise and hope and rejoices with her at once. But the other side . . .

Plummets.

Already sensing—knowing—that this good news for her will be the hammer to my dwindling hourglass.

"What?" Raegan finally prompts. "Whaaaat, Dmitri?"

Even Drue's face is animated. "It's Hemline, isn't it? It's totally Hemline. Look at his face."

"Are you shitting us?" Raegan splits the air with a shrill yelp. "Okay, if you *are* shitting us right now, Dmitri T, speak or forever hold your peace. But if you *are* saying the world's hottest fashion network has finally looked at this girl's audition reel, and—"

"Decided that they want to talk concepts about a show of her own?" Dmitri wields the paper in his hand like a courtesan flicking a fan. "All right. I won't say that. But I'd be withholding the truth."

At once, the two women rush Alessandra with tears and shrieks. I look on, my heart still split open like a melon.

Tomorrow.

She is leaving tomorrow.

If they respond positively, it could mean a reporter job—and in a few years, maybe my own show.

Because her dream is calling.

And now we have run out of time.

I have run out of time.

Bizarrely, the one person who appears to understand is Dmitri himself. When I look up, the man's flamboyance has vanished. In its place is the face of a friend, ready with silent comfort—and a larger message. The resigned set of his face tells me that all the fancy words and humor aside, he wants exactly the same thing for Alessandra as I do.

For her to have all the beauty.

For her to have all her happiness.

But that is where the similarity between us rolls to a harsh end.

Because he will have the miracle of getting to see her joy and success.

And I will be gone.

Hoping against hope that the Almighty will grant a sliver of mercy on my soul, forgiving me for consenting to a witch's hex to get here. Perhaps, if God is truly merciful, he will grant me a glimpse of her elation before I am confined to my eternal fate. I still know naught what that will be—into death, back to the Revolutionary mob, or banished to timeless blackness—but I am absolutely certain of only one truth.

The sacrifice will have been worth it.

She will *always* be worth it.

CHAPTER ELEVEN

ALLIE

Is this what schizophrenia feels like?

I turn the question over in my head while water from the shiny gold bath spigot flows over my raised foot. Lavender-scented bubbles form a froth atop the water around me. Insanity should be the last damn thing on my mind.

But I consider the concept again. Seriously.

I'm certain my brain is on the edge of the break, and it's only been a couple of hours since Dmitri arrived. Every second since then, I've been numb. Locked between complete joy and a solid case of what-the-fuck-do-I-do-now.

Because once I jump, my life will never be the same again.

So much will be left behind.

Including the last forty-eight hours.

Including Maximillian.

Who, two hours ago, kissed me and told me how overjoyed he was for me . . .

Then left the château—

and seemingly disappeared.

My chest clenches. "Damn it," I mutter.

It's for the better. Coming to fairy tale land doesn't guarantee the fairy tale ending. What did you want, anyway? For Prince Amazing to escort you back to Orly Airport in a glass carriage? To kiss you goodbye through your snotty tears and running mascara? There's *a great shot for the social feed.*

I push out of the tub and into a waiting bath sheet. At once, a pleasured groan escapes me. If my mind has to be in turmoil, at least the rest of me is in bliss.

No.

Scratch that.

Bliss is the sight awaiting me in the bedroom. The man standing here, smelling like wind and looking like sin, still dressed in the tight T-shirt and sweats in which I found him earlier. Only then, I was peeved with him. Now, I've just spent the last half hour in the bathtub, trying to rationalize myself out of missing him . . .

"Max."

"Hello, *ma belle.*"

"You . . . you came back."

"Of course I did."

"Where were you?" I punctuate it by sagging against the wall as I ram a wrist against my forehead. "I'm sorry. That's none of my business."

"Of course it is your business." While his syntax is reassuring, his tone is all angry grit. "Sweet *Jesu.* It is always your business, Alessandra."

"Oh, Max." It's barely more than a sigh, and I'm not ashamed. Dear freaking God. How am I going to move on like the man hasn't permanently turned my blood to magma and my mind to chaos?

"Are . . . are you okay?" I ask and nervously resecure the towel.

His eyes cloud over. "Why are you inquiring? Do I not appear . . . okay?"

"Yeah." I purse my lips. "Yeah, of course." I don't know why the point irritates me. I mean, don't I *want* him to be okay? Haven't I been stressing about his okay-ness for every one of the last sixty minutes? "It's just that no one's seen you for hours, and . . ."

I trail off in the wake of his faint yet flawless smile. As he tucks his upper lip into his lower, I attempt to discern even a single thought in his beautiful head. Not happening.

"I had to get away," he finally says, surrendering his smile for the sake of the words. "To think."

"About what?"

Whatever he's feeling, the stuff tempts the corners of his mouth again. "Did you worry, *chérie*?"

I knit my brows until they hurt. "Yes, damn it. Of course I worried."

Worry. That's such an understatement, I almost laugh. That's been just the tip of my emotional iceberg since he bolted out the door after Dmitri's announcement. Not that the bastard has to know that, especially with a ticking clock on my time left here. Metaphorical chit-chat is not how I want to be spending the rest of these precious hours with the man. I want to be reaching for him. Smashing him close. Letting him tear off my towel. Letting him kiss me, caress me, fuck me. Making sure there's nothing between us but breath and heat until Dmitri has to bust in here and pry me off him . . .

And knowing, even then, it'll feel like having my own skin peeled off.

"How are you faring?" He taps nervously at his thighs with his fingertips.

Those elegant, decadent fingers . . .

"Faring?" I blurt it like the absurdity it seems but prepare to save my dignity with a lob of sarcasm. That's before the man glides closer. Closer still. Until we're just inches apart.

His stance is neutral but strong. His scrutiny is fixed and molten. There's a hint of whiskey on his breath. "Just answer me," he rasps, as if the fate of nations teeters on my answer. "Tell me the truth. Are you happy, Alessandra?"

And then he waits.

And I squirm.

And ache. And throb. And need. Ohhh, especially all that.

"Wh-What do you want me to say?" I choke out. "I . . . I don't know what to tell you, Max."

What can I do to make you *happy?*

Yeah. I could say that.

But something ineffable holds me back. Something terrifying. The part my psyche still has in a chokehold, all the while screaming about how a man would never make such a difference to my happiness. That a man wouldn't ever matter enough to.

Damn it.

Here he is . . .

Mattering.

The recognition snaps me. I reach for him as he grabs me in return. He hauls me in hard. At once, he's yanking back my head. My stare is full of him. His sculpted jaw. His regal mouth. His bold nose. His Versailles-gold eyes.

His perfect adoration.

"Just say that you are happy." He dips in, brushing my lips with the hoarse words. "You deserve to be happy, *mon miracle.* You have given so much of it to me. I know that all this has been but a blink of time to you, but—"

"Don't." I nearly growl it, I'm so peeved at him. No. At

the craptastic timing of all this. At the advent of *him*. At the perfect, ironic, what-sin-did-I-commit-for-this glory of him. "*Please*," I gulp against the wet fire at the backs of my eyes. "Just . . . don't."

But he does anyway.

Kisses me. Deeply. Intently. As if it's our last embrace.

No!

But he persists, kneading the seam of my lips with his probing tongue. Absorbs all my confusion with all of his passion, letting me drench his beautiful, ardent face with my tears before he pulls back to show me his own.

"Shit," I sob out. "Max . . ."

My voice dies away as he plummets to the floor with an animalistic groan, pulling my towel free as he goes. I shiver as the chilled night air hits all the damp places of my exposed nudity—and as he clamps his mouth over my trembling mound.

"*Ma raison*," he murmurs, lapping at the dampness between my legs. "My reason. My heart. My calling. My goddess."

"Oh." It's the only sound I can muster as he usurps my sorrow with the ecstasy of his mouth. "*Oh . . .*"

And then I'm gasping without restraint and hissing without shame as he grabs one of my thighs. With a chest-deep rumble, he hitches it over his shoulder. Staccato moans bubble up my throat as his primal groan echoes through my sex, heating me until I rock into him, needing more of his mouth on my tightest, neediest knot.

"I hunger for you," he whispers against my soaked mons. "I will hunger for you for the rest of my days, Alessandra. For the rest of time."

"Then make it stop." I don't hide the prayer in my voice

or the ferocity in my touch, snaking my hands into the thick heaven of his hair. "Tell time to stop, Max. Tell it to *stop*. Now!"

As soon as the words leave me, he halts for a long moment. Jacks his head back, staring up the length of my body until our gazes devour each other.

But only for a moment.

Because after that, he yanks me down to his level.

He keeps my leg pinned to his shoulder, so there's nothing about my body he misses with those blazing sunrise eyes, that ruthless blade of his focus. The same energy defines how he shoves down his sweats and then thrusts up inside me.

"Holy . . . *fuck*." The words shout up from the most wicked, wanton parts of me. I'm sure they fill the room, but I don't care if they bleed beyond that. I don't care if everyone in Paris hears me.

Max pours his stare over me and surges his dick into me. Both are thick and heavy with masculine pride. Every arrogant, decadent lunge is a new testament to how he has captivated me . . . conquered me.

"*Now*," he growls at last, "time can stop."

Together, we fight for exactly that.

As I fracture beneath him.

As he explodes inside me.

Tears burst from me, unhindered and uncontrollable, as the last of my walls crumble beneath his daunting beauty, his desire. He smashes his mouth back to mine, though he doesn't miss a single, perfect pump into me. His thrusts get deeper, stretching me tighter. His lunges spread the heat of his come through my entire womb—and finally out to the quivering pearl at my center. With just those drops, my clit is set off again. Every version of the F-word flies from my lips as my body becomes a puddle of pure ecstasy—and my spirit surrenders for this man, complete and consumed.

Even close to an hour later, after Max pulls out and cleans us both up, I can barely lift my head as he slides the pillow between my hair and his arm. I do, however, screw up the strength to mumble, "No. Want to feel you."

He trails a velvety kiss across my forehead. "Ssshhh, *mon cœur*. The pillow is more comfortable than my arm."

He's got a point. Nestling on his arm reminds me of sleeping on boulders at camp. Raegan was the only one who ever thought that was cool. I, on the other hand, never really liked camp.

Max's soft chuckle makes me realize I muttered the last of that aloud. "Errrrm, Sorry," I add. *Brain. Mush.* "But there it is, dude. You've been bonking a freak who hated summer camp."

He leans on an elbow and angles an adorable smirk. "I am hardly the one to be calling anyone a freak, *ma belle*."

Snorting laugh. "I *wanted* to like it; honestly. But I could never get over why I was being shipped off to some glam camp in the Catskills or the Adirondacks." I trace tiny circles into the center of his chest. As if those are going to erase the pain beneath my next words. "Mom always thought I was oblivious, that I didn't realize exactly why her *man flavor of the month* was paying for it."

The corners of Max's eyes tighten. He feathers his fingers over the damp tendrils along my forehead. "But you did realize." Then curls his hand in to cup my cheek. "Because a doll in a satin carriage is still a doll discarded."

Well, that does it. For as much as I hate camping, he's set himself up in a big one, right in the center of my chest. *Of my heart.* I try telling myself it won't always be this way. Eventually he'll move off to some obscure valley . . .

But right now, everything inside me is just the glow of his campfire.

And the ache of knowing how dark I'll be without it.

I reach up and form my hand against his face, as well. "I don't want to leave you."

A hard gulp undulates in his throat. He pushes his face into my palm. "My sweet little freak. Do you not know yet?" He meshes his fingers with mine and then guides our clasp down to the center of his chest—where his heart beats with the power and passion he's brought to my world in the space of a couple of days. "You will never leave me. You have been right inside here . . . all along."

When I wake up the next morning, I'm in bed alone.

I don't shy away from the urge to tangle back into the empty sheets, drenching my senses in the pine-and-wind scent of him. Nor do I stop myself from wrapping my arms around the pillow, where some strands of his chestnut waves have stayed behind. And yeah, I even close my eyes, stupidly pretending that the pillow is him and he's about to drown me in a breath-altering kiss.

But when the morning sun angles through the window and stabs reality back in, I start drawing boundaries again.

Hard ones.

No moping. No pining. And damn it, *no crying*.

Quitting a man is best done cold turkey. Mom taught me that one enough times. Or maybe it was me who taught her. Clearing that up isn't important. The only priority is the tough-love plan for facing the day.

"You can do this."

I repeat the mantra while kicking my way out of bed. I do it again while marching my ass across the room to pull out my clothes for today. Though Dmitri booked us all on a private charter out of Orly, the earliest departure he could get was later tonight, so Raegan insisted we stick to her plan of a countryside bike ride and gourmet picnic. Granted, we now only have a couple of hours instead of Rae's originally scheduled eight, but that's plenty of time to try filling my head with non-Max memories from the Loire. Something that *doesn't* consist of tumbling chestnut hair, honey-gold eyes, carved god muscles, and a royal velvet voice...

The voice that taunts my memory, replaying so many of his words from our last hours together, in my room...

My reason. My heart. My calling.

I will hunger for you for the rest of my days. For the rest of time.

"Shit." It's more a snarl than a word, and I don't care. Just like I'm over being concerned that my peasant blouse is probably inside out and my Stella McCartney embroidered jeans aren't cuffed right. Just like I screw putting any makeup on besides lip gloss, because what woman in their right mind can think of anything else when their tears refuse to stop?

I meet Drue and Rae for breakfast, though I can't force anything down except coffee and berries. My friends are silent but supportive, giving me room to brood. Damn, how they know me—and how lucky I am to have their strength at times like this.

At times like this?

Who am I kidding? I've never had another time like this.

Not during any of Mom's messy breakups. Or the piles of internet troll emails and comments. Not even after the hundredth time I was told there wasn't a place for curvy girls in high-end fashion reporting. All those instances, I was able to drag myself free of the sorrow. Point myself back on my personal road—because I knew it was the right direction.

But I don't feel right anymore. Hell, I barely know which end is *up* right now.

After Pasca packs the wicker panniers on our bikes with lunch goodies, we set off down the wide paths of the garden. In short time, the pressed gravel gives way to a rugged dirt track. Soon, we're pedaling beneath the thick canopy of the forest, sunlight dotting our leisurely progress. We breathe in a bouquet of wildflowers and listen to soft birdsong. This trail is different than the way we took after I first arrived. Henri calls it *"la route rustique."* Funny, how those French have a poetic way of phrasing everything. After five minutes on the sylvan trail, I'm positive the man really meant *"la route de bruise-your-bottom."*

But dealing with the pain across my backside is way better than coping with the growing ache in my heart. And it's a relief to focus on navigating the rocky trail instead of wondering where Max has disappeared to—*again*. And what he's been doing there. And if he's all right and not lost or confused or—

"Are you even kidding me?" I let my tight lips convey the derision as I stomp harder on the pedals, powering up an incline.

"What?" Rae volleys. "Come on, it's not that big of a hill. We do worse sprints in spin class."

"I don't think that's where she was going with it, missy." Drue gives me a good excuse to admire her ensemble for the day: black velvet culottes and gray pinstriped tights paired with a vintage military jacket and a bright-yellow beret. "And do not bring the sacrilege of evoking spin class on this fine, fine, fine day."

As we cruise down the slope on the other side of the climb, I expel an audible huff. "It *is* a fine day, isn't it? I mean, technically, this should be one of the best days of my life, right?"

"*Pffft.*" Drue takes a swig from her water bottle. "You go ahead and feel whatever you need to, girl."

"We're not here to judge," Rae concurs. "Just to listen."

I shoot her a wry look as we stop in a clearing between leafy alders and oaks. "Just listen, huh?" I tilt back my own water bottle. "So it's forest therapy time minus Henri's Crémant?"

Drue cracks a Cheshire Cat grin while flipping back the lid on one of her panniers. Directly beneath the *très* cute basket top, there's a blue-checkered linen swathed around the neck of a familiar red bottle. "I believe I can assist in the Crémant department."

"Which leaves the therapy duties for Doc Tavish here?" I dismount and drop my kickstand. "Better pour me a big swig of that shit."

"And the problem with that is . . . what, exactly?" Rae flings her mane while getting off her own bike. "Just because I believe in getting the obvious out into the open?"

I grimace as my first swig of the Crémant hits my throat. That's better, though not better enough. "Honey, I know you want to kiss the boo-boo, stop the bleeding, and give me a pretty pink bandage on top, but sometimes, cauterizing the sucker is just a better way to go."

"An amen and a *trés bien* to the sister." Drue clunks her

cup with mine before we both swig again.

Raegan refrains from joining us. Instead, peering at me with a calm that's eerie, she murmurs, "So you're admitting something *is* bleeding?"

Drue beats me to the punch on the exasperated groan. "For the love of the little Lord Jesus, wench. Give it up, okay?"

Rae pouts. "Mmmph."

"Awww." I scuffle over as the lighter fluid in my cup becomes the happy warmth in my blood. "It's okay, little Rae. You can't help it. Hell, for a few hours, neither could I."

The frustration vanishes from her scowl. Open puzzlement takes its place. "Can't help what?"

"Pascaline's story," I clarify. "A secret prince. A clever gypsy. A spell for time travel. It all sounds a hell of a lot better than a delusional actor, a superstitious country woman, and a great piece of folklore."

"Folklore." Rae's lips pinch tight over her echo. "That's how you're labeling the fact that Maximillian De Leon's body was never actually found and buried? And about how that *clever gypsy spell* has only allowed for the guy to live for three and a half more weeks?"

I stumble backward. The thick carpet of slick leaves gives way, slamming me down into the mud, but I ward off both their offers of help. The cold muck is a salve to the fire in my brain and the sprint of my pulse. "Well, crap," I finally stammer.

"Crap *fondue*," Drue elaborates. Her face goes weirdly pale. "So . . . you know that part?" She bugs her eyes at Raegan. "Did you tell her?"

Rae drops her jaw. "You mean you didn't?"

"Stand down, wenches." I slog back to my feet. "I learned it from Max himself." I take a new grateful swig from the fresh cup Drue presses into my grip. "I . . . think."

Drue fidgets with the end of her ponytail. "Which means what?"

"I overheard him yesterday. He was talking to Henri . . . all but emotionally hog-tying the man with a story about how he had limited time. That the curse that brought him here had rules to it."

"Oh yeah, it does." Raegan all but ignores Drue's censuring look, firming her chin and squaring her shoulders. If not for her *Team Bolt* T-shirt, the woman appears like she's about to sit through a job interview. "Pasca filled us in on the rest of the story, after you went upstairs to read Max the riot act."

At first, all I do is glug down more Crémant. I hate the intuition that slams me as vehemently as the alcohol. Still, I force myself to vocalize it. "So you're seriously telling me that there's more to that whole fairy tale?"

Drue leans both elbows on her handlebars. "According to Pasca, yeah. Stuff that's even crazier than what you already heard."

I drink again, floored by the immediate implication of the recognition. That Max wasn't just making shit up as he went along with Henri. But it still doesn't solve, or even narrow down, my dilemma. I'm still pining my soul out over a lunatic who should be committed or a ghost who should be complete ash.

I definitely, absolutely, should *not* be even sniffing at the third option.

That what Raegan's winding up to say is even half of the truth.

"Apparently, the gypsy's curse . . . spell . . . whatever . . . that threw Max forward through time could only be a placeholder for his soul."

Nope. Not even half.

"A *what* for his *what*?" I spit at once.

"A placeholder," she repeats. "Like a spiritual bookmark. Now, Max has to finish the story, so to speak."

With deeper gratitude, I accept Drue's refill to my cup. "And that's accomplished . . . how?"

Rae's gaze narrows as if I've just asked who's buried in Grant's Tomb. "His soul has to find its true match, of course."

"Sure," I croak. "Of *course*."

She goes on as if the snark never left me. "But the deal is, the magic's only good for one full cycle of the moon."

I cock my head. "And how long is that?"

"Twenty-nine and a half days, give or take a few hours." Drue blink-blinks at both of us. "What? I like science."

"And I like reality." I dart a nod of thanks for her being my ongoing bartender but stick to my skeptical glower. "How the hell are you hearing this and believing any of it's possible?" I demand.

Drue shrugs with frightening ease. "How are you so sure it's not?"

"Oh, fuck me."

"The universe surprises us with possibilities every day, honey. When most of the châteaus in this valley were constructed, they were considered the height of man's possibility. If anyone from *this* time appeared in their midst and claimed bullet trains, airliners, and space shuttles were possible, they'd be burned at the stake or tossed in the asylum. So why *not* believe something like time travel can be real?"

I wheel away from them. "Oh, my God." At once, mesh my hands behind my head. "So you're really telling me that if Max

De Leon doesn't lock down some true love in another twenty-six days, he's going to be deported back to seventeen eighty-nine?"

"Exactly." Drue's rejoinder is swift and sharp. "Or maybe worse."

"And what does *that* mean?"

"Pasca couldn't give us the whole scoop on that part," Drue admits. "She simply doesn't know, Allie. Nobody does."

A laugh spurts from me. I yearn to punch it into a scream.

My name is Maximillian George Jean Valence De Leon. I swear it to you . . . on my own life, which is just a pittance now . . .

"Just a pittance." My whisper is muted by my painful swallow. I turn away, struggling not to compare my brain to the chaos of the trees. Massive failure. I'm dizzy, and it has nothing to do with the Crémant in my blood.

Just a pittance.

Was he speaking words of prophecy or lunacy? I've been so convinced of the latter, I didn't stop to consider the fallout of the former. The repercussions of what it would really mean . . .

Not just that Maximillian has actually time-jumped here from 1789.

But that he thinks he's done it because of me.

To fall in love with me.

Incredible.

Impossible.

I don't know how to fall in love.

For the last four years alone, maybe longer, I've done nothing but dream of what's going to happen after that airplane ride back to New York tonight. This is the moment I've been waiting and working for. The affirmation that I *can* bring some beauty and worth to the world—without the conduit of a man.

Even if it means leaving behind the man who brings beauty and worth to *my* world.

Who sees all the beauty and worth in *me*.

But it's not meant to be.

Max needs something more. Some*one* more.

Now, even the metaphorical meaning of the trees is too much to bear. I circle back to Drue and Raegan as the heat behind my eyes becomes the ugly cry on my face. But weirdly, it doesn't come. I'm a damn dryer sheet now, smelling like a forest but feeling like a desert.

A desert hiding a thousand fault lines.

"Hey." Rae's the first to pace back over and gently cup my shoulders. "You all right?"

I jerk my way through a nod. Still, Drue points at my head. "Yeah, but the hamsters in here are still sprinting too fast."

"It's okay." Unsurprisingly, Rae moves in for a full-contact hug. "You can talk to us, honey. What are you thinking?"

Despite their combined care, I hunch in on myself with a leaden gulp. I fight to keep the cracks in check, the fault lines from erupting . . . and my heart from spilling out.

"I'm thinking that irony is a bitch and that I must've really pissed her off this time."

With the words, I've somehow peeved Mother Nature on top of Lady Irony. She splits open the sky on us, sending down a squall that has us shrieking, grabbing the panniers, and dashing for cover beneath a thick oak. The panic takes care of my heartache for a few minutes, at least. I laugh with sincerity while huddling with my friends and tearing into our soggy farewell picnic.

As we savor the sandwiches, cheese, and fruit tarts, I'm secretly glad for the rain. The coincidence has nothing to do with hiding my nonexistent tears . . . and everything to do with exposing the agonized corners of my heart.

CHAPTER TWELVE

MAX

Henri and Pasca have been generous about extending their hospitality, allowing me to stay another night at the château, in Bastien's old bedroom. Apparently my old chamber was gutted and added on to the château's spa—another concept, like so many, that has gained new meaning from what it meant in my century.

My century.

What is the meaning of that anymore?

I pace the chamber, considering the question. My head and heart respond with naught but murky globs.

But the canyons of my soul yield a different answer. The truth of it is like a hawk rising from mist, clear and sure and strong and free.

My century is hers.

My home is Allie.

My time is now.

Even if that means there are but days to now live that truth.

Surprisingly, the chamber has not changed much since the days my brother dwelled here. The furnishings are still defined by his favorite combination: dark blue and crimson. His writing desk is still next to the window, in the position he preferred for watching the sunrise. There are still a few nicks in the wainscoting, courtesy of the fencing battles in which he and I indulged behind Mother's back.

Happier times.

Perfect memories.

I breathe in deep, hoping their comfort will fill the pain in my chest. But newer memories are there now. Better ones.

I close my eyes, holding images of Alessandra in my mind like an engraving. Every beautiful detail. The gloss of her hair in the sun. The perfection of her silken skin. The radiance of her intelligence, always shining in the verdancy of her eyes. The sublime, sensual grace of her curves.

My knees weaken. I plummet into one of the deep wingback chairs before the fire and fix my gaze on the hottest core of the flames, near the tangle of the logs. Though my sockets sting and my body aches, I do not move. The pain brings a consoling numbness. Moving means I must stir the memories once more. I should just remain here . . . for as long as I can . . .

I am so determined to remain my own sentry, I barely acknowledge the chamber door opening. Or the appearance of the two smirking women in front of me, with their hair colors that match the décor.

I jump to my feet with newly fisted hands, until they back off as if having sprung a caged boar.

"Easy, cowboy." Drue raises her palms. "We come in peace."

I slacken my own stance. "Mistresses." I execute a decent if impatient bow. "Your presence is not unwelcome . . . though perplexing." I pivot back toward Bastien's desk to check the time on his treasured clock, and my chest tightens when I realize it has been removed. Or perhaps stolen by the mob from that terrible day . . . "The day grows late. Twilight is near. Should you not have been departed by now?"

"Yeah, well . . ." Drue tapers off the word into a quirk of a shrug. "That was before the raincloud rager kept our asses parked in the forest for two hours."

"Which turned out to be a blessing in disguise," Raegan adds.

I nod, though my perplexity about their intrusion persists.

"Since Dmitri had to move our charter's flight time back, we had time to come back here and change first," Drue explains.

"Ah. *Oui.*" I am still not elucidated.

"And grab the last of the essentials." Raegan inserts a new grin.

"Ah . . . *oui*?"

"Like you."

The women announce it together—and finish with extended giggles.

I do not giggle. Nor, however, have I been cleared from my bewilderment. The duo have freed me from one perplexed mire, only to drag me into another.

"Ladies." Discomfited grunt. "I am afraid . . . I still do not follow."

"We know." Raegan is the one to stride forward now. She leans and gathers up both my hands. "But we're asking you to trust us, Max. You know we want the same thing you do."

"Allie's happiness." Drue underlines it with a nod.

The sincerity in their voices resonates inside me—but settles like thick mud at the base of my throat. "Yes," I finally rasp. "Her happiness."

"Then you'll trust us?" Drue moves over, yanking on one

of my elbows. "You'll come with us?"

I inhale deeply. While expelling it, meet both their gazes. "To the ends of God's earth."

Drue rocks her head back with a wry expression. "Which is what all this might just feel like, buddy."

"Perfect!" Raegan's little hop reminds me of the tiny bird that used to pop up from Bastien's long-gone clock. "But we haven't much time. Stuff whatever things you need into a duffel, and let's get you hidden in the back of the van."

Drue nods. "Dmitri texted right before we came in. Says the fake work visa and ID won't be a problem."

Raegan cuckoo-jumps again. "Sweet. This is epic to the tenth!" She jabs a finger into my chest. "You. Get packing. Now."

I only have to pass three seconds in dazed discomfiture before Henri sweeps in. He's bearing the exact bag Raegan has ordered me to prepare. I have no concept of how to communicate my gratitude as he tells her, "Already handled."

But my dilemma is erased by my shock the moment Raegan thanks him with a firm handclasp. A *full* clasp, palm to palm, as if she is a man and they have concluded business. Henri laughs as if this is normal, causing me to shuffle backward by a step when he turns and approaches me again.

Ironically—or mayhap not—my gawk is cuckoo-bird wide as he reaches into his inner jacket pocket.

Then withdraws a shining object on a chain.

A round timepiece, with a cover made of filigreed silver and a set of initials carved into the back.

I know they are there before even seeing the back.

I know this as my chest tightens into a drum and my heartbeat hammers in my throat. I know this as a stinging pressure builds behind my eyes from the moment Henri pulls out my hand . . . and places the watch into my palm.

My vision blurs while I turn the piece over and run my fingertips over the engraving.

M. G. J. V. L.

For *Maximillian George Jean Valence De Leon.*
Now I have had the biggest shock of my night.

I take only a minute to reassemble my composure. It feels like a year. It feels like two hundred and thirty. Fitting, since that is exactly what this man has just given back to me.

I lift my head. The weight in my throat is onerous, the tears in my vision thick. But I swallow and fumble, scrambling for even a few words of gratitude. They will be paltry, but I must try.

They vanish as soon as I take in his whole face—and behold the glint of tears in his eyes, as well.

In that moment, we are of one mind. One agreement. One message that needs no words—save those he finally delivers to Raegan and Drue.

"*Now* he is fully ready."

ALLIE

I've always been a completely chill flyer.

Until now.

Clarification. The flight itself has been great. With Hemline's permission—and credit card number—Dmitri booked us on the finest luxury charter flight service out of Orly. The aircraft itself is so pristine, it has that new car smell. Dmitri, Rae, Drue, and I had champagne in hand before the wheels ever left the ground. The takeoff was flawless as the pilot guided the sleek white jet into the sunset-stained clouds like a knife through butter.

But that's where the "chill" ends and the "until now" part begins.

While Dmitri and I have let the bubbles do their worthy best on our bloodstreams as we bicker about what movie we're going to watch on the widescreen, my best friends look like the Thelma and Louise of the skies, sitting together and scheming in conspiratorial whispers.

Seriously. The two of them are scheming.

About things I'm not sure I want to know about.

"Hey." My shout is intentionally harsh. I swear, the only thing missing from the air over their heads is a Plexiglass bubble with a sticker reading *Stay out. Evil plans afoot.* "Are you seriously going to let Dmitri call the shots on what we're watching for the next eight hours?"

"Huh?" Raegan blurts. "What who's watching? Where?"

"It's fine," Drue mutters. "Whatever he wants."

My jaw plummets. "Who are you, and what have you done with Eeyore Kidman?" Since we were kids, this woman's always demanded a say in the movie choice.

"Yessssss." Dmitri crosses his long legs at the ankle and hovers a finger over the pad that controls the inflight entertainment system. "If we start now, I can get in *A View to a Kill*, *Octopussy*, and *Moonraker*." With the same finger, he smugly ticks the air. "Ding, ding, ding. Bad Bond fashion shows for the win."

I release my seat belt with a stubborn *snock* and march across the cabin until I'm palming D's forehead. "Out!" I order. "Get thee gone, demon. Return Drue Kidman to me at once!"

"Back. *Baaack.*" She bats my hand away. "Lay off. I'm just tired." She throws a dark side-eye at Raegan. "Somebody subjected me to physical labor in the name of *fun.*" She unfastens her belt with a yawn I don't entirely believe. "As a matter of fact, I'm thinking of going to the back for a nap." The yawn vanishes in favor of her pout. "Tuck me in, wenchie?"

"Fine," I mutter and lead the way to the onboard bedroom. "All right. Anything's better than— Holy. Shit."

My heart is in my throat. My blood rushes to my face. Every thought in my brain is out in the clouds beyond the window next to the bedroom's queen-size bed.

Upon which Maximillian kneels, peering out the wide window like a kid visiting an amusement park.

Though that's where the comparison of him to *anything* childlike has its beginning and end.

To put his own words to good use, *God's freaking teeth.* The flight attendant's black suit, which explains what Rae and Drue have been up to since we left Loire, is the most perfect showcase yet for his long limbs, lithe grace, and courtly posture. Not that he's posturing much at the moment.

He's too busy being adorable. And beautiful.

And the fulfillment of everything my soul has ached for all day.

Maybe for a lifetime.

"*Alessandra.*" A breathtaking smile intensifies the allure of his mouth. "Come and see, *mon miracle.*" He scoots over, making room for me while ripping off his jacket by clumsy hitches. Our arrival has apparently given him permission to shuck the disguise. "Come now and *look.* We are *flying.* Above the clouds!"

For a long moment, I'm filled with too much shock to

move—and too much enchantment to want to. Suddenly, everything's just . . . brighter. Better. Filled with more wonder. He's here. Really here.

"Errrm . . . surprise." Rae's murmur, behind my left shoulder, is followed by Drue pressing in over my right. She notches her chin to my neck before whispering, "Sometimes, great birthday presents *do* come in big packages."

I'd smack her for the snark, but my heart is too busy agreeing with her—in every vibrant way. Instead of the bop, I yank on her wrist and haul her in for a heartfelt mash. After I do the same to Raegan, I swallow to hold in my tears—not that I'm fooling anyone with the effort. The tender focus on Max's face confirms that clearly enough.

"Damn," I finally utter. "I don't know whether to kiss you wenches or toss you both out the airlock."

Drue steps back and links elbows with Rae. "We're not getting a better exit cue than that."

Rae's giggle of agreement is cut short as Drue pulls the door closed with a defined *clack*. A softer *snick* follows as I slide the lock into place too. And why the hell do I feel the need for the extra security when I'm the one sealed in with a muscled hunk staring me down like a hungry lion?

I don't even want to try for the answer.

Just like I shove a lot of things from my mind right now.

Like how they all actually got Max smuggled aboard this thing, posing as a flight attendant. And why he agreed to it, dropping his whole life to hop on a plane with me to New York City. And what the hell I'm going to do with him once we get there . . .

Besides a lot more of what I yearn to do with him now.

Sweet freaking God, especially now. Beholding him here,

with his gaze bright as the sun glinting on the clouds beyond the window. With his smile, potent and powerful and adoring. And oh *hell*, with his breathtaking body, seeming to dominate the whole cabin—let alone the whole bed.

A factor of which I'm achingly aware as he extends a hand out. Bidding—not asking—me to join him.

And I do.

Because I have no choice.

Because this is him. *Maximillian*. This beautiful, powerful, bold, brave man, who has decided to give so much of himself to me...

No. To give *all* of himself.

A concept so daunting, it's painful to think about.

Because I have to admit I haven't figured him out yet. Which should scare the crap out of me but doesn't. Somewhere twenty thousand feet beneath us, there's either a psych ward with a missing patient or a graveyard with an empty coffin. But right now, I don't care about that answer. I only care about how good he feels, so strong and real and right, as he deepens our clinch into a fierce, mashing kiss. As he delves in and fully breaches my mouth. As I clutch him tighter in return and savor his unique essence. Wind, spices, desire, decadence... Holy crap, he even tastes like a powerful prince.

And I want more of the fiction.

So much more.

I open wider as he plunges his lips deeper. Letting him devour me. Command me. Take me.

When we finally part, I move my hands in, bracketing the corners of his eyes with my index fingers. A long breath flows out of him as I rub over his scar and then tangle my fingertips in his thick auburn waves.

"Max?" I finally whisper.

He hums softly, sending fiery vibrations through me. "Alessandra?"

"This . . . is crazy, right?"

"Perhaps." He dips his head until his lips brush my nose. "Likely."

"I don't even care." I lift my head, aligning my mouth beneath his. "My perfect birthday gift."

His smile, in all its captivating glory, curls even higher. "My perfect miracle."

It's all the inspiration I need.

I lower my hands, gently pushing him to his back on the bed. "Lie back and enjoy the view, Hotness. My friends worked hard to make my birthday gift happen. It's bad manners to let their efforts go unrewarded."

At first he only responds with a dark and decadent groan. I'm not surprised, since I'm already unzipping his slacks. He helps me pull them down. His erect stalk surges free, lined with pulsing purple veins. I'm damn sure I've never been happier to greet a man's erection.

"Well," he husks. "Etiquette *is* important."

"Oh, definitely." I say it while whipping off the one-piece knit dress I changed into back at the château—nothing like being prepared without even knowing it—and crawl onto the mattress with him. I stretch out next to him and then press in to feel every inch of his radiating heat. But as hot as his muscled striations are, no part of him is more searing than his sun god stare. I lock my stare with those rich golds while murmuring, "I've been learning that lesson really well lately. You know what they say about spending time in all those French châteaus."

At first, he replies with nothing but a strangled rasp. To

be fair, if the man is capable of coherency while I fist him from balls to crown, I'm not doing something right. But the arch of his neck and the filthy French off his lips are as intoxicating as making the Met Gala's "Best Of" list. I rejoice in the victory by palming the hot orbs at his base and then following the rise of his lifeblood back up his magnificent length. The entire time, I don't drop my gaze from his stunning face. *Damn.* The man is as grand and glorious as a wildcat. A mixture of savagery, severity, beauty, nobility. If he were strutting along a catwalk in Bryant Park, every woman in the tent would want him between their legs. And in their mouths.

Sorry, everyone—but I volunteer as tribute.

The thought really is that smug—and I'm proud of it while trailing my lips down the etched ladders of his brick-hard abs.

"*Alessandra.*"

"Ssshhh."

I whisper it into his skin, controlling the hitches of his hips with my reverent licks and kisses—at least until I dip the tip of my tongue into the hollow of his navel.

And then slide lower.

And lower . . .

"Alessandra!"

"Ssshhh." I issue it past my adoring smile. "Let me do this for you, Maximillian."

"That was an exhortation of praise, *ma belle*, not protest."

I spread my smile wider. And why not? I'm damn sure I've never been happier in my life. I'm on a luxury plane to New York, where the contract of my dreams is waiting to be signed. I'm watching the man of my fantasies get totally naked for me, hauling off his shirt and hurling it against the bulkhead. I'm tossing aside the reminder that he won't be mine forever, but for a little while longer, our paths are entwined again.

That I can do wild, wet, wicked things to him again.

I'm still smiling as I suck at the swollen bulb atop his magnificent penis. He hisses and jolts from the moment I suckle the hot, tangy pearl that erupts there. Holy shit. He already tastes so perfect. So illicit and erotic and intoxicating.

I want more.

So I go for it—inspiring more of the delicious drops by gently palming his balls. Max's hiss spirals into a labored moan. He strains as if I've chained him, his breathtaking muscles stretching at his burnished skin.

In return, I chuckle softly. Wicked? Yes. But justified? Also yes. This moment is a dream. No. Better than a dream. A wanton fantasy come true, with every ounce of his masculine passion now mine. With every spark of his need speaking to my blood, my bones . . . my sex.

But most profoundly, to my heart.

Pushing at it as I lower my mouth all the way over him.

Wrapping around it as he rasps out a string of French that hits me like both prayer and penetration.

Filling it as he lifts me free, drags me back up his body, and aligns my stare with his.

I'm inundated by gilded magic. Overtaken by the tingles of his touch. Awash in shivering arousal and reawakened lust . . . Especially as he swings my body across his and fits my aching apex against the throbbing ridge of his.

"These must be gone." He clarifies with a brutal twist of his free hand into the lacy band of my panties. "*Now.*"

"Unnnhhh." It's all I manage for a long moment. After just a few rubs along his hot shaft, I crave every inch of it inside me. "Okay, tiger. I'm right on that page with you. Just give me a second to— *Oh!*"

My exclamation coincides with the distinct sound of rending fabric. *Holy crap.* The man has officially lived up to every speck of his bodice-ripper romance allure. I know that as fact the moment my underwear—well, what's left of it—slips down the back of my legs.

And is followed by the push of his cockhead at the entrance of my tunnel.

I take him in with a welcoming clench of my pussy. Seal the deal with a new mash of my mouth to his. His lusty groan vibrates through my entire being. Floods me with the sunburst of his passion . . . and soon, the streaming, searing torrent of his come.

As he groans through his orgasm, I scream through mine. I can't tell the difference between the sun's glow on the clouds and the orgasmic blaze inside me. I'm quivering, pulsing, exploding, flying . . .

Complete.

Well, that does it. Sex is officially never going to be this good again.

Because sex with Maximillian has so little to do with sex.

He pulls up a little, his eyes filled with amber adoration—though he balances that innocence with a wholly insolent smirk. I want to bop him but don't. I can't even form half a laugh without it threatening to become a sob instead.

At once, he seems to read every speck of that thought. He turns his head, capturing a couple of my fingers between the firm surfaces of his lips before murmuring, "What is it, *mon amour*?" He dips lower, brushing his mouth over my palm. "It is all right, Alessandra. It is just us. Whatever you say—"

"Won't count." The second I utter it, we both stiffen. But

it's not like I can take it back or make it less true. "Right? That *is* the way this thing works, yes? I have to return your love, and really mean it, and then declare the whole damn thing in public, or you'll be gone. Whatever the hell that means."

Uncertainty casts new shadows across his face, dimming the radiance of his gaze he now averts out the window.

"How did you learn that information?" he finally murmurs after a tense minute.

"If it's true, does it matter?"

He scrubs a hand over his face. "It does not matter either way, I suppose."

"So it *is* true."

He grips my waist with both hands, gently lifting my body off his. As soon as his cock falls free, he twists and leaves the bed. "It does not matter because you do not believe it, *chérie*."

I scramble around to sit up straight. All my frustration and confusion finally bubble to the surface and spill out. "Just because you say so?"

"Because I know so." With two brusque steps, he clears the space to the bathroom. After a few moments, he reemerges, bearing two clean cloths. As he sits and offers me one, he utters, "I have not come on this trip to try to make you believe, Alessandra. I only want to keep loving you for as long as fate will let me."

I do nothing to hide my growing conflict as he brushes back my sweaty curls with his fingertips. My scalp tingles as he threads his touch deeper. A weary sigh escapes me. I force my eyes to close, afraid his incisive gaze will easily read my answer to his confession.

But maybe that's exactly what I want.

More than anything.

Make me believe, Maximillian.
Please make me believe.

CHAPTER THIRTEEN

MAX

Bastien.

Mother.

Father.

My soul cries with their names. My muscles coil, battling not to throw off the cloak that Carl lent me to disguise myself in this crowd.

Crowd?

No. It is a mob, succumbing to the most terrible rules of mob mentality. They are vicious. Violent. Bloodthirsty. Animals.

"Off with their heads!"

"Off with their heads!"

"Off with their heads!"

My father, barely recognizable because of their beatings, looks as if he desires the same thing already. Bastien, two years my younger but five times the warrior I shall ever be, glares into the throng as if mentally severing their heads.

But the sight of Mother incinerates my soul the most.

Her head is bowed, her posture defeated. They have stripped her to her night shift. Her stooped shoulders shake. Though I have never seen her like this, I know every drop of what she is feeling. Confusion. Grief. Betrayal by so many standing here. People whom she has personally helped in so many ways over the years. People she has even called friends.

All calling for her head beneath the ax.

All cheering even louder as Father is led to the block first.

All bellowing in triumph as the executioner swings the blade high.

And brings it down with a sickening thunk.

"No." *I grab the cloak's cowl.*

"No, milord!" *Carl stays me, his fist tight on my wrist. "They will revolt and be after your blood!"*

"Better mine than theirs."

"It will change nothing, Maximillian."

"Maybe they can escape."

"It will change nothing, Maximillian."

"Better mine than theirs!"

The ax falls again. The mob celebrates louder. Bas is gone now.

"No. No!"

"Max. Max!"

I whirl, glaring at Carl. Why does he sound so strange? Why has his voice gained such entrancing music? Why does he sound like . . .

"Alessandra?"

"Max." She calls to me through the dark—of my mind as well as my soul. "Wake up. It's all right, Hotness. Wake up. I'm here."

"My blood for theirs," I mumble. "Take me instead. My blood . . ."

"Ssshhh." She strokes warm fingers against my clammy forehead. Her sheets smell of strawberries and vanilla. In the distance, a vast city rumbles and churns and honks and clamors through the night. There is a louder thunder. The train going by. How do I know that? "You're safe. Listen to me. You're safe, Max."

"But they are not."

She slides closer, wrapping a soft thigh over mine. "Baby, it was a dream."

"It was my life."

I hate myself for the snarl, but it is unavoidable. I already know she forgives me for it—as she has done countless times over the last ten days. She has led me from the hell of my memories with her comforting kisses, sweet caresses—and tight, welcoming body. That perfect sheath to which my cock has grown hopelessly addicted.

That miracle of connection . . . that my soul cannot exist without.

I cannot think about that right now. Any of it.

I kick back the bedcovers and rush to my feet. There is a chill in the night air, but I am still sweating from the dream. I stomp, clammy and naked, into Alessandra's living room. While stepping through the shafts of moonlight, I rake my hands through my hair. Well, what Dmitri's barber left of it. They are called stylists in this age, and I have subjected myself to having two inches shorn. I am not certain I enjoy the feeling—but after two centuries without a trim, I was likely due. Not that the choice was truly mine. Dmitri was accepting naught but compliance. There is a grand soiree in two nights, being hosted by the Hemline nobility. An advent far too important for Alessandra. Everything and everyone must be perfect, especially the man with whom she has chosen to attend.

Me.

But thinking about the party is not the reason for my disquiet. Nor are the waning recollections of my nightmare.

I pace the length of the room, taking in its exposed brick walls and sleek aluminum fixtures. When I first arrived here, Allie joked about my stunned stares. *Well, Hotness, it's not a palace. But if you squint real hard . . .*

I did not squint. But then, just like now, I did struggle to accept it all as more than a grand, glorious fever dream. All these wonders . . . Television. Laptop. A furnace in the floor. A bookcase with hundreds of tomes in it. I ponder the resplendence of it all. The complete insanity. And yet I am still considered the lunatic here . . .

A rustle from the doorway jerks me out of the ruminations. Allie, wrapped in the throw blanket from the bed, is the heart of my frustration but also my fever. She is softness, skin, cream, luxury. Her curves are a captivating rival for the swaths of the blanket, which dip low enough to snare my attention. As she readjusts the cover, I am given a fleeting glimpse of the crevice I love most on her body.

"It was the same scene, wasn't it?" Her husky voice chases the cold from the air. "You were thinking of your parents and Bastien."

"People you do not believe in." I turn from her, attempting an impassive shrug. "So let us not speak of it further."

"Max—"

"Let us not speak of it, Alessandra."

"Then come back to bed and let me help you forget it." Her voice is no longer on the air. It heats the breadth of my back as she steals a hand around to my front. Despite my clenched effort at control, a hiss bursts off my lips as she circles my shaft. She pulls and squeezes in all the right ways, filling it with more blood.

"*Ventrebleu,*" I choke. "By every saint there was and is . . ."

The blanket whispers to the floor. With her other hand, she reaches between my legs from the back. Once she finds my balls, she massages them with hot, perfect little circles.

"And all the angels too." There's an irresistible tease in her murmur. "Don't forget them. Especially this one."

"The one with her horns holding up her halo?"

"Something like that."

With a grunt, I wrap a hand around her wrist. Though she does not release me, I can at least halt the insanity-inducing strokes. "I will surely fuck you until dawn, *mon petit* demon, and you need your rest. You have appointments all day and night tomorrow. Your preparations for the party are too important. The Hemline nobility will decide upon your fate with them. You must be prepared."

"Psssshhh." She cups my balls with more determination. "I can sleep when I'm dead."

The air between us stops.

The flames between us freeze.

The time between us races. Not enough. There will never be enough time . . .

I step fully away from her. The seconds speed by faster.

"Shit." She thumps a nervous toe against the floor, punctuating her gritted tone. "Shit, Max. I'm . . . sorry."

I push out a hard breath. "Why?"

"Because even if I don't believe in the freaking curse, you do, and I . . ."

She ceases the toe jabs, replacing them with a frustrated snarl. If she believes that will exonerate her from finishing the statement, she is gravely mistaken.

"You what, Alessandra?"

As I turn fully toward her, my arms stiff with challenge,

she chews the inside of her lip. Her nudity increases how tiny and vulnerable she seems. I steel myself against that heady allure. Barely.

"I . . . care for you, Max." *Thump, thump, thump.* She puts her toe to work again. "You have to know that by now." She attempts a soft laugh. "Hell, I rode the Bryant Park carousel for you. And nobody ever gets half my street cart gyro wrap."

Then why will you not admit that you love me? Preferably in front of a hundred witnesses? Or even three?

Perhaps my stillness speaks the words for me. Perhaps she simply senses them after her intense glance across my face. Either way, she grabs up the blanket and sweeps it around herself once more. "Despite all that, I know how this will end, okay? Believe me, damn it. I have a lot of experience with exactly how this will end, and—"

"Is that so?" I slice her short with a bitter bark. "*Exactly* how shall it end?"

She tightens the blanket like a queen with her robe. "Don't growl at me, buddy. I don't know any other woman who would give you leeway like this with the time-traveling fantasy, okay?"

"Ah." I step back as if she has driven a fist through my chest. "So it is still my . . . fantasy."

"Which I'm not knocking you for." She approaches with an entreating voice and soft steps—and I yearn for a fist between my ribs instead. "But Max, one of us has to approach this thing from the real world. And in that world, I've watched a long list of amazing women throw away everything they are in the name of true love—which never turns out to be as true or as magical as they claim it will be."

My body tenses as she draws near, but I make no move to

halt her. I am certain my next words will perfectly accomplish that purpose.

"A list of amazing women . . . led by the woman you call mother?"

My prediction bears out to truth.

She stops so suddenly, her feet chirp on the wood floor. She shivers so completely, I yearn to gather her into my arms again. But I do not. She has issued her hard truths to me. It is time for her to receive the same. "I am not the only one who fights memories in their sleep, *ma chérie*."

She dips a curt nod. "Fair enough."

I almost dice the air itself with the sharpness of my new laugh. "*Brava*. You found one fair thing about all of this."

She blinks. The new sheen in her gaze reminds me of moss on a battle turret. "You know what, Hotness? I think you're right. Maybe we should just go back to bed."

I nod tightly—while fighting every urge through my body, a thousand claws strong, to pull her back. But what will be achieved save the satisfaction of our lusts? How will that change the fiber of who she is? How will it heal her heart's wounds and smooth her soul's scars? The damage she carries from a long and painful war—against the enemies she must overcome in order to save me?

Her own logic.

Her own will.

Her own fears.

The answer is already agonizingly clear.

She cannot.

I see that now, as clearly as the skyline of the city across the river. I confront my terror of it as I did when first seeing the Isle of Manhattan at night, jutting against the stars in its brutal brilliance. But on that night, Alessandra had tugged me onto the balcony upon which I walk now. She took my hand, making me view the sight with different eyes. The bold glass angles of 30 Hudson Yards, the Bank of America Tower, and the Nordstrom Tower. The historical icons of the Chrysler Building and the Empire State Building, which she coaxed me to the top of a few days ago.

And then, the most meaningful spire of them all.

The gleaming silver beacon at one end of the island. The tower called Freedom—and the story she relayed, explaining exactly how it came by the name.

And suddenly, none of it was so fearsome anymore.

Just as the certainty of my death can no longer be.

The moment I come to the admission, the fear starts to lift. My conflict clears. Even the constant pressure in my chest, denoting my struggle to let her go, is a little lighter.

Fate has saved the most difficult part of my journey for the end, and for that, I am thankful.

I can do this.

How agonizing can two more weeks be?

ALLIE

"The hem needs to be taken up here . . . and here."

I use the salon's mirror to meet the scrutiny of the woman at my feet. She lowers her wrist, adorned with a bright-pink pincushion, and blinks past trendy glasses that double the size of her caramel eyes. I arch my brows and nod, making certain she comprehends my instructions. Not expecting miracles on the answer. Though the advisors of the Maison Magique are some of the top fashion consultant salons in the city and I was damn lucky to snag personalized appointments for Max and me, that *magique* just isn't happening during our final fitting before the big Hemline gathering at the Hotel Obelisk tomorrow night.

In short, the most important meeting-not-a-meeting of my life.

Which means my head needs to be fully in this game.

Not that luscious little Refinna the seamstress is helping in that department. The observant little woman widens her smirk, completely wise to the friction between Max and me—and there's nothing I can do to stop her snark. The energy she's sensing is real. I have no right to keep asking him to play my dutiful boyfriend, even when we both know what's at the end of this little life episode. For us both.

Goodbye.

That's all I can give him. That's all I know how to give.

The coffee and yogurt in my stomach start to curdle. This time, the nausea has nothing to do with Refinna—though her pout makes me feel like a brat who's asked for thousand-dollar tennis shoes instead of alterations at three hundred bucks a stitch.

"Is mademoiselle quite certain about the higher skirt?" She peers through the trendy lenses, theatrically perfect about her bafflement. "The dress's color is already a risk factor. Lavender is a fleeting trend, *n'est-ce pas*? And if the event is at the Obelisk, then perhaps black—"

"Will be what everyone else in the place is wearing." I sweep a polite smile. "So you see ... *oui*?"

She purses her lips, making it obvious she doesn't. I sigh, almost wanting to let her win. The fate of nations doesn't rest on the color of my dress for tomorrow night. By next week, the

Hemline party will be a distant memory for many.

Next week.

My belly sours more painfully.

Hemline's decision will be final by then, with the new shows for the fall season to be announced live on Connie Filigree's prestigious morning show.

And as Max himself still maintains, his last week of mortal life.

It's only a few details worse than the hard truth Dmitri brought me this morning. Though the man has been my unexpected yet invaluable knight in shining armor through all of this, putting off the authorities with swagger that's worthy of bedazzled trophies for miles, he's told me that the jig is nearly up. The ruse must come to an end.

And of course, Max keeps saying it won't be an issue. That he'll be a ghost soon. Trouble is, he's got even Dmitri convinced about his tale, and now my self-involved assistant has become committed to Max's plight. In Dmitri's own words, I've got to either propose to the man or buy him a one-way ticket back to the Loire.

In short, the whole situation sucks elephant balls—which Refinna looks like she's rolling around in her cheeks as she plays with the tuck points I've indicated along the dress's front hem. "The front . . . It is cut like elegant drapes, *oui*? And thus, the leg is highlighted like so . . ."

"Understood," I return. "But—*respecteusement*—I'd like it shown off like so." I grab a couple of pins off her wrist and poke them through the fabric, demonstrating exactly where I want the alteration.

She flairs her sleek eyebrows. "That is a daring hemline to commit to, mademoiselle."

"All the better, since she is a great deal of beautiful woman."

Refinna and I pivot toward the man who's quashed our ovaries in the span of one sentence.

If Maximillian De Leon was my addiction before now, he's just become my obsession. Every tissue between my thighs clenches. Every cell of my pussy demands carnal knowledge of him—especially if he's wearing *that* suit.

Holy shit. That suit.

Yeah, I hit a home run on picking out this one. Even snooty Refinna won't be challenging that fact. Crazily, the choice took all of five minutes, since we came in for his fitting right after leaving the Empire State Building. I'd been certain Max would love the experience after his giddy excitement during the plane ride, but he'd lasted less than a minute on the building's famous observation deck before turning three shades of green. He was still squeamish when we got to the salon, so I followed instinct and selected the ensemble that captured my eye first. The slimmer-cut pieces, designed by a new Italian stud with Prada, are a shade brighter than navy but darker than cobalt. The jacket is lined in a luxurious fabric blending shades of plum and—yessss—lavender.

Yeah. I'm already obsessed.

And everyone in the Garment District will have to take a number in line behind me.

Except, it seems, for little Refinna.

The little bird pops to her feet and struts over to Max as if she's holding the big Number One instead.

"Hmmmm." The peevish diva I've been dealing with has been replaced by the flirty creature who struts a full circle around my man. Okay, not my man, but the hell if he'll become hers. "My, my, my," she croons, deliberately coy—a guile I now see he's familiar with. Maybe even enjoying a little.

Down, Allie.

I back up the command by crucifying my palms with my fingernails. Then deeper. *What the hell is going on with you? He's just being nice—in an eighteenth-century French court kind of way.*

"Êtes-vous d'accord?" Max casts a smooth but friendly smile across the showroom.

Because he's polite like that. Because he believes everyone gets to have kindness, even if they're a condescending snit.

"Oh!" Refinna jumps up to respond. "*Oui, oui!* I do approve! The man must always wear the suit, not the other way around. And monsieur, you do wear this suit."

The praise rolls out of her like a satin ribbon. She starts touching him in the same way, disguising her seduction as an assessment for the suit's fit. Max hardly flinches, which jolts my tired mind in all the wrong places. Refinna's strokes get bolder, making her look like a desperate dollar-beer-bar babe from this angle, but Max doesn't seem affected in the least. Not even as she runs a long, defined finger up and down his fly.

Until he turns to her with a dark stare and an extended growl.

What the living hell?

His expression, which could mean anything from illicit invitation to blatant caution, has been one of my favorites for the last month. I'm not sure how to feel about it now—but I'm damn well going to find out.

I kick off my heels and then push off the fitting box. I'm glad for the few steps necessary to get over to the cozy pair. The jabs of the pins in my thighs help to clear the red haze from my vision. I'm not so fortunate with the conflict in my blood, which is slathered in a layer of thick confusion.

This scenario isn't new for me. I'm practically a pro at it. And sometimes—most times—I'm even relieved when one comes along. It's easy. Clean. An ideal excuse for justified outrage. A perfect opportunity to plate up a big, juicy buh-bye to a man. Best of all, the problem can be his, not mine. No messy self-esteem issues. No sleepless nights inspired by Launette Fine, wondering what I did wrong and what I could have done to save things.

As they'd said in the Loire itself, *voilà*.

But *voilà* doesn't have a contingency plan for a piece of work named Refinna. The same Refinna who tucks her fingertips into Max's waistband while batting her honey eyes up at him. The woman who's clearly going for the gusto with one end goal in mind. To drag him off to her personal fitting room.

"What an astute woman you are, mademoiselle." I'm sweet about it and even stop myself short of the girlfriend lemur latch on his arm—though inwardly, I consider it. His natural pine-and-wind smell, combined with the crisp newness of his custom suit... Not a soul in Manhattan would fault me for going full lemur. "He makes the suit his, doesn't he?"

"Hmmm," the bird croons. "Ohhh, yes."

"Max enjoys making things...his."

"I am most certain he does."

I want to roll my eyes. The woman isn't giving up. Worse, I see that Max knows it too—and stifles a smirk as a result. For all the man's gee-whiz reactions over the past twenty-two days, he picks now to transform into the Marquis de World-Wise? I'm not sure whom I'm peeved at more now.

"Well, thank you for your help." I'm sure she notices the clench of my smile. "And since there are only the few alterations on my dress for you to handle, perhaps we can come back in a few hours to pick up—"

"Oh, no no no."

"Excuse me?"

"We do not know if yours are only the alterations." She gives the answer to me but locks her gaze on Max. "So many hidden challenges with suits. I believe I shall require a closer perusal of Monsieur De Leon's . . . fit."

"Of course you do." I grit it out so hard, it's an incoherent mumble.

Once more, Max battles back a grin. "*Mademoiselle*," he soothes. "*Tout va bien. Je ne souhaite pas vous déranger.*"

"It is no trouble." Refinna translates his words with the simplicity of her reply. She goes for the big-eyed blink-blink again. "In fact . . . it is my pleasure."

She enforces every illicit subtext of the words by dropping her stare south of his trendy belt. I re-twist my hands into fists. If this wench is all for scrapping decorum, so am I.

"Mademoiselle," I level. "Even in your native land, shit like this isn't close to acceptable." I step in, nearly taking Refinna's eyes out with my breasts. I don't care. Max presses against me from behind, soothing a hand down my arm, but I resist. "Stay out of this," I snap and backhand his chest.

"*Ma femme.* This is not worth—"

"Stay out of this."

Refinna rocks back on one of her skinny gold stilettos. "Perhaps that is not the only thing you have ordered him out of—which is why he is growling for the chance to get into me."

One punch.

That's all it requires to send the girl down for the count.

One punch.

But undoubtedly, the beginning of a thousand repercussions ...

Including what is going to be my very short career.

Holy. Crap.

What have I just done?

And is it too late to beg Max just to zap my ass—along with the rest of my short-tempered, career-burning self—out of this time period altogether?

CHAPTER FOURTEEN

MAX

"Alessandra."

"*What?*"

"You must come out of the shadows, *chérie.*"

I almost regret saying it. Truthfully, the shadows are a magnificent place in which to find her, especially in this little grotto tucked away from the bedlam calling itself a "quiet but formal party."

I cannot admit that I initially shared her excitement about the Hemline event, having dismissed it with cavalier pride. Even after twenty-plus decades, I'd assumed no *fête* on earth would rival the carnality of the French Court masquerades. But the people of this Obelisk Hotel have proved me wrong. In grand and magnificent ways.

The hotel, owned by an entity called Richards Resorts, has employed a small army for the event. Yet none of them are attired in matching uniforms. The luxury of their unique vestments is outshined only by the serving trays they carry, illuminated from within by some hidden magic. The food tables, brimming with luxurious fare and encircling the long rectangular swimming pool, are bridged to each other via long clear tubes filled with running water and teeming with living fish in every color imaginable.

But I am doubly dazzled by the crowd.

At court every year, I could walk through one room and know I might as well have viewed the whole throng. The women with their high wigs and low necklines, the men with their brocades and buckles. Nearly everyone with skin the color of milk, a status symbol of its own—and usually not in the best ways. But at this gathering, there are interesting faces everywhere. So many textures and hues and expressions.

While Alessandra was correct that most would opt for some form of black with their attire, the variations on that theme are astounding. From nearly naked nymphs to mummy-wrapped Amazons, my fascination has been completely conquered. If my days in this realm are truly numbered, at least I have the memories of the last two hours to take with me.

Two hours.

Another comprehension I cannot fully grasp.

Somehow, the time feels like twice as long—a sensation for which I should be grateful, since fate has conspired to hang the moon large and luminous over the city tonight, a glaring reminder of the time I have left to exist. But I cannot celebrate as long as Alessandra stays glued to that bench. Or refuses to touch the delicacies I have brought for her. Or even peeked at the glamorous crowd beyond her discreet hiding place.

"I'm good right here, Hotness." At least a smile glimmers in her kohl-lined gaze as she gratefully accepts the new libation I bring for her. "Mmmm. A fresh cosmo and a hot date. What more could I want—except to not be here?"

I settle onto the plush couch she has commandeered since sneaking off after her greetings to the Hemline nobility. I cannot stay a hand from wandering to her nape, exposed because of her upswept coiffure. Tiny tendrils wrap around my fingertips. She is exquisite, and I want the entire crowd to know it, but her terse profile betrays exactly what she thinks of that notion. In the woman's own words, it is a *hard no*.

"Perhaps we should leave." By New York standards, the night is still young, and she is imbibing her third pink drink. She should be comfortably buttered soon. "We can go back to your condo, and I can show you how delectable you truly are in that dress . . ."

"You mean the one I altered myself because I decked the seamstress so hard, she threatened a lawsuit if I didn't leave the shop?" She sends me a grimace identical to its fifty predecessors. "The seamstress used by half the damn industry in this city? Maybe the entire East Coast?"

"And, apparently, hated by all of them as well." I add my palm to the gentle rubs at the back of her neck. "Did you not see the backlash to her rant on her Twatter page?"

I fathom not why that makes her choke on her drink in laughter, but my chest warms with the success of eliciting her happiness.

But only for a moment.

Her face twists once more. A defeated sigh rushes from her. "But now, the Hemline guys will only think of me as the badass vlogger who laid out the bitch seamstress and nothing more."

As I watch her swipe at the drops leaking from the corners of her eyes, I gather her close and caress the side of her neck. "I confess, I am confused," I murmur. "Is badass not a *good* thing?"

She swivels her head, attempting a nod. "Technically, yes—but not when it's the only thing. Not when that's the only category I fit into for them now. Not after years of working so hard with Dmitri to do things in a better way, to make a bigger difference. Facing up to so many who wanted to write me off for my double-digit dress size." She sniffs, eyeing me wryly. "Little hoochies just like Refinna."

I tighten my frown. "So, the hoochies are the ones who consider it acceptable to play the strumpet with another woman's man?"

"No." She pivots around by the waist, sloshing part of her drink on her hand. "Of course not."

"So Refinna was different than the others."

"Yes." She squeezes her eyes shut. "*No*. I mean—what she did shouldn't have set me off that way, because technically, you're not—"

"What?" I scoot a finger beneath her chin and gently lift. "I am not . . . your man? Is that it, Alessandra? You do not want to assign that to me? It feels better not to?"

"That's not what I said."

"But it is all right if you want to, *ma chérie*." I curve my hand up to stroke my thumb across her cheek. "Or even if you need to. I am not here to frighten you, *mon miracle*. I only want you to feel adored. Beautiful. Protected. Safe."

Her nostrils flare. Her fingers tremble as she sets aside her drink. "I'm not sure I'll feel safe about anything again, Max." With her head still ducked, she whispers, "Especially after you're gone."

She finishes by lifting her head, though instantly attempts to hide from me again. To shield her tears, now glistening tracks down her cheeks, from me. I refuse to accept that. I need to see all of this.

I need to see all of her.

I lift her chin once more.

"*Ma femme.*" I adore her with the words.

"My man." She caves me in with hers.

I tug her closer to me. Let her cry against me. Just before I gather her in for a desperate, desiring kiss.

She is lavender silk and cosmo-tinged tears. Sweeps of tongue and sighs of surrender. Connection and conflict and curves and craving, until I am lost in her all over again. So sure of her all over again. So sure of *me* and this complete reality of my existence.

I am Maximillian George Jean Valence De Leon, born in seventeen sixty, a secret dauphin of France—and the man kissing the soul out of my soulmate at one of New York City's hottest parties of twenty nineteen. The soul so bruised, she does not know how to open it to me. A heart so hurt, she is terrified to declare it to me.

And that is all right, because I love her anyway.

And that is all there is. That is all that matters.

Even if I must die to prove it.

But this moment has not been given to us for those morose thoughts. It is a gift from the Creator, crafted with intentions of seduction, connection, and ultimate consummation.

So my cock keeps reminding me. With throbbing urgency.

I shift my embrace to the sides of Alessandra's waist—and then commandeer her body over mine. My angle on the couch lends naturally to her straddling me, with the damp triangle of her underwear riding the demanding bulge at my crotch. Our mouths meet in a juicier, deeper kiss. Our gazes tangle in darker, hotter connection. I reach in and cup her face, capturing more of her diamond tears with the pads of my fingers.

"Max," she sighs against my lips. "*Max.*"

"Alessandra." I grate it against her mouth as she dips in to press our foreheads, noses, and lips. She tastes like the fruit of her drink and the spice of her passion. My senses are drunk on the heady mixture. "You have entranced me. Called to me. Possessed me. And given me the grandest, most spectacular adventure a man could ever ask for . . ."

She cuts me short with a heady new kiss—and the mesmerizing heat of her body. As she rocks her thinly clad pussy along my jolting cock, my senses are dazed with desire. *Jesu.* She is softness and silk and passionate perfection.

She is everything.

"Damn it," she gasps, spreading the petal-shaped layers of the dress that has made her the most succulent goddess at this gathering. The triple-jeweled band atop her head, arranged like Venus's own headpiece, picks up the dim lighting in our corner as she tucks in her head. At once, she focuses on unlatching my pants. "I need *this* adventure, man of mine. Right now."

"Then take it." My voice is a low dictator's growl. I crave the proof of what my command does to every inch of her body. "Take my cock out of my pants, Alessandra. You know what to do with it then."

Wordlessly, she obeys. After freeing my shaft, she feverishly works my pre-come from my head to my balls and then back again. The entire time, she rolls her hips with mesmeric insistence. She gasps and whimpers, clearly encouraged by the urgency of my savage grip.

I swipe my touch inward. She cries into my mouth. I groan into hers.

At the same moment, I yank her panties to the side. I have to have her now. Have to feel her naked pussy against my hard flesh . . .

"I want inside."

I shove up, angling for the slit that already drips for me. She grabs at my jacket lapels, using the purchase to help align the penetration—but the moment before she sinks fully down, her attention rivets to the area above my waist. She wraps one of her hands around one of mine. With determined intent, she guides my fingers to the silken valley between her breasts.

"You already are inside," she whispers. "Right here."

And for a moment, as our bodies fully join, time stops.

And when it does, I see it all.

With every new thrust into her center, I remember it all.

The forests of her gaze in the eyes of a village girl with whom I once played. The curve of her smile in the Loire hills at sunrise. The perfection of her passion in even my earliest, self-given orgasms. In all of it, I see her—realizing now that I have *always* seen her. She has always been inside me too . . . through my entire life. Through all of hers. Through the hundreds of years that have separated us. The essence of my heart. The substance of my soul. The reason for the miracle.

And now, the seed of my life . . . spilling from my body into hers.

"Max." She twines the breath of it with my harsh moans. Then repeats it as her walls convulse around my cock. "*Yes.*"

I envelop her in my embrace, clutching her close. "I love you, Alessandra. No matter what."

"And I—"

"Ssshhh," I soothe when her own sob is her interruption. "You do not have to say it."

Because I already know it.

Because I always have.

"I—I *want* to say it," she whispers. "But . . ."

"But you have only known the words to bring sorrow." I kiss her with steadfast warmth as our bodies merge with persistent fire. "I understand why you do not trust them."

More moisture wells in her conflicted gaze. "Oh, Max." She wraps her arms around my neck as she molds her delectable body against mine. We rock together, treasuring the feel and fit and perfection of each other. "Can't . . . can't we just . . ."

"Can't you just *what*?"

She and I freeze. Also together, we snap our heads toward the human willow reed standing before us, impatiently tapping his black-booted foot. He pins us with a brilliant glare from beneath his dying flower hair.

"Dmitri." Alessandra's voice is still woozy, as if he's merely walked in on us slumbering late. "Wh-What're you—"

"No, missy. What are *you*—" His jaw falls as soon as his stare does. "Balls of Jesus. At the most important soiree of your life, are you out here fornicating with your boy toy?"

"Is that really any—"

"And if you are, why didn't you notify the press first?"

"No!" She lurches to her feet, leaving my erection exposed. "No press!" With a fresh gasp, she plops back down. I groan from the impact in tandem to the approving jump of Dmitri's brows.

"Well, fuck a goddamn duck." He chuckles hard enough to spill his drink. "Though I've never seen a duck built like *that*."

I narrow my gaze with insolent intent. "And you have . . . observed . . . that many ducks in such a state?"

The man snorts out a louder laugh. "Quackity quack and get back, baby. I really like him, Allie." He licks some of the cosmo off his hand. "Still, you really owe me for this one, wench." He dumps the remainder of the drink into the fountain and then clunks his empty glass down on the ledge, freeing a hand to beckon to Alessandra. "But we're making the next round champagne, as soon as you come with me."

"I don't think so." She huffs and folds her arms. The motion ensures that every inch of my cock is brutally aware of her backside's perfect cushions. I grunt to restrain my fresh groan.

Dmitri's lips twitch again. "Well, think again, sassy," he says. "Because the Hemline crew wants to talk some hard business with you. Right now."

Alessandra pops back to her feet. Fortunately, I am ready this time. While I stuff myself back into my trousers, she blurts, "Are you seriously shitting me, mister?"

"Uh-uh." Dmitri copies her pose, one hand on a cocked hip. "You're coming with me, Miss I-Just-Hit-A-Million-Followers." He tosses his head back as she gapes again. "Close your mouth, dear. Flies in the teeth aren't sexy."

But it is I who finds the wherewithal to speak next. "A million?" As I rise, I throw my stunned stare between them.

"Yeah." Alessandra nods, tearing up again. "That's a lot."

"Ding, ding, ding." Dmitri taps the air with his forefinger. "And *that's* our magic word for negotiating the salary for your deal with these bad boys, okay?"

She stumbles, grabbing at me for support. "D-Deal? As in . . . for the show? It's still on the table?"

"Not just on the table, gorgeous." Her friend flounces his head back. "Right now, you're the fucking fabulous centerpiece."

Alessandra steadies herself enough to pin him with a full gape. "Wh-What do you mean?"

Dmitri rolls his head back into alignment and then fans

his feathers, savoring his full peacock mode. "Just what I said, darling. They want to talk to you about headlining their fall lineup."

Alessandra grabs my hand with one of hers. With the other, she leans and seizes Dmitri's. "Are you freaking kidding me?"

ALLIE

Dmitri wasn't kidding.

Yet now, a week and a day later, I'm still struggling to believe it.

Struggling to wrap my brain around the fact that this moment is truly happening—and damn near like I always dreamed it would.

With getting into the city in a town car sent by the studio instead of having to take the subway.

With my name embossed on the name plate of a private dressing room door at Hemline's midtown studio.

With Drue and Raegan arriving at said dressing room, bearing celebration champagne and flowers. There are flailing arms and screams from Rae. A way-to-go-wench hug from D.

Dmitri arrives next, his hair sprayed as high as his ego, ordering around his new boy-toy assistant like the diva manager he's always dreamed of being.

And yes, there's even a phone call from Mom, who's "so proud" of the "little girl" who's now made her look smokin' hot to the guy she's been crushing on at the gym. I shock myself by simply laughing at her antics this time. Yeah, she'll probably get her heart shattered again. Yeah, she'll probably be a mess about it for a while. But hell to the no will she stop trying to chase the damn prince just because Dad couldn't stick it out and be that for her.

And just like that, as I meet my own excited gaze in the bright-lighted mirror, I'm pierced by a crazy bolt of comprehension.

Because right now . . . Launette Fine is kind of my hero.

Better yet, it's awesome to be hers too.

"Go out there and wow 'em, honey." Her voice drips with tearful maternal pride. I yearn to talk to her longer, but the styling team enters, laying out their brushes and creams and sprays, to transform me into Hemline's newest *It Girl*. "I'll be watching every second of the broadcast from Bubby's Diner. Wolfe and I are going out for breakfast. The man likes taking me to breakfast, Allie. As in, sitting down and ordering stuff and then talking. *Talking*. Can you imagine?"

"I totally can." I give in to a soft smile.

"I have you to thank for all of this, honey," she gushes.

"Errrm." Suddenly, I frown. Though I'm afraid to ask, I go ahead and do. "And how's that?"

"If you hadn't encouraged me to get over Ralph by signing up at the new boxing gym, I wouldn't have met Wolfe."

At once, I'm back to a grin. "Aha. Cupid's arrow in the shape of boxing gloves."

"And a pair of biceps to stop traffic." She bursts with a girlish giggle. "And some other . . . notable body parts."

"Okay, Mother . . . *ew*."

She mellows the snicker. "Sorry, baby. I'm just so happy."

"And I'm just so glad." And it feels good to really mean it. To hear her hope. To recognize her resilience.

To understand the truth of my epiphany.

Sometimes—a lot of times—courage isn't about

identifying fear.

It's about knowing the bastard—and then doing crazy stuff anyway.

"Hey, Mom?"

"Yeah, honey?"

"I'm proud of you too." Before she can go all teary-mushy-sappy, I rush on. "Have fun. I love you."

"I love you too, my epic Allie."

As I end the call, Drue sidles up next to the director's chair in which I'm perched. For a second, all she does is check out the asymmetrical black-and-red suit that took me ten hours of shopping to finally pick out for this occasion. Through every moment, there's a proud smirk across her lips.

"Boom," she finally murmurs. "The outfit slays, baby."

"Thanks." I return her smile via the mirror. "Guess the all-day shopping marathon was worth it."

"Especially because I didn't have to go on it with you."

I widen my smirk and roll my eyes before concurring, "Max was a trooper. It was pretty grueling."

And just like that, the demon hovering on the outskirts of the perfect day has invited itself back into the party. Closing my eyes to let the makeup girl do her thing with shadow lends an ideal excuse to start up my mantra.

Don't. Think. About. Him.

Not his decadent gold eyes. Not his hypnotic waves of honey and cinnamon hair. Not the smiles that take over every crease of his face. Not the kisses that consume every inch of your body.

Not the ten thousand versions of perfect he makes you feel.

Don't think about him. Don't think about him. Don't think about him.

With that effort logged into the Fail column, it's impossible to hold off the shittiest thought about him too.

That he isn't here.

That I've known he wouldn't be from the moment he pulled his body out of mine for the last time last night.

That in that unmoving, unbreathing moment, in which our stares were illuminated by the moonlight through my skylight, I simply knew already . . .

I knew.

That he'd be gone by the time I woke up in the morning.

Not just because he'd shown me as much, with his packed bag on the couch and the charter jet confirmation Dmitri had personally brought over.

Not just because he barely ate anything when we decided our perfect celebration would be Chinese takeout and a *Terminator* bingefest.

Not just because we only made it through an hour of Schwarzenegger's finest glowers before screwing like horny teenagers on the couch. Then the floor. Then the kitchen counter. Then finally the bed.

None of it sank in . . . until the moment, with our breaths still mingled and his body still buried in mine, that he dipped his head and pressed the softest of kisses into the space over my heart.

The final kiss he'd ever give me.

And, what he'd still clearly believed, of his life.

Like a stubborn idiot, I'd still refused to accept either—at least verbally. In the depths of my soul, the dread had already begun. Had scratched and crawled at me, battling my senses for control, screaming at me to stay awake and squeeze every moment of magic I could get in his arms. Somehow believing that if I didn't let sleep win, the night would last forever.

But, at least for an hour or two, sleep had won.

And when I woke up, he was gone.

Now, he's probably already cleared security at Teterboro and is likely on the Hemline jet, waiting to be cleared for the nine o'clock takeoff.

The exact same time Hemline will be debuting me to the world.

"Everything okay with Ms. Launette, maternal unit from outer space?"

Drue's query yanks me back to the bustle of now. The question's a filler, and we both know it. She sees the puffiness I've fought by slamming ice cubes over my eyes. She also sees the tight lines at the corners of my mouth and the stiffness of my shoulders, even after the makeup crew throws on a plastic drape to cover my clothes.

"She'd kill you for not calling her Launi, you know," I quip.

Sharp chuff. "And *I'm* known as the evasive one."

"If you must know…" I kick up one side of my mouth. "She's out with her new boyfriend, whom I'm apparently responsible for helping her nab."

"*There's* the bonus."

"His name is Wolfe."

"Bonus revoked." After we both giggle, she slides a hand over mine. "So. How are things really going?"

"With Mom? Actually, pretty good."

"You *know* the subject of her was dismissed at Wolfe, right?"

"Yeah." I go ahead and pour all the dismal drops of my heart into the syllable. "I know."

Drue folds her other hand over mine. She squeezes so hard, my plastic cape crinkles from the movement. "It's going to ache for a while, hon."

"Thanks, Eeyore."

She smirks. "But you also know it'll turn out all right."

"But will *he* be all right?" I sit up straighter just for the benefit of filling my lungs with more air. Wasted effort. My chest burns. My throat swells. The awful pressure rises, threatening to overcome every inch of my sinus cavities. With all the cosmetics they're shoveling onto my face, I can't even blink the tears away.

When the makeup gals step away for a second to debate my lip color, I use the moment to attempt a full stop on my emotional bullet train. Instead, I lock Drue's gaze with the intensity of mine—and pin her with the question I swore I wouldn't wield.

"What do you think?" I get down another hard swallow. "Did *you* ever believe him?" I rasp. "I mean, did you ever seriously believe he was . . . that he came from . . ."

My tightening throat makes it impossible to say the rest. Drue helps the effort by scooting a hand under the plastic and clutching my hand again. With the purpose of her grip, she's already rendering her reply to me.

That her reply doesn't really matter.

That at this point, even if I choose to believe Maximillian De Leon's insanity, that doesn't matter either.

But there's no more time for moping.

At once, the universe punches into fast-forward mode. The makeup team whips away the plastic cover, and I look up—

Into the face of an utterly glam beauty.

My skin is dewy and flawless. My eyes are smoky and expressive. My hair is teased and luxurious.

Holy shit.

I barely recognize this stylized siren. I mean, I'm *gorgeous*—but I'm a stranger.

But before I can get nuanced to the point of morose about that, Dmitri sweeps in and helps me out of the chair. I step into the red-bottomed shoes I also splurged on for this outfit, and we're strutting out for the grip-and-grin with Hemline's corporate honchos. Flashbulbs pop. A small crowd starts clapping. Dmitri's boy toy posts a video snapshot of the moment and excitedly reports the skyrocketing Likes figures.

It's a dream. A crazy, colorful, beautiful dream.

But not a dream come true.

Not anymore.

Not without the man of my dreams here too.

No. Not just the man of my dreams. The person of my heart. The match of my soul . . .

What's he doing right now? Is he thinking about me too? Is he watching the planes on Teterboro's tarmac and thinking about how we spent the flight over here from France? Does he miss me yet? Does he miss me at *all*?

All those questions, and so many more, bombard my brain as I'm guided to the "Hemline Daily" set. Dmitri delivers me to the seat next to the show's anchor, a vivacious blonde with legs to her neck and a face full of Botox. All hail Connie Filigree. The woman maintains that's her real name, but she's also told the world she's only twenty-six. Whatever. More power to her. Why is everyone so hung up on those numbers, anyway? In the end, isn't time the ugly rival we all want to punch like a snotty seamstress? I mean technically, Max is two hundred fifty-eight . . .

I laugh at that musing.

Until I don't.

ANGEL PAYNE

Fate decks me in the face. And the mind. And the heart. And every one of my senses careening in orbit around one exploding star of a realization.

Max is two hundred fifty-eight.

I believe it.

I believe *him.*

Which means . . . what?

It means nothing.

Not now.

It means I'm too damn late.

Lights flare brighter—as my soul dives into horrible, haunting darkness.

"Gooooood morning, fashionistas! Where's *your* hemline today? It's right *here,* you sweet little monsters, where we're excited to bring you all the sizzling hot news from fashion fronts around the world."

It means he's not watching airplanes at Teterboro.

Or thinking of me at all.

"But today, the hot flash *you* want is originating from right here, at Hemline Central, in the heart of New York City—and it's all about this badass babe sitting next to me, Miss Alessandra Fine!"

It means he's dead.

And I killed him.

"Allie has just signed a fab contract to host one of our new fall shows, focusing on the best trends and killer looks for girls with boobs and booties. Personally, I'm excited as hell about this. Tell us what you have in store for us, missy!"

That's it. I'm officially up. The moment is here. The chance has come.

And if I open my mouth, I'm certain only one sound will tumble out.

A sob. Then another. And another.

"W-W-Wow," I stammer. "Oh, God. I'm … uhhh … so sorry. I'm just so happy that I'm overwhelmed. Just give me a minute, please?"

"Of course." The woman's lips and cheeks might be fake, but her compassion isn't. I'm grateful for the true kindness of her handclasp. "Take all the time you need."

All the time.

That I need.

But time has turned traitor on me, and I know it. And it's going to take more than a few verklempt seconds to get over it. Judging by the helpless twist of her face, Connie knows it too. These are tears I've never cried before. Tears beyond the realm of ugly. They're heavy and silent, full of emotions surpassing what they represent on the outside. Sorrow scooped from my darkest wells, where the rain of my fears has become the depths of my grief. It pours in a wordless, frozen torrent from eyes no longer blinded by the lights or even conscious of the cameras …

Now, I'm staring beyond the cameras …

Into the shadows.

The darkness that's filled with people.

Stunned people. Gawking people. Disappointed people.

My manager. My friends. All the suited dudes who have ponied up a shitload of money for me. I'm letting them all down, but I can't summon the will to care.

Because he's there too.

Oh, holy *shit*.

I swipe both palms at my face, dragging and smearing makeup as I go, but I still don't care.

He's there.

He's...

Here.

I stagger to my feet, tossing aside the red-bottomed stilts.

And he's still here. Lighting up the studio's darkness with the resplendence of his full, warm smile. Filling the air with his rich, indulgent chuckle. Conquering every scrap of my awareness with his perfect, potent presence.

But is he?

This can't be real...can it?

My senses don't care. My mind explodes with how real he seems. My heartbeat triples with how real he feels. My every instinct is seared from the golden brilliance of his gaze.

Damn it.

The confident, arrogant, persistent man is already haunting me with his hotness.

Fucker.

Beautiful, incredible ghost man...

Who makes the crowd part as he moves forward.

Who takes my breath away with his strong, measured stride.

Wait.

He *parts* the crowd?

Because *they* see him too?

Because...they...*feel* him?

Because...

I don't waste time with another moment of stupid theories or useless what-ifs.

I don't waste time. Because time sure as hell isn't going to waste me again. Or him. *Especially him.*

I run, forgetting about the cameras tracking me, the gasps surrounding me, even the director yelling at someone to get more light on me. It's all background noise and worthless chaos. It's as insignificant as the insecurities that have stopped me from believing in him. From believing in *us*.

I crash against him with a painful cry.

I grab his hair with painful twists.

I smash my lips to his with painful force.

And yet, none of the pain is enough. I want all the agony this man will bring me. And all the ecstasy too. All the regrets of his yesterdays, and all the hopes of his tomorrows—

But most of all, every drop of the joy of *now*. Of having him *here*. Of having him *real*.

Of having him *mine*.

I let that elation flood the tearful smile I lift to him. Our bond intensifies as his brilliant gaze pulls mine in. Flips my psyche end-over-end. Steals my breath until I'm gasping for breath between the thankful chokes of my sobs.

But somehow, at least half-aware of the crowd gawking around us now, I find the fortitude to push words to my lips. "You're not at the airport, Hotness."

"Did you really think I would leave like that, Alessandra?"

Inexplicably, my jaw clenches. So does his.

Unavoidably, my lungs start pumping on rapid breaths.

So do his.

At alarming speed.

"Max?" I grab again at his hair. It's thick and soft and full between my fingers—but something still isn't right. He's not solid anymore. Not sure. He's battling to lift his arms, to hold me in return, but they're limp as soaked silk, dangling at his sides. His breaths are shallow. His big body starts to sway.

"*Max?*"

He dips in, taking my lips in a soft kiss. Too soft. *Fuck.*

What's going on?

There's pain. A lot of it... inside my heart. The air in my lungs feels like the ash now defining his skin tone.

"Max. Damn it. Wh-What's happening to—"

"*Désolée, mon miracle.* I... I am so sorry."

His voice doesn't seem real anymore either. I stretch my mind out, fighting to keep its substance on the air, but he's fading. The ghost I've refused to believe in...

For too damn long.

"I did not want you to see this," he stammers. "For it... to end like this. But I was selfish. I knew I needed to see this... before I..."

"Max!" I sob harder. Desperately clutch at his shoulders. "No. Damn it, *no!* St-Stay with me. Stay with me! We'll get you help—"

"Too late," he interjects. "But that is... all right, my love. I just wanted to see you find your dream and know your happiness. I knew if I could see that, I would be able to face this."

"Th-This? This *what?*" It's broken up by my tears and frustration and confusion, as my mind struggles to grasp what I'm seeing.

No. What I'm *not* seeing.

Him.

I don't see... him.

While I still cling to his head and shoulders, Maximillian De Leon has vanished from the knees down. As his gorgeous thighs turn into sparkling ash as well, he reaches toward me, seeking purchase.

He crumbles to the floor anyway.

"N-N-No!" I fall to my knees and throw myself on top of

him. I wrap my arms around his waist, my tears soaking the ash-gray T-shirt he wears. Inch by inch, Max's face turns the same color.

"Alessssss . . . andra . . ."

"No, no, no, no!" The words are agonizing in my throat, every syllable a newly burst fault line in my heart. They widen by the second, exposing the dark loneliness beneath.

The darkness he endured . . . for me.

For over two hundred years . . . for me.

And I ignored his sacrifice. *Chose* to ignore it. Threw his gift back in his face, so many times. The treasure I see, embedded in his amber-diamond stare, has been squandered by my own fears, doubts, angers, and insecurities.

My inability to accept the unreal. To grasp the ungraspable. To see my fear and move past it.

To admit that I've fallen in love with him.

Too late.

I'm too damn late . . .

"Max! Max, *please!*"

But his life force continues to drain. I don't just see it happening before my eyes, as his body continues to vanish. I feel it too. Feel him disappearing like my tears on the air, which also keep falling like ashes. I feel it like the huge half of my heart that he's taking with him.

That time is ripping from me.

Just like it's stealing him.

"No! Nooo!"

His eyes roll back in his head.

"Alessssss . . . andra . . ." he repeats, though the word is barely a breath anymore.

"No!" I scream it now. Pummel his chest with the

sobbing sequences of it, hating how I can feel every labored, desperate breath limping through his lungs. "Stop screwing with me, you asshole! Don't do this to me!"

He curls his hand down, brushing feeble fingertips across my soaked cheek. "I . . . love you."

"And I love you too, goddamnit. Do you *hear* me, Maximillian George Jean Valence De Leon? I fucking *love you*, so stop this bullshit and come back to me!"

I'm nothing but grief now. And humiliation. And desperation. And fury. And loss. And draped across the man who has made me feel more whole and alive and loved than anyone in this time or any other. My heart roars with loss. My mind rages with disbelief.

Which is probably why I don't hear everyone's stunned gasps at first. Or even the awed cheers and then the rise of applause.

What the hell are they . . .

His hand, sprawling against the back of my head, is the beginning of a damn good answer to that. So is the resurgence of his torso beneath my cheek. And then the sleek striations of muscle that lead toward other . . . *surging* things.

Thank God for miracles.

A miracle.

Yeah. That's exactly what I mean this time.

Exactly what I choose to believe, working my way back up the solid sinew of this man's body until our lips are sealed and our tongues are twirled in what everyone in the room concludes is a grand finale to this newest PR stunt in the "Allie and Max Show."

And maybe I'll just let them be right about that.

Because the *Allie and Max Hour* does have a cool ring to it . . .

A lot of minutes later—but not nearly long enough—I reluctantly slide my mouth away from his. But only far enough to ensure he's still all here. That he's still the miracle that isn't going away.

Once I establish every flawless inch of the man is still in place, I finally allow him to roll up into a kneel. I do the same, butting my knees against his, mirroring the double-handed hold he has on my face, before whispering, "I do, you know."

He ticks up one side of his mouth. "You do . . . what?"

"Love you."

"Oh. Well . . . that."

"Well *that*?" I bop his shoulder. "Like I've said it a thousand times already?"

"Because you have, *ma revelation*." He pushes in, kissing me tenderly again. "Now I simply have time in which to catch up."

I smile and nip at his bottom lip before echoing with meaning, "All the time you need, Hotness." I turn my whisper into a full kiss, savoring every warm, perfect corner of his mouth before finally pulling back. "All the damn time you want."

As his hold tightens and a beautiful smile breaks across his lips, I'm damn near able to read what his mind does with that offer. Probably because mine does much of the same thing. Time, once the miser that held me back and the adversary I had to beat, has suddenly given me the best gift of my life. Sunrises and sunsets. Castles and bell towers. Good days and bad days. Seconds and minutes and hours and years with the man who defeated it to get to me. To get here and love me . . .

I guess I'll give time another chance.

Just like I'll dare to give love a chance this time.

To look beyond my fears . . .

And believe, for once, that maybe there's some merit to this fairy tale crap.

Now *there's* an idea for a new vlog . . .

Just after Max and I finish with the mushy kissing part.

And maybe a few other things.

Because now, we have all the time in the world.

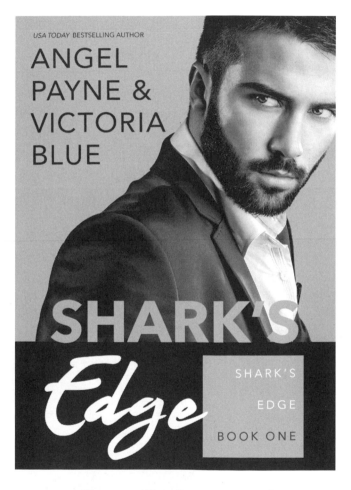

EXCERPT FROM

SHARK'S EDGE
BOOK ONE IN THE SHARK'S EDGE SERIES

A king.

My kingdom.

I'd earned every bit of it.

Every. Single. Bit.

But now someone was messing with me, and they wouldn't get away with it. I barely recalled the woman's name, even though it kept popping up on the news reports. *Tawny Mansfield*. But really, in a sea of Candys and Sugars and the occasional Minx or Jinx, Tawny didn't seem all that special.

I wasn't doing much better with her face in the grainy photo that flashed across the screen repeatedly. Dancers and escorts had a certain look in common. A little too much makeup, a little too much hair product, clothes that were worn a little too tight. Nothing really stood out about her appearance either.

What did it matter?

What did they matter?

Well, of course they mattered, but not to me. That was my issue. Mine. I wasn't interested in getting attached. I didn't have time for relationships, and I certainly didn't have time for emotions. I stuck to secure sexual transactions.

Uncomplicated arrangements where both parties knew exactly what was—and wasn't—expected.

"Do you think she was one of LuLu's girls?" my best friend asked, as if he had a direct link into my thoughts.

"I don't think so. I imagine LuLu would've already been breathing down my neck by this point if she were. She's fiercely protective of her assets." It wouldn't hurt to confirm the thought, though.

"Siri, page Terryn."

"Do you mean fucking Terryn?" the disembodied voice volleyed back.

"Yes!"

Grant's face split in two with a wide grin.

"Yes, Mr. Shark?" Terryn's voice came over the intercom speaker.

"Get Louise Chancellor on the phone." I didn't bother with "can you" or "please." Just merely stated what I needed and expected my assistant to make it happen.

"I can, but I may be able to save you a call. Ms. Chancellor left a message about fifteen minutes ago. I'm sorry I haven't been able to give it to you before now, sir. It's been a bit hectic out here."

"Cry me a river, Terryn. Just tell me what she said." I scrubbed my hand down my face, hoping to hell Tawny Mansfield hadn't worked for the high-end madam I regularly used.

"Ms. Chancellor said, and I'm quoting . . . " Terryn inserted a dramatic beat. "'She wasn't one of mine.'" She paused again before adding, "Uhh, I'm guessing that makes sense to you?"

"Terryn?" I queried, impatience oozing from my voice.

"Sir?"

"Is it your job to play superspy decoder ring or just give me my phone messages?"

"Uhh. I was just trying to make sure—"

"Terryn?" I cut her off before she could stammer any longer, wasting my valuable time.

"Yes?" she answered timidly. *Christ.* I'd break this one too. It was just a matter of time.

"Just answer the question so we can both get back to work."

"To give you your phone messages, sir." Her voice had gained strength as she repeated the answer option verbatim.

"Perfect. Now where's my lunch?" I switched topics, ready to move on to the next item.

A soft knock sounded on the door, and just like that, my dick twitched in my slacks. It was like my goddamned body sensed the young redhead was within a fifty-foot radius.

"Never mind," I said, disconnecting the intercom. "Enter!" I shouted toward the door, the way I always did when Little Red Riding Hood came by with my lunch.

Most days, I attempted to appear occupied with my work as she set up my meal, but since I was already standing in the middle of the room, there'd be no way to avoid her today. Maybe that was a good thing. It just meant I could sneak in a few glances of her glorious, lithe body from a new angle. I'd been getting more obvious with my staring lately, but it couldn't be helped. The air thickened between us the moment she walked through my door. The thrill of the hunt, maybe?

"Oh. Well. Hi. Hello," she stammered, taking in my looming form from head to toe as she came into my penthouse office. Gazes locked. Breaths stuttered. Cheeks flamed.

And then my annoying COO cleared his throat, tramping through our moment like a wayward puppy through a newly planted flower bed. I gave him a sideways glance, and Ms. Gibson slipped past me while asking her daily inquiry.

"Where would you like me to set up lunch today, Mr. Shark?"

On your flat stomach. Between your milky thighs.

"Here, let me help you with that." Grant, a warm smile on his face, all but tripped over himself to take the large tray from her.

"Sit down, Twombley. Let the girl do her job." *Because you're spoiling my view.*

He glared at me over his shoulder and continued taking the burden off Little Red, ignoring me completely. "This looks fantastic," he said, giving her the full force of his pussy-slayer grin.

"Thanks. I tried something new with the dressing today. We've been working on a few new recipes." She gave an impish shrug toward the food before looking back up to Grant. "Are you having lunch in this office today, Mr. Twombley? I can get your tray off the cart and set it up in here as well." As they moved deeper into the penthouse to the area I used for meetings, they continued chatting. She tilted her head way back since he towered over her by a solid twelve inches. Then they both swung their gazes to me.

"Well, shit, don't let me interrupt." I threw my hands up, unexplainably pissed after watching their exchange.

Who was I trying to kid? It was completely explainable.

It's called jealousy, motherfucker. The good old-fashioned green-eyed monster.

But what the hell was that about?

I didn't experience jealousy. I inspired it.

I narrowed my eyes at the young caterer and then shifted my stare to Grant. "We need to strategize about this Mansfield situation. More specifically, how it might delay progress on the Edge. We can do that while we eat."

Grant pivoted smoothly back toward Abbigail. "If it wouldn't be too much trouble, then . . . I'm sorry. I don't think I've ever caught your name." He set the tray down on my sleek stainless-steel conference table and offered his hand. "Grant Twombley."

I continued to stare in borderline fury while my chief operating officer gently caressed the inside wrist of the intriguing redheaded sandwich girl. Her lips parted slightly while she stuttered to form her own name, wholly affected by his attention.

"Abbigail Gibson. Abstract Catering. It's very nice to meet you, umm, Mr. Twombley." She smiled shyly, causing me to suck in air sharply. The woman yanked her hand from Grant's at once, darting her eyes in my direction as if caught doing something she shouldn't be doing.

Grant leaned down, sharing a conspiratorial murmur. "Ignore him. Nearly everyone does."

"I find that hard to believe," she replied quietly.

This story continues in *Shark's Edge*!

ACKNOWLEDGMENTS

They say every book has its own special background story that one never sees on the page—and never has that been more true for me with this book. What began as a germ of an idea so many years ago has finally bloomed into Maximillian and Alessandra's love story—and I am so happy that you all finally get to read this little project of my soul!

The completion of this years-long journey would not have been possible without some amazing people to help guide this crazy tale. First and foremost, to the god of an editor who has been there from Day Freakin' Zero: Scott Saunders, you are the hero who's been through this book so many times, you can probably recite it by heart—and yet you are so steadfast and supportive through every pass and every revision. I am so grateful!

Developmentally, this story wouldn't be what it is without Felicity Carter and Jeanne De Vita, both of whom went "above and beyond" their job parameters to impart their wisdom, talent, and exceptional skills to not just this project but my journey as a writer overall. I have learned so much from you both and feel so thankful to have benefited from your knowledge. *Goddesses!*

Everyone who knows me is aware of what a special tale this was (and still is!) for me. To see a story of one's soul come to fruition like this...is truly a miracle and a blessing. I am beyond blessed to thank the team at Waterhouse Press for being on this journey with Max, Allie, and myself. Thank you to Meredith Wild and Jon McInerney for believing in the story from the very start, and also to the fabulous team who have helped to breathe life into this crazy cast of characters: Robyn Lee, Haley Byrd, Keli Jo Nida, Yvonne Ellis, Jennifer Becker, Jesse Kench, Amber Maxwell, Kurt Vachon, and Dana Bridges...you all rock my world so hard! *Merci* to the Creator for all of you!

Thanks to the writing nation friends who kept me sane through this process! Victoria Blue, Shayla Black, Rebekah Ganiere, Jenna Jacob, Julie Kenner, Sierra Cartwright, and Jodi Drake. You women are life. Thank you!

To every single goddess of the RAWR sisterhood: I'm fine. Just fine. Honestly; I'm *fine*. I love you zany goddesses!

To every member of the Payne Passion nation, wherever you are: I love you, I see you, I appreciate you. And *very* special thanks to Martha Frantz for keeping it all organized and churning. I love you, girl.

To Diana Gabaldon, Herself! You broke the mold and made us all believe. I'm so grateful.

MORE MISADVENTURES

MORE MISADVENTURES